JANE MCGARRY

Also by the Author:

A Maiden of Snakes
A Prophecy of Wings

The Stewartsland Chronicles
Not Every Girl
Unexpected Rewards
A Betrayal Exposed

Hope is the last thing ever lost.
Italian Proverb

PROLOGUE

So much of what they speak about me is false, fabrications and exaggerations propagated by both gods and men. A pretty pretense to cover their own pettiness and desire for revenge. Still, some truths linger in the tale, distilled to legend now, but with enough of the kernel intact to resonate as genuine.

The notion I was the original woman? A silly hyperbole. How could there be life without women? Many existed long before my story played out, and many will live long after I am gone. The significance of this false embellishment adds to the gravity of the blame others attempt to lay at my feet.

I was not the first—nor, I suspect, the last—to be used as a pawn in the games of the gods. The same powerful beings whose complicity led to the misery of many. Their cunning guided me right into the trap, a moth to a flame, exactly as they meant it to be. In me, they found the perfect scapegoat, the one whose name others will link to this catastrophe for eternity.

How much of this blame do I bear? This question haunts me, forever my shadow. I could have been more mindful, more observant of the warnings of Athena, the only immortal who tried to aid me in this fate. But alas, the will of Zeus is a force above all others. Even had I known his plan from its inception, the outcome would not have changed. A mere woman is no match for the King of the Gods. Nor were any others involved in this account. We were but instruments in the orchestra he conducted.

I record this story with the wish that one day my words will be passed down and among the inevitable elaborations and enhancements, a core truth will remain—that the

Olympians unleashed this misery on humankind, not I. May these words absolve my daughter and her daughter's name so our descendants can once again hold their heads high. The disgrace of blame expunged. Perhaps I aim too high in my expectations. Women will ever be the sinful ones in the stories of men.

My hope, the only gift to prevail after the tragedy, is that my story will infuse into the essence of all women the understanding of their inculpability. My hope is women will see themselves as worthy in their own right. My hope is women will rectify this deceitful narrative thrust on us by both gods and men.

Yet, as I sit here all these decades later, I often wonder if hope is not the cruelest gift of all.

ONE

The dragonfly flew a fingertip's length out of reach, weaving among the bright flowers in the meadow. Behind it, a girl chased, her toddler legs too chubby and clumsy to keep up. With a lunge, she dove forward in a final effort to grab it, but with no luck. The insect's translucent wings powered its cobalt body high over the child's head and off into the summer sky. With a stomp of her tiny foot, the girl let out a shriek of frustration.

"Now, Pandora," her mother admonished, "there is no need for such a ruckus."

"But it got away," she protested, the dragonfly but a speck in the sky now. "I only wanted to see at it up close."

"Didn't Auntie paint you the beautiful dragonfly picture in your bedroom? You can see that one up close." Danae stopped and kneeled to her daughter's level, the sun warm on her cheeks.

"Oh, mama, it's not the same," Pandora wailed, brimming tears wiped by her tiny hands. "I wanted to touch it and smell it and see how it's put together. I wanted to follow it home to see where all the dragonflies live."

"Your curiosity will be the death of me," her mother chuckled as the girl crumpled into her arms. "So many questions in that little head of yours all the time. Come, it's time to go home."

Danae held out a hand to Pandora, who toddled out of the meadow with a reluctant glance back in search of more quarry. A soft breeze fluttered their loose hairs across their cheeks, a calming caress in the spring heat. All around them, the meadow hummed with life. Clusters of bees hovered above newly opened flowers. Birds sang in the dense cover of bushes, their occasional flutter rustling the young leaves. Fluffy clouds like tufts of wool glided across the pristine blue sky.

"Papa said it's good to ask questions," the girl asserted, stopping to smell a newly opened hyacinth. "That it is the best way to learn new things."

"Yes, but papa isn't the one who has to spend all day answering them," Danae muttered to herself.

"What mama?" Pandora asked, tugging her mother to a stop.

Danae gazed down into her four-year-old's eyes, round and full of innocence, and sighed. "Nothing, sweetheart. Papa is right. Questions are a good thing."

From the day she could talk, Pandora's inquiring mind, coupled with a reasoning ability beyond her years, defined her personality. Danae watched her daughter interrogate adults, who suddenly found themselves on the losing end of a debate with a mere toddler. Lycus admired this trait in his daughter and laughed outright at the people who fell prey to her examinations, particularly when it was not him. Danae, on the other hand, worried this characteristic would eventually lead to trouble. After all, society encouraged women to be amenable, not inquisitive.

The meadow gave way to a dirt road compacted with wheel ruts. Pandora preferred to walk right in the middle, where the ground bulged higher. Here she pretended to be a wagon laden with merchandise from faraway lands. She marched between the parallel grooves with purposeful steps, snippets of imaginary tales tumbling out of her mouth. Every day, she made up far-fetched stories about the world outside of Lemnos and asked her mother to write them down. Danae worried the house would run dry of ink from all her daughter's fanciful notions.

"I am a great caravan filled with spices and fabrics from Thessaly," she told Danae. "Or better yet, from Aegyptus."

"Wow, you must have some fascinating items," her mother said, a smile tugging at her lips.

"Tell me again about Aegyptus. How far is it? Are there truly giant pyramids? Are there crocodiles in the water? Do they eat people? Or are they mad when we swim in their water? What about mummies? Are they really dead people who chase you?"

"My, that is a lot of questions, Pandora. Let's save some for your father."

"Daddy will know the answers. He knows everything," the girl gushed.

A full grin broke across Danae's face. Lycus never left one of his daughter's questions unanswered, even if it meant making up the most outlandish fact he could conceive to placate her insatiable mind. Pandora never suspected. In her eyes, the man was a genius.

Along the route, small paths branched off. Modest homes lay tucked around orchards of stout olive trees and vineyards, the immature buds only small inklings of the ripe fruits to come. Flowers bloomed in vibrant bursts of color along the earthy landscape. A flock of doves scattered off the path, but hurried back to continue pecking for insects when the duo passed.

Up ahead, an old man lounged on a stone wall, whittling a piece of wood. Shavings fell around him, a miniature storm of flakes, some taking residence in his long white beard. When he noticed them, he stood, his crooked back matching the contours of the uneven wall, both worn with age. The man stuffed the knife and wood into his pocket, lifted the brim of his hat, and waved.

"Grandpa!" Pandora cried, breaking from her mother's grip, and hurtled down the path to him.

"How's my little love today?" he asked, bracing himself against the wall when she crashed into him.

"Good. I almost caught a dragonfly," she said, then added with consternation, "but it got away."

"Ah, yes, that will happen. Dragonflies are as quick as the gods they are," Myron consoled. "But don't worry, one day you are sure to get one."

Appeased by this statement, Pandora launched into a series of questions ranging from insect types to the possible number of stars in the sky. Myron, ever indulgent, was ready to address each one. He smiled at Danae over his granddaughter's head.

"I can walk her from here," he told his daughter.

Relieved to have a few moments of quiet, Danae leaned against the wall and watched the two continue down the path. Pandora stopped every few feet to pick something up or point something out, her little lips moving a mile a minute to her ever-patient grandfather.

Danae loved her daughter, though her excessive curiosity was exhausting on a day-to-day basis. For a moment, she wondered why the gods chose her for the challenge of this child's unquenchable spirit. At this thought, a force overtook Danae, the sensation of being pulled down a tunnel at the end of which she saw a grown Pandora engulfed in chaos. A pit of fear filled her stomach from the sheer terror the image emitted. Danae stumbled and sank to her knees, small rocks digging into her legs. She gulped for air as the horrific sight dissipated back into the dirt path in front of her. Blinking a few times to center herself, she stood and brushed the pebbles off her shins. Her eyes rose to Pandora, rounding a bend out of sight.

Was it an omen of her daughter's fate? Was there any way to protect Pandora from it? Whatever it signified, Danae pushed the vision to the back of her mind and refused to think of it again. Over the years, she kept the memory at bay, but for a few times when it crept up on her, unannounced and unwanted. On these occasions, she tamped the thought down once more; however, the clarity and dread did not fade over the years. It remained as potent as the initial stab of alarm on that summer afternoon and while she worried for Pandora, she never spoke of it to anyone.

TWO

Epimetheus paced the main room of his house, the dirt floor packed tighter with each worried step. Prometheus had gone too far this time. The last thing Epimetheus needed to contend with was the wrath of Zeus, but his elder brother reveled in the thought of one upping the King of the Gods. Despite Epimetheus' warning that any success over the Olympians would be short-lived, Prometheus disregarded his concerns.

The door burst open and his older sibling stomped in, arms full of thick pork ready to be cured. He plopped the bundle on the table with a satisfied smile. Though large, the room contained little furniture, and every sound reverberated like the toll of a bell. A goat lay on a pile of rags in one corner. Bothered by the noise, the animal rose at Prometheus' entrance and hurried outside. Epimetheus wished he could follow.

"See," Prometheus gestured to the pile, "the best part of the meat for us, not the gods."

"Because you tricked the gods," Epimetheus countered, not sharing his brother's excitement.

"You say *trick*, I say fair play. I gave Zeus the choice. It's not my fault what he decided."

Prometheus pulled out a chair and sat, the picture of calm. He nudged the chair next to him for Epimetheus to sit, but the younger Titan continued to pace the room.

"*Decided* because of your deception. Honestly, Brother, you act as though you've won, but no one wins against Zeus in the end." How could Prometheus fail to understand this?

"Ah, Epimetheus, the Olympians respect us because we fought with them in the War of the Titans. Besides, they appreciate my cleverness. It's why after the war they trusted me to create humans," he chuckled and added, "especially after your folly."

"You never miss a chance to mention that do you?" Epimetheus growled.

Many years ago, the siblings had been the only Titans to side with the Olympians in battles which saw the triumph of the younger generation immortals over the older. Prometheus, certain the immortal Titans would lose to the children of their chief god Cronos, allied himself with Zeus. After the war, the Olympians entrusted the brothers with the creation of inhabitants for earth. Zeus provided a pithos full of gifts for the duo to embellish their handiwork. Epimetheus set about quickly making a variety of animals, assigning each one a positive attribute, such as speed, wings, fur, and strength. Prometheus took time creating humans, but when he finished, few good qualities remained in the pithos, as his brother had used most of the desirable ones on the animals. Incensed about what little characteristics remained, Prometheus berated his brother's rashness. This amused the Olympians, who thereafter deemed the name Epimetheus synonymous with foolhardy. Prometheus devised other ways to improve his humans, teaching them craftsmanship and arts. Thus, his name became associated with shrewdness. A detail Prometheus lorded over his brother.

Epimetheus trudged over to the table and cut off a slab of pork. Grabbing a large skewer, he stabbed the meat and put it over a spit on the fire. The rest he cut into strips for salting. Soon, the aroma of roasting pork filled the room and his stomach rumbled. While the meat cooked, he cut up some artichokes and asparagus. The goat returned from outside and trotted over. Epimetheus set down a plate of vegetables and gently stroked Rhea's head before giving her an asparagus spear, the animal his far preferred dining companion.

"There now. The meat smells delicious, right?" Prometheus crowed, as drops of fat crackled into the fire. "You will thank me once you've had a bite."

Epimetheus only shook his head at his brother's bravado. Part of him admired Prometheus' cunning, another part resented it. Though his brother was often at odds with the Olympians, they showed Prometheus a level of respect, yet granted Epimetheus no such esteem. He glanced at his sibling, who sat confidently, assured of his charm, which not only kept him in the gods' favor, but also attracted countless women. Epimetheus looked back at his large hands, how clumsily they chopped the food, his entire being ungainly. The complete antithesis of his charismatic brother, Epimetheus was inelegant, even awkward around both deities and humans. His solitary existence on this hilltop, with only his animals for company, was his place in this world.

The sting of humiliation troubled Epimetheus when his brother bragged about his deeds and popularity with humankind, along with his popularity with the gods. However, Epimetheus worried his brother remained too complacent when it came to Zeus. This latest ruse with the meat was the second time Prometheus crossed the king of the Olympians and the god had been infuriated enough the first time.

When his brother realized there were no decent gifts left for his humans, he went to Zeus to request a choice one, specifically fire. But the King of the Gods refused, declaring fire belonged to the gods alone. Undeterred, Prometheus came up with a plan. He threw a golden pear into the midst of all the gods and goddesses labeled: *For the most beautiful goddess of all.* Naturally, a fight broke out among the goddesses as to whom the pear belonged. The gods sat back and watched the chaos unfold with glee. During this distraction, Prometheus snuck into Hephaestus' forge and stole fire, along with some crafted implements which he brought to his humans, who celebrated the miraculous gifts. Fire to keep them warm and cook their food, along with various tools and weapons for building and protection. Furious, Zeus demanded the humans sacrifice animals for him as payment for the fire. Prometheus should have stopped dallying with the gods then, but of course he did not.

When Prometheus saw how much food Zeus required his humans to forfeit, he worried they would not have enough to eat. Recently, he came up with a plan. He slaughtered a cow and made two piles. In one, he placed the best cuts of meat hidden under bones, in the other, entrails and scraps covered with juicy fat. He asked Zeus if the god would be kind enough to let humans offer one of the piles to the chief Olympian and keep the other for themselves. Zeus gave his word that this arrangement would be agreeable. The god came down to earth and selected the pile of fat, deeming it the more valuable choice. When the deception came to light, an angry Zeus realized he could not break his word. He returned to Mount Olympus, but Epimetheus doubted the King of the Gods would let this offense stand.

"You must be careful," Epimetheus warned. "This is the second time you have deceived the gods. They will try to make you pay. You must be watchful."

"My brother," Prometheus laughed heartily, "I am way too clever for them to deceive me. You, however, are likely to walk right into their trap. So perhaps you are the one who should be watchful."

"Have you no faith in me?" Epimetheus chafed at his brother's ability to turn the situation around on him.

"You always act on impulse, without proper consideration. Remember that the next time the gods offer you a gift of any kind so we don't have a repeat of the animal fiasco."

Epimetheus only huffed and returned to salting the meat. He knew his brother loved him. They were all each other had. Prometheus worried for him, but his lack of confidence in any decision Epimetheus made hurt. After all, it had been Epimetheus' idea to join the Olympian's side of the war, a fact his brother never gave him credit for. Perhaps it was a slight consolation that the all-seeing gods knew this. Epimetheus was true to them, and respectful—unlike his brother.

With this thought in mind, he removed the pork from the fire and divided it into two plates for dinner. Surely, of the two of them, the gods saw him in a more favorable light. Epimetheus was not the one who needed to worry about their vengeance.

THREE

High on Mount Olympus, Zeus raged at the treachery of the crafty Prometheus. Storm clouds rumbled above his head, soaring off to beleaguer the world below. His footsteps thundered against the heavy air. This was the second time the Titan tricked him. Against his better judgment, Zeus had not retaliated the first time. His fellow Olympian had reminded him of how Prometheus betrayed his fellow Titans, the ruling gods, and helped install Zeus as King of the Gods. But now, the Titan pushed too far and Zeus would have revenge. Various torment alternatives played over in his mind, none deemed harsh enough for the transgressions. After the war, Zeus had shown the brothers favor, only to be repaid with this duplicity. He would make sure the punishment for Prometheus was as carefully thought out as one of the Titan's own schemes.

"Problems?" Ares asked, strolling into the columned room.

Twelve golden thrones ringed one-half of the chamber in a semi-circle. Each bore the symbol of their owner, gods on one side, goddesses on the other, meeting in the middle with the two raised seats of Zeus and Hera. Above, the open sky roiled with dark clouds punctuated by streaks of lightning. Ganymede, Zeus' cupbearer, was the only other present, cowering behind the highest throne.

"I will not be made a fool!" Zeus bellowed at his son in a voice that would make most gods shudder.

Ares merely removed his shield and sword and plopped onto his own throne. As the god of war, rages and violence were his companions. He did not fear this behavior, not even from his all-powerful father, whose near daily tantrums were far from a novelty. Ares wondered who upset him this time—Hera, another god, a disrespectful human. The choices were endless.

"That Titan has deceived me for the last time and I will have revenge."

Zeus took a sip of nectar from a golden goblet. He slammed the cup down with such force on a table, its marble top shattered. Ganymede raced to catch the goblet before it clattered to the floor. Moments later, the boy had the table mended, and the cup refilled, everyone accustomed to the aftermath of Zeus' outbursts.

"Ah, Prometheus," Ares deduced, raking his hand through his shoulder-length hair. He waved away a drink the boy offered. "What trouble has he caused this time?"

"He wanted his humans to have more of an animal to eat instead of sacrificing all of it to me as I instructed. He asked if I would consider an arrangement where they only kept some for themselves. He set out two piles and told me to pick which one I wanted to be the share of the gods."

Zeus did not continue. Ares watched him pace in anger, hiding the amusement from his face, before prompting, "And?"

"He tricked me into picking the worst parts while his retched men get to keep the better parts for themselves," Zeus yelled and lightning flashed across the sky.

"Is everything all right?" a smooth voice inquired.

Athena, goddess of wisdom, glided into the chamber. She gazed between her angry father and bemused brother. She needed little of her wisdom to assess the familiar situation and shared a glance of commiseration with Ares. Her father did not let any perceived slights go unanswered, which meant they could be here for a while.

"Father is mad at Prometheus again," Ares informed her. "Perhaps you should have brought Athena with you. Certainly, her great acumen would have noticed the deception."

Athena scowled at her brother, who always belittled her gifts. Ares thought the answer to every problem was battle and death, whereas she knew many circumstances required a more subtle touch. While he craved blood, she saw war as a last measure, preferring to settle matters if not peacefully, then wisely. She sometimes marveled they were relatives, even as only half-siblings. Where she inherited her father's sagacity, Ares received his hot temper.

"What has he done?" she asked, slipping onto a throne on the opposite side of the semi-circle from her smirking brother. The goddess removed her helmet and laid it next to her spear. Ganymede brought her a cup of nectar.

"I gave him my word about which pile of a sacrificed animal the gods would take as an offering. Prometheus hid the best cuts under a mass of bones while covering entrails in the thick, juicy fat." The trick appeared all too obvious now that he explained it to his children.

"Now his precious humans get the meat while I am stuck with a pile of offal," he railed, the heavens flashing above him.

"So, kill him and be done with it," Ares suggested with a dismissive wave of his hand.

"And what of the other gods and goddesses?" Athena asked, her measured voice tinged with annoyance. "We swore to protect Prometheus and his brother when they sided with us against their fellow Titans. Poseidon, Hades, and Hera will not approve."

"Since when does Father care about *their* approval?" Ares countered, delighted at the thought of turmoil among the Olympians. Any fight was a good fight, as far as he was concerned.

"Athena is right," Zeus interjected. "Besides, death is too easy a punishment. I want him to suffer eternally like his brother, Atlas."

After the war, holding up the sky became the burden of the enemy Titan, the weight of the world on his back for all days to come, a fate worse than death. Watching Atlas suffer every day brought the King of the Gods a measure of joy. Zeus had banished the fourth brother, Meneotius, to the depths of Tartarus. To this day, he wished he had exacted a more brutal retribution.

"Then we must think of a fitting punishment," Ares said, mirth apparent in his tone at concocting a plan for the ceaseless torture of Prometheus, or anyone, for that matter.

"But a careful one," Athena counseled. "He will expect payback from Zeus and will be cautious."

"What do you suggest?" Zeus asked, finally taking the chief seat in the room. The sky above cleared from menacing black to hazy gray, subdued, for the moment, by its master.

A few moments of silence followed, the storm subsiding further as Zeus pondered the situation. Ares drummed his fingers on the chair's arm, bored with such strategizing. Killing enemies was much faster. He lifted his shield to admire his reflection. Athena sat, head down, lost in thought, her gray eyes closed. She examined the situation from all angles, searching for the right approach. An idea came to her.

"I think we are correct in assuming Prometheus will expect revenge to come directly from you, Father," she stated. "However, I think we may be able to punish him indirectly through his greatest weakness—his brother, Epimetheus."

FOUR

Pandora chewed her lip in concentration while she knotted off the blue thread. Satisfied with its tightness, she clipped off the excess string. She placed the shears back in the sewing basket, where they nested among the brightly colored spools. Turning the veil over, she admired her work. A pleasant breeze wafted across the covered portico where she sat with her classmates, each with a pile of garments at their side. Clematis vines twined up the columns and across the pergola above, bursting with a riot of pink and purple blossoms.

"There. It's finished," she declared.

Cyane, who sat next to her, took the soft material and ran her fingers over the intricate blue stitching. "That's so pretty, Pandora. My embroidery resembles something Tiresias would sew."

The young woman giggled but quickly made the sign to ward off evil. Better not to incur the wrath of Apollo by jesting about the blind Theban seer, one of the sun god's favorite prophets. Nerida, the instructor's assistant, gave them a stern glance, and they quieted. At least Madame Tullia could not hear them. The teacher stood across the room, showing another student how to sew a perfect chain stitch. Madame Tullia was not one for jesting, smiling, or any other frivolity.

"Your embroidery is wonderful." Pandora put a reassuring hand on her friend's arm.

"But your garments are as fine as though a goddess sewed them herself. Your dowry will be exquisite."

For that is what the young ladies made, clothes for their dowry. Pandora smiled, her eyes falling to petals scattered on the stone floor like vibrant spots of paint. She remained unsure how stitching pretty borders on veils correlated to being a good wife. Her mother, always busy running after Pandora's younger brothers, never had the time to sit and embroider. But the skill was an integral part of their schooling, along with reading, writing, and trying to master an instrument. Despite this compulsion to educate young women, the teachers tired of Pandora's endless questions, as though her knowledge should be limited to what they wanted her to learn and no more.

"Hopefully, we have some time before our dowries become necessary," Pandora huffed, chafed by the thought of marriage. She could not imagine leaving her parents, even if they were still close by. Her father indulged all her questions, a trait any new husband may not share.

"We will have to make sure Hephaestus doesn't notice us," Cyane teased.

The girls belonged to a select group of families who lived on the island of Lemnos. Here, Hephaestus, the god of fire and artisans, kept his forge in a towering volcano that sprung from the center of the island. Black plumes swirled out of the peak when Hephaestus worked, which was most of the time as he was not a deity prone to travel. The god used his powers to keep breezes constantly blowing to the north, which kept their village on the southern shore free of the eternal smoke.

Years ago, Prometheus had stolen fire from the forge to give to mortals, greatly improving their quality of life. As retribution against the Titan, Hephaestus selected ten men and ten women, the smartest and fairest of them all, to live on Lemnos under his protection. According to legend, Prometheus had railed against this unfairness, claiming the Olympian stole the best of his creations. Only when his brother, Epimetheus, convinced him the punishment could have been much worse did Prometheus finally relent. Over the years, the population of Lemnos had grown to a fair number of inhabitants, blessed with fair weather, ample food, and little misfortune.

"Yes, we must keep our heads down," Pandora agreed, "and forestall the inevitable as long as possible."

Both girls knew they would likely be wives within the next two years, though it was not a horrible fate. Hephaestus almost always married his women to men from the island. Rarely did a person have to leave the special place to live among the ordinary Greeks. Pandora and Cyane planned to have matching houses built next door to one another where they could continue their friendship. The idea of their children growing up to be friends warmed both their hearts. These thoughts brought solace to Pandora, as she yearned for a life where she could contribute something meaningful instead of simply obeying her husband's instructions. But such was the way of the world.

"Ladies." Madame Tullia's voice made the two girls jump. "It's time to pack up for the day."

The friends exchanged a quizzical glance. The sun, discernible through the slats in the pergola, was higher in the sky than when the teacher normally dismissed them. Confused faces rose from laps, followed by chatter. Madame Tullia held up her hands to silence the young ladies.

"Yes, it is earlier in the day, but all of Lemnos is to report to the amphitheater this afternoon for a special announcement from Zeus himself," the instructor said.

She whispered the last two words with a reverential awe; they hung in the air, thick with meaning. Pandora and Cyane clasped hands in excitement. Occasionally, Hephaestus would announce things to his people through his oracle, such as changes in offerings for a god or simple municipal decrees. Never had there been a proclamation from the King of the Gods. Pandora sometimes wondered if Zeus even remembered they lived on Lemnos where it lay hidden from Olympus in the heavy smoke of the forge.

Piling their embroidery into baskets, the friends hurried to leave with the rest of their animated classmates. The group made its way across a small atrium, Madame Tullia for once too flustered to admonish the girls for their lively babbles. Nerida trailed the students, her efforts to maintain a line in vain. The girls rambled in disorder, a flock of errant hens. In the main school building, Pandora stowed her basket in her cubby. With a small burlap lunch sack in hand, she met Cyane at the door and they headed out into the warm sun. A few girls pushed past them, eager to get home and learn if their parents knew more about this intriguing turn of events.

"What could Zeus possible have to tell us?" Pandora pondered, her curiosity piqued. "Do you think there is another war? Do you think they need a hero for a grand adventure? Do you think they need some resource only found on Lemnos?"

"Leave it to you to come up with a million possibilities," Cyane teased.

"Maybe he needs someone to embroider a dress for Hera, or someone to teach Madame Tullia to smile," Pandora quipped.

She tossed out a few more ideas, one more unlikely than the next. By the time they reached the fork in the path which led to their respective residences, the duo doubled over with laughter. They parted with a customary hug, one they enacted since their earliest school days.

"I'll see you at the amphitheater later and hopefully all questions will be answered to your satisfaction. Though that rarely happens with you," joked Cyane.

Pandora chuckled and waved, her heart grateful to have such a wonderful friend. On the short walk home, even more ideas danced around her mind. Whatever the news was, she could not wait to hear it.

FIVE

Hephaestus paced the floor, his forge spitting black fire up the shaft of the volcano, annoyed at the disruption of his sister and her news of the proclamation. Unlike his father and uncles, he did not enjoy meddling in the affairs of men, even the inhabitants of Lemnos, whose governing he left to the prefect and priests. Still, he had a protective affection for his people, doting on his special enclave, and did not appreciate interference from Olympus.

Athena waited while her brother digested the news, unbothered by the sweltering room, a cool aura of gray surrounding her. Deep in the bowels of the mountain, Hephaestus had set up his forge. An enormous blemish on the tranquil island, with its soft, white beaches and lush greenery. The goddess of wisdom always marveled at this juxtaposition of the island's beauty and blight, and its odd parallel to the marriage between Aphrodite and Hephaestus. Aphrodite, the picture of loveliness and Hephaestus with a deformed foot, inflicted by Zeus when he threw him off Mount Olympus as a baby.

"Are you sure this is a good decision?" he asked, hammer still in his hand, anxious to return to work.

"A good decision? I do not know. But Father has made it all the same." Athena stated.

Hephaestus shook his head. Frazzled at the unwanted distraction, he went to the anvil and swung his hammer high. When it pounded down on the sword, sparks flew into the air, dancing around him like a swarm of gnats. After a few more hits, he plunged the sword into a bucket of water, its contents sizzling with frenzy. One of his two golden handmaids poured cool water into the bucket until the bubbling abated.

Athena watched the girl's fluid movements, impressed with her brother's creation. Hephaestus had fashioned the maid and her sister automaton by molding pure gold into their forms and immortalizing them. They were elegance in motion, singular works of art. She preferred them to his Cyclopes, who trudged in and out of the workroom, their single eyes unnerving. How these ungainly creatures crafted such delicate jewelry and golden embellishments was beyond her. Still, their hands had helped shape the prized aegis of the gods, a shield with a hundred golden tassels. Athena loved how it roared with the sound of ten-thousand dragons when she raced into battle.

"He should have asked me before sending a message to my people," Hephaestus complained, the hammering doing little to relieve his anger.

"By all means, try to reason with him. You're lucky I brought the proclamation and not him or you would know nothing of it," the goddess of wisdom countered, patient with her brother's outburst.

Hephaestus rounded on his sister, hammer held out accusingly. "Why can't he use a mortal from elsewhere? He still blames me for the fire incident, doesn't he? So, he will take something I cherish."

Athena only shook her head at the memory of Prometheus' theft. "I think he blames us all for being easily tricked. Besides, whatever his reasoning, the plan is already in motion."

"To get to Prometheus by targeting Epimetheus." Athena saw his shoulders sag in acceptance with his statement. "I suppose is a wise plan. Did you have anything to do with it?"

"Yes, to go through his brother was my idea. Rewarding Epimetheus for his loyalty will surely cause vexation for Prometheus. Zeus insists on a coveted maiden to exact his revenge. You rarely send yours out into the world. Their existence remains shrouded in mystery and lore. It will be an honor for Epimetheus to be offered a maiden of Lemnos." Athena put a hand on her half-brother's arm.

"And wouldn't you enjoy imposing vengeance on Prometheus? The idea of us favoring Epimetheus over him will accomplish that."

The god of fire sighed. He limped to the other side of the forge, his maimed foot dragging slightly behind. Donning a pair of huge leather gloves, he pulled another red-hot sword from the flames and took it to the anvil. Athena watched a shower of sparkles fly down in illuminated raindrops. Pity filled her heart at the sight of her deformed brother, the only non-perfect deity of Olympus. He asked for little and never caused strife among the gods, instead enjoying his solitary life in the peace of his mountain forge. The world of Zeus' intrigue did not interest him. His heart was too kind. Guilt twinged in her at the thought of this plan causing him pain.

"You are to have the final say in the selection," she consoled. "It is ultimately your choice to make."

The god stopped mid-stroke and turned to Athena. "What do I know of such matters? I am no judge of what maiden would satisfy Father. In fact, of all the gods, I am the least qualified to make such a selection. Isn't stealing one of my humans enough? Don't make me choose which one."

Regret filled Athena. The people of Lemnos not only revered Hephaestus, but genuinely loved him and he returned that affection. In addition to his benevolent rule, the god was a patron of the arts. Every citizen afforded the opportunity to learn a craft. Beautiful sculptures, paintings, and metalwork graced every corner of the island. The god truly did his best to foster a society based on creativity and kindness. When Zeus suggested one of his maidens, Athena, knowing their value, immediately agreed. Now, the defeated expression in her brother's eyes made her heart heavy.

"I can observe your maidens if you let me. I will select the one who is best suited for the task," she offered. It was the least she could do.

"Yes, Sister," he said with pleading eyes, "please do me this favor."

She nodded her assent, and he bowed his head in thanks. The two golden handmaidens glided to the forge, casting more iron into the melting pot. Thick smoke rose between Hephaestus and Athena. When it cleared, she was gone. Hephaestus threw himself back into his work, black smoke pouring from the forge as hot and thick as his resentment.

SIX

The amphitheater burst with spectators, the air abuzz with anticipation. Pandora and Cyane squeezed into a row alongside their fellow students. Each had taken the time at home to don a dressier chiton. A few sported elegant hairdos and makeup. They clustered in the front few rows of one section, specifically designated for maidens—an unusual occurrence as on most occasions, they sat with their parents. The girls whispered with fervor to each other behind their hands, trying but failing to appear dignified, while they speculated on what was to come. Madame Tullia, who sat at the end of one row, shot them her '*Stop acting like a bunch of petty gossipers*' glare.

Women comprised most of the other seats, many with babes clinging to their hips. Small children clambered about them, their energy amplified in the crowded theater. Men spread out along the curve of the walls. Work gloves and other implements dangled from their hands, most coming directly from the vineyard or the shop. On stage, the high priest sat with the island's prefect, each dressed in full splendor. They exchanged private comments, both chests puffed out with pride. Several of the island's most noble inhabitants came forward to greet them.

Pandora noticed a dark spot against the clear blue sky. It drifted and wheeled, becoming ever larger until it landed on the pinnacle of the amphitheater walls.

"Look!" She grabbed Cyane's arm and pointed. "An owl. Strange for one to be out during the day. It must be a sign from the gods. But a good omen or a bad one, I wonder?"

"Maybe it's merely as curious a creature as you," her friend teased. "Or maybe it's Athena herself in disguise."

Pandora knew how the wise goddess sometimes took the form of an owl, but before she could say anything more, the high priest rose. He strode to the front of the stage and raised his arms for silence, the multicolored sleeves of his robe fluttering around him. The buzz of the crowd dissipated, only the cry of an infant piercing the air. The priest savored the moment of expectancy, the sun glinting off the golden thread in his cap. Pandora leaned forward, not wanting to miss a word.

"My fellow citizens, the oracle has received a message from Zeus, greatest of all gods."

A murmur of excitement rippled through the crowd. Bastian gestured to a veiled priestess behind him—the oracle. She spent most of her life in a deep fissure in the mountain where she inhaled a sulfuric steam that emanated from deep within the earth. Through the entranced state this smoke induced, she received messages from the gods or visions of the future. The priests depicted her fate as one most fortunate in the eyes of the gods. Yet seeing her in person, her frail figure supported by two attendants, Pandora was thankful they did not grant her such a blessing.

The high priest held up an arm and the crowd fell silent. He joined his hands together in front of him, eyes skimming over the crowd. Satisfied he was the center of attention once more, he announced, "One of the unmarried maidens of Lemnos is to be chosen for a special task. A task that will bring fame to her name for all eternity, as deemed by Zeus himself."

All the girls in Pandora's section gaped at one another, wondering which of them would receive this honor. Hair was smoothed, shoulders were straightened, while they waited in rapt attention. As excitement filled the air, Pandora's stomach churned with unease, suspecting the gods' generosity may come at a cost. Cyane grasped her friend's hand and gave it a tight squeeze. At her radiant expression, Pandora could not help but smile back, despite her misgivings.

"Over the next few weeks, we will question and observe all eligible maidens and determine our selection. Thank you for taking time out of your schedule for this afternoon. May the gods be blessed." Finished, Bastian turned his back to the crowd and shuffled off the stage in the oracle's wake.

His abrupt ending confused the audience for a moment before voices erupted all around. The young ladies near Pandora squealed and shrieked at each other. She could not hear whatever Cyane tried to say to her over the tizzy. They funneled out of their rows en masse into the heaving tide of bodies leaving the amphitheater. Danae found her daughter, and with hands on Pandora's shoulders, guided her outside to the road. They walked together, animated groups scattering past, until the crown thinned enough to give them breathing room. Still, Pandora said nothing.

"Why so quiet, Pandora? What did you think of the announcement?" her mother asked, surprised a river full of questions had not flowed from the girl's mouth already.

"It's exciting, I guess."

"You guess?" Danae retorted, wondering what had become of her curious child.

The girl walked, her eyes glued to the stones on the path. She tugged at the shoulder of her dressy chiton, which hung looser than her everyday one, a soft breeze caressing her face. The sense of disquiet at the high priest's words had not dispelled. Her mother remained silent at her side, their steps in time with one another.

"Has anything like this ever happened before on Lemnos?" she asked her mother.

"No." Danae sounded surprised at the question. "Not to my knowledge. But the gods are unpredictable, aren't they?"

Pandora stopped in her tracks, all the worry erupting from her. "But why now? What exactly is the maiden being selected for? Why were they not specific? What if it's some sort of trick? What if you're selected but don't want to go?"

Danae laughed. "There is my inquisitive daughter. I knew there must be a million questions in your head."

Her smile faded when she saw the concern in Pandora's eyes. Cupping the girl's chin in her hand, she said, "Do not worry. Hephaestus watches over us. No harm will come to anyone. Trust in the gods."

Pandora nodded, but could not shake the uneasiness that accompanied the announcement. Sensing her daughter's mood, Danae put an arm around Pandora's shoulder, who nestled her head close. Her mother's kiss brushed the top of her head while they walked along the path toward home in the warm afternoon sun. Neither noticed the owl sitting in a nearby olive tree, whose wise, gray eyes took in the entire conversation.

SEVEN

Epimetheus stroked the mane of the skittish horse in front of him. Having created animals, his touch calmed any beast, his spirit inherent in their instincts. Several more horses scattered amid the enclosure, which ran up to the stable, sizable but modest. It was the largest edifice on the flat crest near the top of a mountain. Epimetheus' hut sat at the far end, the fired clay roof bricks sagging on one side. Between the two buildings, chicken coops dotted the meadow where goats and sheep grazed.

With gentle hands, Epimetheus examined a stone wedged in the front left hoof of the wary horse. He popped the culprit out using a small knife and tossed it aside. Pulling an apple from his sack, he rewarded the animal, who chomped it up in two bites. After the treat, the steed nudged Epimetheus with its head and galloped across the paddock to join its comrades.

"Nice work."

Epimetheus, sure he was alone, startled at the voice, out of place on his solitary property. On the fence rail sat a sprightly figure, a young man with an almost feminine litheness. He wore the garb of a peasant, a floppy-brimmed hat hiding most of his face except for a knowing smirk. Though in the clothes of a worker, his smooth hands and pale skin belied such an occupation.

"Oh, it's you," mumbled Epimetheus, not fooled by the disguise. He put the knife back in the burlap sack of tools slung over his shoulder.

"Surely, I merit more of a gracious greeting than that?" The guest asked with mock indignation.

"What do you want, Hermes?" Epimetheus shook his head in annoyance. The messenger god never visited without a purpose, usually a mischievous one.

Hermes hopped down from the fence and tossed aside his hat and cloak. As a Titan, Epimetheus would not perish if the god took his immortal form, but Hermes preferred the simplicity of this human veneer, where much less effort was required. Besides, the horses may not fare as well if he chose his divine appearance and that would put Epimetheus in a fouler mood, the opposite of what he needed.

"Perhaps I love to watch you with your creations. You did such a good job inventing all the different animals. Maybe I came to admire your work," he drawled, gesturing to the herd meandering the paddock.

The mended horse returned to nuzzle Epimetheus, who absently pet its nose, never taking his eyes from the god. "I think we both would find that hard to believe."

"Always so dour," Hermes cackled. He reached to pet the horse. Not knowing what to make of the god, the animal backed up before running away.

"You should go see my brother. Whatever you want, I assure you, Prometheus is far better suited for the task."

Epimetheus lived on this remote hilltop for a reason—to stay out of the affairs of gods and men. His animals were all the company he needed. Unlike his brother, he did not crave any recognition from the gods, even if they thought him foolish, as Prometheus always suggested. Epimetheus saw no point in trying to get the better of the Olympians. A quiet existence was all he desired, days filled with hard work and little drama.

"Ah, but Zeus is somewhat irritated with our Prometheus at the moment. Surely, your brother mentioned that?" Hermes stated, conjuring a bunch of grapes. He popped one in his mouth and juice ran from his lips.

"Yes, he told me," Epimetheus replied. "And I warned him about playing tricks in the past. Why he continues to instigate Zeus is beyond me, but if you think I can reason with him, you are going to be disappointed."

"Yes, his antics are troublesome," the god sighed, ready to set the bait. "Which is why Zeus wishes to reward you."

"Reward me?" Epimetheus found it hard to hide his incredulity. "Since when does the King of the Gods dole out rewards for nothing?"

Hermes knew the remedy for conquering skepticism varied by whom he dealt with. He knew the right buttons to push, the most flattering phrases to utter. It was why he always delivered this type of news, after all. No one could resist the urgings of the divine trickster, a fitting epithet. It was almost unfair, but that was not for him to judge. Hermes needed to convince Epimetheus of the good fortune about to befall him. He knew he could not find a more gullible mark than this senseless Titan.

"Oh, but how can you say nothing, my dear Epimetheus? You helped the Olympians in our war against your fellow Titans, did you not? Such a display of loyalty is not forgotten. And you haven't done a thing to arouse the anger of the gods, nor do you seek the spotlight as your brother does. That is far from nothing, wouldn't you agree?"

Epimetheus scrutinized the god, who leaned against the fence in his unassuming disguise. Hermes twirled his hand and in place of the grapes, an apple appeared. The god leaped over the fence onto the soft grass in the paddock and tried to tempt one of the distrustful horses, who shied away. Prometheus' warning about the gods rang in his brother's head. However, the messenger god made valid points. Unlike his sibling, Epimetheus had kept out of trouble. If the gods punished Prometheus for his bad behavior, it may follow they would recognize his obedience. He always assumed the gods overlooked him, but perhaps they appreciated his fidelity.

"What is this reward offered so freely?" he asked, curiosity getting the better of him.

"So untrusting, Epimetheus. It hurts my feelings." With a dramatic flourish, Hermes placed a hand on his heart. When the Titan merely stared, he continued, "Look at this magnificent home you created. The grand manor, the manicured gardens, the well-built stables, and the burgeoning fields. Anything you could ever want for, but for one thing."

Epimetheus gazed at his humble estate, confused by the line of conversation. "And what would that be?"

"A wife, of course."

"A wife?" the Titan spluttered. "What on earth would I want with a wife?"

Hermes ambled over to him and through the slats in the fence, put a hand on Epimetheus' arm. "Companionship, support, dare I say … love? Are you not lonely here?"

The crease between the Titan's brow furrowed. He had never considered any of this. Prometheus was the only one who visited him, otherwise, he spent all his time alone.

"Perhaps it would be nice to have the company of another. Someone to help you watch over all the animals," Hermes continued. "And have you not earned a reward for not angering the gods as your brother does?"

Epimetheus could see the reasoning behind this argument. For a moment, the memory of his brother's warning battled with the words of the messenger god. Though he had never thought of it, perhaps a wife would add something to his life.

"And it would be no ordinary woman," Hermes whispered, as though confiding a deep secret, "Hephaestus has offered one of his favored mortals to be the bride."

The Titan, flattered at the generous offer, tried to think of an evil motive from Zeus. He weighed the idea from a few angles, but could find no gain for the gods in the proposal. Prometheus' voice rang in his head. *Do not trust the Olympians*. But as Hermes pointed out, Epimetheus had done nothing to incur their wrath.

"Maybe you are right," Epimetheus surmised, pleased at the deliberation he put into the proposition. No one could accuse him of rashness. "And Hephaestus' people are as near to perfection as humans come."

"Exactly," Hermes agreed, mischief flashing in his eyes at the ease of accomplishing his task. "Do you accept this most generous gift from the almighty Zeus?"

"Yes," he declared, a sense of certainty and entitlement welling in his heart.

"Excellent. I shall let him know." The god smiled, knowing his enchanted words hit the mark.

The horse nudged Epimetheus, who searched his sack for another apple. When he turned back to ask for further details, Hermes was gone.

High on Mount Olympus, Zeus sat on his throne, drumming his fingers on the armrest. Hermes flitted down on winged shoes in front of him.

"Well?" the King of the Gods demanded.

"It is done."

A broad smile filled Zeus' face and his thunderous laughter pealed across the sky.

EIGHT

"Girls, please try to settle down," Madame Tullia implored.

The instructor shook her head at the commotion in front of her. Ever since the announcement two days ago, focus eluded her students, making them all but impossible to teach. With her hands on her hips, she stared at them, romping about the field as spirited as a herd of sheep. Instead of helping to burn off some of their rampant energy, her idea to let them out here only induced a further supply of vigor. *Such is that age*, she thought with resignation. Someone approached from the building. Madame Tullia shaded her eyes and was pleased to see Nerida. Perhaps she could help round up the students.

With her typical straight-backed posture, the assistant marched up to her cohort and thrust a missive at her. "Here."

"Who is this from?" the instructor asked, taking the thick parchment envelope in hand.

"The high priest. New information about the observation process he mentioned at the announcement." Nerida tried to keep her voice low, but a nearby student somehow caught the words despite the surrounding cacophony.

"Madame Tullia has a message about Zeus' proclamation," the girl screeched and her peers shrieked louder than the two women thought possible.

Her assistant cast an apologetic expression at her colleague. Madame Tullia pinched the bridge of her nose, all hope of a productive afternoon dispelled. She imagined what the high priest would think if he saw the chaotic behavior of these chosen maidens and her resolve steeled.

With her hands held high, she let out an uncharacteristic bellow, "Ladies!"

Silence fell, the students shocked by the outburst of their stoic teacher.

"Let us go inside calmly and take our seats. Once I have your attention, I will read the letter, but if you continue in such an immature manner, I will tell High Priest Bastian none of you are suitable for this venture."

The abashed group hurried toward the building, Nerida shepherding them along, with only quiet murmurs among them. Madame Tullia brought up the rear. When the last of her charges scurried inside, she joined them with missive in hand.

"Now that you are all finally paying attention, I will read the letter."

Since the scroll had arrived from the chief priest, Madame Tullia and Nerida had spent the last quarter of an hour attempting to quiet the girls. The moment they thought the mission achieved, one girl would whisper something, setting off a chain reaction of chatter. When Madame Tullia, in a rare display of anger, threatened them all with expulsion, the girls sat, hands folded in front of them, in deflated silence. The instructor unrolled the parchment and cleared her throat for the full effect.

"It says 'The oracle spoke words yesterday, a direct communication from the almighty Zeus, King of all Gods.'" She paused at the gravity of Bastian's words. A soft breeze filtered through the open window slats, wafting a small white cloud of dandelion seeds around the expectant audience. "'Let the maidens of Lemnos be told the news. Zeus seeks one of you, a special one, for the honor of becoming a Titan's wife. You will live out your days in luxury, your name remembered for all time. Observers from the temple will come to judge each of your abilities at school through a series of tests. Moreover, each eligible girl is to write an essay on why we should select her for this esteemed distinction. The god will choose based on all the collected information.'"

A moment of stunned silence filled the room before chaos erupted. Madame Tullia shook her head, discouraged by the emergence of further commotion, one that even the soft-spoken Nerida now joined in on. With a heavy sigh, she rolled up the scroll. She sank down at her desk, thankful that no temple observers were present, for surely, they would find none of her charges an appropriate choice in this state of disarray.

"Can you believe it?" Cyane exclaimed, grabbing Pandora's arm. "What an amazing honor."

"Yes, quite an honor." Pandora smiled back at her friend, though she did not share the same enthusiasm. Unease filled her yet again, questions piling up in her mind.

Nerida calmed herself and took her seat next to Madame Tullia. They sat back and waited for the tidal wave of noise to subside. Years of teaching had taught the instructor when attention was irretrievable. The unruliness would settle eventually, like silt in the bottom of a turned-up puddle, and then there would be questions. After a while, the chattering dissipated and Pandora raised her hand.

"Yes?" the instructor asked, happy to have her patience rewarded and not surprised from whom the first inquiry came.

"Does it say when the temple observers will be here?" Pandora asked the least important question of the jumble in her head.

"No. But you are all quite lucky they were not here to see the display of childish behavior. If any of you take this matter seriously, you will come to school tomorrow ready to impress rather than distress any temple personnel." The girls' cheeks reddened, and Madame Tullia smiled inside, knowing her words hit the mark. "Now, let us get back to work."

Over the next two days, three priests from the Temple of Zeus visited the classroom. One observed the girls performing embroidery, weaving, and drawing. He was a stout man with a belly that suggested he did not miss many meals. His eyes, though slightly bulging, were kind, and he was quick to compliment any talent he detected before noting it down on a list. Though Pandora was not the best in her class at these skills, she outshone most of the others.

The second man, with a wiry frame and a shock of gray hair, tested each girl on mathematics, science, and languages. Where his colleague was full of encouragement, the older priest lacked any sign of praise, his bony hand scratching harsh strokes on a piece of parchment. Some girls left his presence with unshed tears brimming in their eyes. Pandora, not cowed by his severity, answered each question with pride and confidence. These areas were her strong suit, and it showed.

The third man had hair so blond and eyes so pale, they blended into his skin, leaving his head a large white blob with a pink slash of pursed lips. He stood at the front of the room and watched, never uttering a word. Pandora found his penetrating stare unnerving whenever his gaze fell on her. At the end of the second day, Madame Tullia ordered the girls to their seats and ceded the floor to him.

"Now, we will discuss the most important aspect of this process, the essay," he said, in a high-pitched voice that Pandora never would have placed with his face. "You will write a list of reasons you think you are the right maiden for this honor. You will sign your name and seal this essay in an envelope with your name written on the outside. Bring them here in the morning and I will take them and pass them along to the high priest, who will leave them for the almighty Zeus."

Pandora, fascinated by the way his red mouth punctuated his pallidness behind crooked but equally white teeth, barely heard what he said. The maidens held their excitement in check until dismissal, when they clustered together outside the academy to exchange ideas. Pandora listened to their exhilarated notions, relieved this ordeal was nearly over and life would return to normal.

NINE

Cyane repeated the words of the third priest over and over on the walk home. Sensing the significance of the essay, she ran through a list of ideas about what to write, but dismissed each one as unoriginal. Pandora concentrated on the familiar crunch of the stones beneath their feet. Why would anyone desire to be shipped off as a bride based on such mundane requirements? Why would any groom, Titan or otherwise, require such a list? She had no desire to enter this type of arrangement. Yet clearly, Cyane yearned to be selected as much as the other eligible girls. At sixteen, marriage was not only inevitable, but loomed closer every day—whether it involved a Titan or not.

"The essay is important," her friend declared, hand tightening around Pandora's arm. "It has to be different enough to stand out, don't you think?"

Wispy gray clouds blotted out the sun, the smell of rain in the air. Up ahead, a group of classmates huddled, their excited squeals echoing back. Pandora wished she could conjure their enthusiasm, but her heart remained as muted as the sun's hidden rays. She could not embrace the idea of being auctioned off as though she was chattel, moreover consider it an honor.

"I suppose," Pandora answered, but at Cyane's pleading eyes added, "You are a gifted embroiderer, weaver, and the best lute player in the class. And smart. Also, you are from one of the noblest and wealthiest families on Lemnos. Surely, there could be no better pick than you."

"Thank you, Pandora, but we both know that you excelled at all the tests too. We have an equal chance of being selected. Can you imagine? The wife of a Titan." Cyane's sky-blue eyes grew misty at the thought.

Better you than me, Pandora thought before adding aloud, "I hope I can visit you wherever you go."

"Oh, I will make sure of it," her friend vowed. "My dearest friend will always be welcome in my home."

"I wonder if it's Prometheus or Epimetheus?" Pandora remarked.

"Prometheus is said to be extremely handsome," Cyane said. "I don't recall much mention of the brother."

Nor did Pandora, except for the tale that Prometheus was the wiser of the two. Epimetheus' foolhardy reputation preceded him.

"Think how famous you will be. Prometheus is nearly as revered as the gods. There will be statues and portraits of you adorning every wall in Greece," Pandora said.

"Do you really think I have a chance?" Cyane asked.

"You are beautiful and dutiful, the perfect qualities for a wife. Either Titan would be lucky to have you," Pandora assured.

The girls reached their parting spot on the path, neither noticing the owl who watched them from above. After a hug, they turned in different directions toward home. At first, Pandora thought of how disappointed Cyane would be if she were not the selected maiden. Pandora would need to comfort her friend from the blow. Yet, of all the maidens, Cyane was the prettiest and the richest. It made sense for her to be chosen, if these were the merits Zeus sought. But what if he wanted something else? Pandora was by far the smartest and most educated among them. What if that swayed things in her favor? A pit of dread pooled in her stomach at the notion. She had no desire to win this contest, and the only way left to ensure she would not was the essay. What had Cyane said? *Different enough to stand out.* Pandora agreed, but not in the way her friend meant.

Danae and Lycus knew of the testing at school and of the essay assignment. Parents of all the maidens had strict instructions to let the girls perform the tasks on their own, with no guidance or counsel. Pandora had little to add about the essay when she returned from school.

"Do your best," Lycus had told Pandora, unbothered by the entire affair. She spent her afternoon curled in a chair in the yard with her cat, Rex. Her mother had watched Pandora carefully, worried about her daughter's lack of questions.

"How did the testing go?" Danae asked at dinner.

"It went well enough," Pandora muttered. "All the maidens have the same skills, after all."

"I suppose that is what makes the essay so critical," her mother ventured.

Pandora only nodded her head. Her father soon spoke about a broken olive press and a missing replacement part. While he discussed it, Danae kept her eye on the way Pandora only moved her food around with her fork. Lycus remained oblivious to his daughter's sullen mood.

"Do you want to talk about the essay?" asked Elara, her beloved maid since birth, with a conspiratorial wink.

The heavyset woman brushed out Pandora's hair after a bath. Elara wiped an unruly gray tress of her own off her cheek. Of all the home's residents, the girl confided in Elara the most. From the location of hidden childhood contraband to the names of her teenage crushes, the maid faithfully kept all her charge's secrets.

"No," Pandora replied, her eyes downcast. "Though I do think it's a silly way to pick a wife for someone."

"Yes, I suppose it is." Elara stopped mid-stroke, her eyes becoming solemn. "But that is the way of the gods and we must obey."

When Pandora's eyes filled with uncertainty, the maid hugged her shoulders tightly. "Don't worry. Pray to the gods and lay your worries at their feet."

Their eyes met in the mirror, Elara's crinkled in consolation and Pandora's aswirl with doubt. The maid helped Pandora into her nightgown with no more mention of the assignment. With a gentle kiss on the girl's forehead, Elara took her leave.

Alone at her desk, Pandora stared at a blank sheet of parchment in front of her. A soft wind billowed her curtains out like air-filled sails and crickets chirped in the darkness. She shut her eyes to enjoy the moment of tranquility. Reality set back in. How could she write the essay to guarantee she would not be chosen? The thought had plagued her since parting with Cyane.

Her mother drifted into the room and sat on the edge of the bed. Rex, who lounged across it, stretched out his paw and yawned. All tan with black-tipped ears, nose and tail, Pandora found him quite regal when her father brought him back from a trip east, thus earning his kingly name. He had been small enough to fit in the pocket of Lycus' cloak and had been but a stunning pair of blue eyes in a tiny ball of fur when she first held him.

Danae tried to stroke his head, but finnicky, the cat moved it out of reach. The contest worried her. Its mention stirring up the terrible memories of dread from that day long ago. She wavered over whether to finally share it with Pandora, but decided the girl had enough on her mind. Still, Danae sensed something was amiss with Pandora, but could not put her finger on it.

"Having trouble with the essay?" she asked.

"I'm not sure what to write. Honestly, I have more questions about the matter than I have to say about myself," Pandora admitted, coming to sit next to her mother.

"I would expect nothing less," Danae chuckled. "If this Titan only knew all the questions he would face in a lifetime with you, it would likely scare him off."

The two shared a laugh, and Danae put her arm around Pandora's shoulders. She kissed her daughter on the top of her head, as she always did when her child needed comfort. Pandora relaxed against her mother's side, content with her life and not wanting anything to change. For a few moments, they listened to the cricket serenade until her mother rose.

"There is no pressure on you to win this, Pandora. Your father and I only want you to be happy. I know it must be hard to be pitted against your friends. The outcome will disappoint more than a few. It will be over soon and the entire event will be behind us. I know you want to excel at everything, but try not to worry if you aren't chosen." Danae assured.

"Thank you, Mother," Pandora said, not correcting her mother's assumptions. "I will figure out something meaningful to write."

Danae kissed her daughter's cheek. At the door, she turned and said, "The best advice I can give you is to write what's in your heart."

When the door shut softly behind her, a cryptic smile played across Pandora's face. Her mother's words gave her an idea. She dipped her quill in the inkwell and wrote.

TEN

Athena paced the hilltop, where the bright sunshine glinted off a pristine meadow. A few sheep dotted the green grass as white as fluffy clouds. Far across the field, the satyr, Pan, lolled under a tree, his goat legs neatly tucked beneath him, keeping an eye on his charges. Soft music floated across the air from the flute at his lips. Hermes enjoyed meeting his sister here, as it gave him a chance to see Pan, one of his favored sons. A rustle of air brushed Athena's cheek and the messenger god came to rest beside her on his winged shoes.

"Here they are." He flourished a pile of envelopes held fast by a blue ribbon in front of her face.

Athena took the bundle and untied them. She thumbed across the edges of each letter, some thin, some thick, each holding the hope of a mortal for an honor from the gods. Did none of them realize the selected girl would be nothing but a pawn? She suspected not. Lemnos was far removed from the usual scheming of Olympus in deference to Hephaestus, who doted on his people. Still, a marriage with Epimetheus was an honor, even if the reason was more to upset his brother than reward a particular girl.

"Why do we need the letters?" Hermes asked, leaning on his staff of entwined snakes. "We can watch mortals ourselves. Shouldn't that be enough to decide?"

"We can watch them, but people sometimes reveal more in writing than they show to others. Besides," she added, "if we simply chose one, the others would clamor for ways to prove their selection would be better. This gives them a sense of involvement, as though they have a say in the outcome."

"Well, they are all merely trifles in my eyes. I would throw those envelopes in the air and pick one at random, but I suppose you are the wise one."

"And I suppose that is the reason Father asked me to choose the girl and not you," Athena retorted.

Hermes opened his mouth to speak, but stopped himself, a wicked glint flashing across his mesmeric blue eyes. Athena took note. Her brother knew something more about this matter, for good or evil. Before she could ask, the wings on his shoes fluttered, and he rose skyward. He circled his sister from above, tapping her head with his staff. She swatted up at him, though he remained slightly out of reach.

"I'm going to say hello to my son. Good luck to you with your dreadfully boring assignment." He darted across the meadow, landing at Pan's feet.

Athena had to clutch the envelopes against her chest to keep them from scattering in the ensuing breeze. She sat on a nearby boulder to read them. Fifty girls sent letters for consideration. Zeus left it to her to select the maiden for Epimetheus. The King of the Gods' instructions were clear—make her attractive, but compliant and dutiful, so she would give no trouble. Though it had been her idea to get revenge on Prometheus through his brother, Zeus could only extract such pleasure by finding the most enviable maiden. Athena sighed at her father's unfathomable ability to hold grudges.

Each envelope bore the writer's name on the front in fonts ranging from swooping to constricted. Athena, who spent the last few days observing the maidens in her owl form, eliminated almost half without opening them. *Definitely not up to the task*, she thought, tossing those envelopes to the side. Zeus wanted compliant not frivolous. She opened the first letter, written with the most practiced script.

To the most auspicious gods and goddesses,

I am humbled by the opportunity to vie for such an immense distinction. My father, Cosmos, is the wealthiest banker on Lemnos. We trace our family roots to the original selection of Hephaestus. I am highly educated in both domestic affairs and the arts. I am an expert weaver and lute player. My keen grasp on politics and household management makes me an optimal candidate for a Titan's wife. I am both beautiful and dutiful. I can think of no greater honor than to humbly serve in such a prominent role.

Thank you for your consideration,
Lysandra, daughter of Cosmos

The goddess placed the paper down, a shake of her head at the haughty tone. Four nearly identical letters later, Athena rubbed her temples. At this rate, she might as well toss the letters in the air and randomly pick one, as Hermes suggested. These mundane mortals wrote such cliched phrases she could scream. Across the meadow, Hermes hovered above Pan, who proudly showed off a few of his prized sheep. The god would take the finest one as a sacrifice. Athena noted the similarity to her current undertaking. She would change life's course for whomever she selected. With a determined resolve, she read on. Several banal letters later, she opened another. The crisp clean penmanship impressed her, but it was the words that caught her attention.

To the selectors,

I am supposed to write why the gods should choose me for their magnanimous offer, but after some thought, I wonder why I should accept any such offer? Who is the Titan in question? Why does he deserve a wife delivered from the gods? Why can he not choose for himself? Where would I have to go? Why would I desire to leave my family? What other strings are attached? Perhaps this is

*all a test by the gods to measure our loyalty. I can tell you
with a clear conscience that I have been devoted in my
worship to all the gods. I have performed all the necessary
rituals and tributes. At this time, it is not my wish to be
married and leave Lemnos. There are many other maidens
far more worthy of this proposition than I.*

With greatest respect,
Pandora, daughter of Lycus

Shocked by the impertinence, Athena laughed aloud.
Having spied on this maiden a few times, she already
marked Pandora as headstrong and precocious. That the
girl would be this blunt intrigued the goddess. Athena
smiled to herself at the thought and laid the letter aside.
Her diligence demanded she read the remaining letters. She
found one more monotonous than the next, a never-ending
list of credentials. The last letter read, she tossed it on the
pile, happy to be done with them. How could most of these
girls behave with no more agency than the sheep in this
meadow, docile and unquestioning? Pandora stood out
among them for better or worse. By the mischief in her
brother's eyes before, Athena knew Zeus had something
more planned. This girl may make things somewhat
difficult for him and Athena would love to watch that
unfold.

"Find one?" Hermes burst down from the clouds above,
landing in the soft grass.

"I believe I have." Athena tucked Pandora's letter under
her breastplate. With a point of her finger, the pile of
unchosen letters dissolved into nothing.

"And will Zeus be pleased with your choice?" he
inquired. He rested his back against a boulder, tossing an
apple in the air.

"He trusted my judgment on this," the goddess of
wisdom stated, "and it was not a hard task. Most maidens
long for the honor of such a prestigious marriage."

"True. Mortals are easily pleased. I'm sure the matter will go as Father plans." Hermes glanced up at her, a conjured cup of nectar in hand, still not telling his secret.

"I'm sure they will," Athena agreed, turning to hide her sly smile.

ELEVEN

"And you *agreed* to it?" Prometheus bellowed. His voice echoed across the hilltop, startling birds in the nearby trees, who flew off in a dotted clump. In the paddock, the few brave horses who stood by their master ran to the other side, panic in their eyes. Epimetheus shut his eyes, annoyance taking hold at his brother's ravings.

"Yes," Epimetheus stated calmly, hoping Prometheus may simmer down.

He wished he could join his horses where they stood against the far fence, nervous tails swishing. Though he did not turn around, he knew his goats would have raced up the steep incline behind the house, all the way to the craggy summit. Not a sound emanated from the chicken coop, the inhabitants all taking cover inside the henhouse. Loud at the best of times, Prometheus always put the homestead on edge, but his fury induced concealment.

A bright sun shone over the mountaintop. Puffy clouds drifted casually across the azure sky. Mild weather graced Epimetheus' estate year-round, which he enjoyed almost as much as his privacy. He rarely ventured off the property, content with what he had. Unlike his brother, who now paced behind him, with angry steps shaking the ground. Prometheus basked in the adulation of humans, never missing an opportunity to draw notice to himself. Epimetheus willed his horses to relax, but they wisely remained on the other side of the paddock.

"I can't believe you would accept a gift from the gods," Prometheus shouted, color high in his cheeks. "After I warned you *not* to."

"Brother, they are not upset with me. In fact," he added with a hint of pride, "they see it as a reward for my respect for them.”

Prometheus kicked a pile of chopped wood. Pieces of timber scattered in all directions with explosive force. Across the enclosure, the horses stomped, several emitting nervous whinnies. Epimetheus worried they would hop the fence and run up the hill with the goats. Truthfully, at the moment, he would consider joining them.

“You fool! They are using you.”

“Please calm down, you’re scaring my animals,” Epimetheus implored.

“You and your blasted animals. The perfect example of your impulsive stupidity.”

Epimetheus bristled at the comment, though unsurprised his brother again threw the incident in his face. His creation of the earth’s creatures was a source of many arguments between the siblings over the years. Prometheus never once admire the amount of thought he had put into each and every animal. Instead, he branded Epimetheus as foolhardy.

Did he not appreciate the graceful curve of a swan’s neck? Or the majesty of a lion’s mane? Could he not marvel at the speed of a gazelle? Or the resplendent plumage of a peacock? Even the goddess Artemis had praised his efforts once, yet his brother continued to mock him. Heat rose through his body and he fought to calm himself. The last thing his animals needed was two screaming Titans.

“Remember how you left me with nothing to work with?” Prometheus goaded. “How I had to cover for your poorly thought-out decisions? It was only due to my quick wit and ingenuity that I was able to make something worthy of the gods. If I had not thought of language and the civilized arts, what would have been left for man?”

Epimetheus knew he sometimes made rash choices, while Prometheus used deliberation and wisdom in all matters. The gods always commended Prometheus on his cleverness, while treating Epimetheus as though he was a useless second son. Until now …

"It's not my fault you angered the gods by stealing fire," Epimetheus pointed out, irritation lacing his words. "And instead of leaving it at that, you pulled the stunt with the sacrifice of meat."

Somehow, they never dwelled on Prometheus' mistakes despite the wrath it brought down on both of them. Naturally, Epimetheus sided with his brother during these blunders with the Olympians, which could have left him on the wrong end of a horrible punishment. His support had been out of familial respect, but if he was to receive none back, why should he bother?

"The gods now appreciate my honor and respect and they wish to reward me. I'm sorry if that makes you jealous," the younger Titan declared.

"Jealous?" Prometheus spat out. "You're an even bigger fool than I thought."

Anger clouded Epimetheus' sight, a blurring rage filling him. He grasped the rail of the paddock with such force it splintered, slivers of wood hurtling through the air. The panicked horses jumped the fence and raced farther across the hilltop, but their master did not notice. Prometheus fancied himself the savvier one, saw Epimetheus' simple life as a sign of a simple mind. Maybe he was right, but the gods may value these unpretentious ways. He rounded on his stunned brother, who rarely saw his sibling show any emotion.

"It's hard for you, isn't it? To believe they may favor *me* now?" He could barely keep his voice in check.

Prometheus, mollified, inhaled deeply. He walked to stand in front of Epimetheus and grasped his shoulders. "Brother, I beg you, turn this offer down. Any offer from the gods comes with strings attached. It is a trick."

"If the gift of a wife and companion is a trick, why did they not offer it to you?" Epimetheus asked.

Granted, Prometheus had a relationship with the water nymph Hesione, but that would not preclude him from this offer of the gods. Epimetheus pushed his brother's hands away and bent to pick up the broken wood. The repair to the fence would be easier than convincing the animals to come back. The horses were out of sight, and it was his fault. Cursing his outburst, he rose to face Prometheus, who regarded him with pity.

"Because they know I would expect treachery. Don't you see? That is the only explanation," Prometheus replied.

Epimetheus' fury turned to resolve. He would show his brother that he merited this reward, that it was not a foolhardy decision, that for once, the gods chose him over Prometheus. In a steely voice, he said, "The gods have made me a generous offer and I do not intend to turn them down."

Turning his back on his brother, he walked along the paddock rail in the direction the horses fled without a glance back. Prometheus, who had never before failed to make his brother see reason, watched him stalk away, knowing his misgivings were correct. Now, he needed to be extra vigilant until he understood the Olympians' end game. Epimetheus' hulking figure disappeared behind the barn. Perhaps Prometheus should have tried a less angry approach, but by the tone of Epimetheus' last remark, he knew his sibling's decision was unequivocal. All he could do for the time being was let things play out.

"So be it," Prometheus whispered to himself and left the hilltop.

TWELVE

"I hardly slept last night. I was so excited," Cyane exclaimed.

She and Pandora walked hand in hand behind their parents toward the amphitheater, their steps in unison. Today, another achingly perfect day on Lemnos, the high priest would announce the gods' selection for the Titan's bride. All around the duo, other families walked, the parents ahead in one orderly group, followed by a disarray of girls. Where the adult heads bent together in soft conversation, the overwrought girls clucked like anxious hens. Pandora noted the anticipation in each maiden's eyes at the prospect of being the chosen one.

Cyane wore a chiton of luxurious blue silk which flowed in a waterfall down her body. With her dark hair wound into a crown of braids atop her head, she rivaled the beauty of any goddess. Pandora never saw her friend appear more beautiful or nervous. The bangles on Cyane's free arm jingled with every fidget and uneasy gesture. Her other hand gripped Pandora's as her comments ran between giddy and apprehensive.

A group of younger children, free of any anticipatory anxiety, ran past with a ripple of giggles. Two small boys bumped into Cyane, nearly knocking her down. She dusted off her dress with a huff. Pandora helped straighten her friend's garment. She took her hand again and squeezed it. Cyane smiled, but even her makeup could not hide the dark circles under her eyes. Her dear friend longed for the high priest to say her name today, as did every other girl.

Not Pandora.

Her mother's words about scaring the Titan off gave her an idea of how to formulate a letter which would eliminate her from the process. She dared not share this secret with Cyane, who would have been appalled to know Pandora filled the missive with questions for the gods and a slate of reasons why she did not want this so-called honor. Thankfully, no one checked what the girls wrote. Madame Tullia had only bundled them together in a bright blue ribbon and sent them to the temple. Surely, whoever read the letters had discarded hers at once. In the two weeks leading up to the announcement, she played her part well, acting as though she wrote the same sentiments as the other girls. But while they fretted over today's decision, the empowerment of freedom flowed in her veins.

A bottleneck at the entrance to the amphitheater slowed them down. Scents of flowers strewn through hair and liberally applied perfume overwhelmed Pandora. Though she wore her best chiton, she had done little else to embellish her ensemble, leaving her a dull green leaf among the vibrant flowers. She followed the eligible maidens to the front row, an amorphous mass of whispers and giggles. They smoothed each other's hair and adjusted chitons to perfection. *Quite a pretty flock of sheep*, she thought, *all subservient and compliant*. She fought to keep a smile from her lips while all around her, agony grew with each passing second.

When High Priest Bastian climbed the stage, a hush fell. A group of four temple maidens with a tottering gray-haired chaperone came behind, ushering the heavily veiled oracle. The priest waited for the women to reach him, the elderly one stopping on unsteady feet at his side. Bastian enjoyed a long moment of expectancy, his gaze sweeping the crowd before landing on the restless maidens. With practiced hands, he unfurled a scroll of parchment and paused for effect.

"The oracle has dictated this petition to me from the gods." His sonorous voice reverberated off the stone around the packed semi-circle of seats.

The moment had arrived, all eyes riveted on the high priest. Silence hung in the charged air as if time itself waited for the announcement. Every maiden leaned forward in her seat, eager to hear the next words. Cyane unwittingly dug her nails into Pandora's hand, who, despite her wish not to be picked, found herself swept up in the spectacle. After all, it would be an exciting day for someone.

"By decree of the mighty Zeus, king of all gods, and with the blessing of Hephaestus, our benevolent guardian, one maiden will be chosen as bride to the Titan, Epimetheus."

A murmur ran through the crowd. They revered Epimetheus and his brother for their help in the War of the Titans. Several shrines in their honor decorated the island, and they held an annual torch race in honor of Prometheus, considered cunning and wise. Pandora knew little about Epimetheus except for his rashness, but understood the esteem which came along with his name.

"This maiden will henceforth leave the island of Lemnos. She will be escorted to Mount Olympus, where the gods and goddesses will bestow gifts as a dowry for the new bride."

A louder rush of voices swirled through the crowd. This was an unprecedented honor indeed. Cyane clutched Pandora's hand even tighter while another girl nearly swooned. The high priest waited for the buzz to quiet before he continued.

"After careful consideration by the gods, they decree that the maiden shall be—Pandora, daughter of Lycus."

At the mention of her name, a ringing filled Pandora's ears, tunnel vision sucking her into an abyss. Foreboding visions of grief and suffering played out in her mind, cries of despair and hatred which rose in intensity and dread. From far away, she heard her classmates say her name, but her eyes could not focus on anything. A forceful grip on her shoulders brought her back to the present, where the amphitheater rang with applause. Cyane held her, her lips moving into sounds that finally turned into words.

"Pandora? Pandora? Can you hear me? They want you to go up on stage."

With a mechanical nod, she walked on wooden legs to the stairs and climbed to the top, numbness still ringing in her head. Bastian motioned her over and offered his congratulations. Pandora stared at the veiled oracle, swaying between the temple maidens, whose wishes in life were as irrelevant as Pandora's would be now. This thought sobered her, and she regained her senses. The high priest spun her to face the crowd.

"May the gods bless you, Pandora, daughter of Lycus. You are the chosen bride."

A rousing ovation rang throughout the theater. Bastian smiled in satisfaction and led his entourage off the stage. Alone, Pandora's eyes sought her parents, who applauded dutifully though not excitedly. She would have to leave home, leave them, an unbearable thought. Cyane mounted the steps to usher her stupefied friend down. Madame Tullia hugged Pandora before her classmates mobbed her with congratulations. Pandora nodded to them all, still unable to speak. Feigning a smile, she pushed her way forward.

Danae grabbed her and pulled her close. The crowd gathered around them as though they were a circus sideshow. Lycus cleared a path for them out of the theater, where more well-wishers waited. While her parents accepted all the felicitations, Pandora walked with her gaze down, her mind fixated on one question—how could she get out of this?

THIRTEEN

"I refuse to go!" Pandora shouted from behind her bedroom door, which she had slammed and locked for good measure. At sixteen, she knew better than to behave this childishly, but anger and fear got the better of her.

After several sickening hours of congratulations from every possible inhabitant of Lemnos, her family was finally in their private confines. While in public, Pandora contained her rage, enduring both the happy sentiments of the genuine, and the contrived wishes of the envious. Once inside the privacy of their courtyard, she exploded. Lycus shook his head and hurried away to the safety of his study, but Danae and Elara tried to reason with her until she fled to her room.

Now, face down on the bed, Pandora fumed, too angry to even cry. Fury, as she had never known, coursed through her veins. How dare they pick her? How dare they give her no say in her future? She would not go. They could not make her.

The mattress bounced when Rex jumped onto the bed. He rubbed against her side. She sat up and stroked the length of his back, which arched in pleasure. The cat allowed only Pandora to touch him. Besides Danae, who the animal tolerated, everyone else in the household earned hisses and swats. He curled up against her leg and purred. In the midst of her rage, panic set in. Who would Rex have if she left? He would be lonely without her. Fat tears brimmed in her eyes, splashing down her cheeks.

"Pandora, please come out so we can talk about this," Danae implored, with soft knocks on the door.

"Please come out," Elara pleaded. "I'll bring you your favorite honey cakes."

She did not answer, even though she could tell her mother wept. Instead, she picked up Rex and cradled him against her chest. His purring soothed her, and she calmed. Then, an idea hit—she would run away, her and Rex. They could live in the hills out of sight. It was the only option. Placing the animal down, she went to her closet to gather the needed items. While she grabbed a satchel, Rex sauntered in to watch. Besides a change of clothes and some food she could sneak from the kitchen later, she could not think of much else to bring. Her mother's rapping grew louder. After more thought, Pandora realized she would need a blanket. She folded an extra one up and set it on the floor next to her bag. Rex climbed on it and, after some kneading, curled up. The pounding stopped outside and Pandora went to grab her comb.

Her bedroom door flew open with a bang, an angry Lycus filling the frame. Rex leaped up from his comfortable spot and scrambled under the bed, his tail twice its original size. Pandora stood frozen at her vanity.

"Get out here this minute," her father ordered. "You have upset your mother enough."

Pandora trudged out of the room, head held high, arms crossed in defiance. Elara wrung her hands in dismay. Danae, who stood behind Lycus, could not help but marvel at the resemblance in posture between father and daughter. This would be a difficult battle.

"I realize this situation is not to your liking, but we are in no position to defy the will of the gods," he reprimanded. "Do you want to bring misfortune down on this entire house? On your family?"

Pandora shook her head and tears welled once again. She could not live with herself if she cursed her family or anyone else. Though she hated to admit it, her father was right. Flouting the will of the gods never ended well. The vision of hatred and despair she saw when the high priest read her name must have been a warning from the gods, who knew she would rebel against their decision. Her destiny foretold, the current of fate now swept Pandora along, no longer the captain of her ship. Sobs of defeat filled the air.

"There, there, girl, it will be all right." Lycus patted her arm awkwardly, never one who could handle tears. "I'll leave you ladies to talk this out."

Lycus turned down the hallway and disappeared. Danae stepped forward to embrace her daughter. Pandora sank into her arms, the smell of roses in her mother's hair bringing back childhood memories. Rex poked his head out from under the bed. Ever the consoler, he rubbed against his mistress' leg. Danae guided her to the bed, and they eased down onto the soft mattress. Rex jumped up to join them.

"You have been chosen for a great honor." Danae pushed a matted lock of hair off the girl's tear-stained cheek. "I know it doesn't seem that way to you right now."

Pandora shook her head. She thought she wanted freedom and control, not a simple life on Lemnos, a life like her mother's. Yet now, the thought of leaving the sanctuary of the island terrified her. Few inhabitants ever left, and those who returned confessed to terrible homesickness while away. Few mortals lived as comfortably as the residents of Lemnos, doted on by Hephaestus in every way.

"I don't want to go somewhere new. I don't want to leave you. I want to stay here in peace," she stammered.

"The world is bigger than this island," Danae said, as if reading her thoughts. "But Titans are divine beings. Epimetheus will protect you. Try to consider this as a big adventure."

"I can't leave. Who will take care of Rex?" she sobbed.

"Rex will be fine with me. Isn't that right, Rex?" her mother held out a hand and the cat nudged it with his head.

Still unconvinced, Pandora asked, "But what if Epimetheus is as dense-headed and lacking in foresight as they say he is?"

"Then he will need a strong girl to help him. People will know the god's marked you for this honor. Your name will be famous. You can use that to benefit mortals out there, especially women, who are never seen as the equal of men."

"I never thought about that." Pandora let out a ragged sigh and absently stroked Rex, who had curled up beside her.

"I believe big things await you, Pandora," her mother avowed. "Big things you could never achieve on this island. You are far too curious to be stuck in this small place forever."

Lycus peered in. His face brightened at the absence of any hysterics. He took a few cautious steps into the room and when no shouting ensued, asked, "Have you decided to accept your fate, daughter?"

"Yes," Pandora replied, a sense of purpose filling her. "I am ready for my future."

"That's a good girl," he said, opening his arms.

As Danae watched the two embrace, she fought to hold down the monstrous dread which had haunted her since that long-ago afternoon. Although she spoke confidently to Pandora, from the moment Bastian read her daughter's name, fear nestled in her heart. Tomorrow, she would make offerings to all the gods and goddesses beseeching their protection for her daughter.

FOURTEEN

Only two days later, Pandora arrived at the temple on Lemnos, one small bag slung across her shoulder. The high priest told her to travel light. She only brought a change of traveling clothes, one finer tunic, and a few small keepsakes. How she wished she could have snuck Rex into the bag as well. Because he could not understand the finality, parting with the cat had been harder than saying goodbye to her family and friends.

"I hope you can visit me someday," she said to Cyane last night.

They sat in the back courtyard of Pandora's house, the sky darkening from deep pink to dark blue. Pandora gazed up at the pinpricks of starlight. Would she see these same stars at her new home? Would she ever feel as secure as she did here? A hollowness filled her inside as the inevitable rushed toward her.

"Yes, I hope for that too," her friend agreed, "and I am sure you will come back here to visit."

In the end, the words rang hollow between them, the likelihood of either event slim. Neither knew exactly where Epimetheus resided, but it must be far away. They embraced, each filled with the sense their girlhood relationship was over. This morning her mother and brothers wept at their farewell. Danae wiped tears on her veil, the children clinging to her leg, too young to understand what transpired. Pandora kneeled, took the hand of each one and asked them to take care of Rex. With solemn eyes, they nodded. Elara fussed over her tunic and hair until the last moment, words of encouragement falling from her quivering lips. Lycus remained stoic, his final words a command.

"You have been given an honor by the gods, dear daughter, represent our family accordingly."

Bastian met her outside the temple with four veiled companions, three other maidens, and an older woman. The high priest inspected her and apparently found her appearance satisfying, because they set off at once in a wordless parade. On the walk to the pier, she tried to take in every small detail of the island—the rolling meadows, the stumpy olive trees, the white beaches all beneath the great forge of Hephaestus, which stood sentry in the background. In her sixteen years, she imagined leaving a thousand times, but now the comfort of these shores beckoned her to stay. Her stomach grew tight at the thought of the wider world. The tang of salt grew stronger in her throat as they made their way down to the pier, where a mighty trireme bobbed against the tide. Dwarfed by the vessel, Pandora stared up the keel, where three rows of oars hung out of symmetrical ovals. Her gaze drew up to the high railing on the top deck and finally to the enormous sails, now rolled up in large cylinders. How something this large could remain afloat was beyond her ability to grasp.

The gangplank creaked underfoot as the small party ascended, the ground receding with each step up the uneven wooden boards. Swarthy sailors pulled them aboard, greedily surveying the women, who, including Pandora, pulled their veils farther over their faces. Bastian walked over to confer with a man whose white beard glistened against his dark, weathered skin. By the deference paid to him by the crew, Pandora assumed he was their captain. After a brief consultation with the high priest, the captain called, "Lift anchor."

A bustle of activity followed, men scurrying in all directions like bees from a disrupted hive. The boat swayed and Pandora clutched the rail as the vessel pulled away from the shore. With each row of the oars, the island grew smaller. Men released the sails, and the ship sped across the calm sea. Pandora watched as the details of Lemnos blurred until it was but a speck on the horizon.

Only a plume of smoke from the forge remained visible, but it too faded. Heaviness filled her heart.

"Praise the gods, we have favorable weather," a kindly voice observed.

Beside her stood the attendant from the temple, an older woman whose plump face broke into a wide smile when Pandora met her eyes.

"I have never been on a ship of this size before," Pandora said, knuckles white against the dark wood of the rail.

"You could not ask for a more seaworthy vessel. I'm Galena. The high priest and I will chaperone you and the other maidens to Thessaly." Sensing Pandora's melancholy, she placed a hand on the girl's arm. "All will be well, young lady. Your fate is a great honor."

The ship cut a smooth track across open water until it came to the mainland, where it followed the coastline north for most of the journey. The other maidens came over and Galena pointed out landmarks during the trip, one she had made several times. Her constant chatter eased some of the tension in Pandora's body. In the late afternoon, the ship docked in the port city of Araphen. Pandora gaped at the activity all around her. Boats of all sizes lined the docks, workmen loading and unloading cargo. Crates, barrels, and fabric bolts swung on cranes to and from the storage holds. Sailors climbed masts to make repairs while deckhands scrubbed the boards.

Once on dry land, the bustle grew. Merchants hawked an array of products, from sailing gear, maps, and trinkets to fresh seafood laid across large slabs of ice. They hollered over one another along a block that held more people than all of Lemnos' citizens. The noise and the air, filled with the scent of fish, sweat and unknown spices, sent Pandora's head spinning. Galena kept a steady hand on her elbow as she guided the girls through several streets around the shoppers and stalls to the steps of a large inn. Here the ladies remained on the porch while the high priest went inside.

"It's a lot to take in your first time," Galena commented. The gawking maidens clustered around her, watching the commotion of the city.

"How many times have you been here?" Pandora asked.

"I escort two trips a year. These girls," she said, with a gesture at the rest of their party, "are bound for Thessaly where they will serve in their chosen temple."

Thessaly, the site of Mount Olympus, was their final destination. From what Pandora recalled from her schooling, it was much larger than the city of Araphen, a thought she could not fathom given all she had just witnessed. How sheltered her life on Lemnos had been, far from such an influx of humanity. Facing the gods on Olympus should be her greatest fear, but the idea of a life at odds with the familiarity of her tranquil island worried her far more. Beside her, the other girls giggled at a magician who performed tricks for them below the railing. *They will live out their days in the safety of a temple*, Pandora thought with a pang of jealousy.

Bastian came out of the inn with the keeper. "Our rooms for the night are all arranged. Come, we will dine in a private room for supper."

After a hearty meal, the ladies retired. The three young maidens shared one room, while Pandora and Galena took the adjoining one. The small chamber held a bed and nightstand, with an open window providing a pleasant breeze. Galena drifted right off, but even though she was exhausted, sleep eluded Pandora. Half the size of her bed at home, the lumpy mattress and the older woman's snores did little to settle her troubled mind. In the dark, with the strange noises of the city wafting in, she missed Rex's small body curled against her leg with the soothing sound of his purrs. Pandora prepared herself for a long night.

FIFTEEN

Next thing Pandora knew, Galena shook her shoulders. Dawn filled the sky with streaks of bright pink against the steel gray. Pandora rubbed the fitful sleep from her eyes and splashed some water on her face from a pitcher on the nightstand. Upon further examination, she noticed rudimentary figures painted on the porcelain. A large man held up a burning torch while smaller figures prostrated around him. Prometheus, her soon-to-be brother-in-law, a foreign term in her already muddled mind.

Two horse-drawn litters waited outside the inn. The temple girls piled into one, a clear camaraderie having developed among them, leaving the other for Pandora and Galena. The men, including the high priest, rode on horses whose saddlebags burst with provisions. There should be an inn as well-stocked as this one to stop at on each night of the journey, but the escorts came prepared in case an unforetold event befell them.

Galena settled on the puffy cushion, a basket of food from the innkeeper balanced on her lap. She motioned Pandora to sit across from her. Servants lowered the linen curtains, creating a comfortable cocoon. With a small jolt, they were off.

"Here, have some grapes and cheese," Galena offered. "You look as though you did not sleep much and you must keep up your strength."

"How long of a journey is it to Thessaly?" she asked, biting into the fresh grape.

"About six days," the woman replied. She broke a loaf of bread in half and held one portion out to the girl. "Thankfully, there is a road the entire way and we need not venture into the wildlands."

Pandora nodded while she ripped off chunks of bread and ate it with some cheese that had a pleasant nutty flavor. With a full belly, the swaying litter lulled her to sleep. She woke at midday refreshed when they stopped for lunch on the banks of a stream. While the men ate and watered the horses, the women found a secluded pool nearby where they could bathe. Galena supplied them with towels and soap, then she sat on a rock to keep watch.

"Hi, I'm Larissa," one girl said to Pandora. "This is Daphne and Melete."

Pandora recognized the latter two. The twins had finished school a couple of years prior, but she had never seen Larissa, who either received her tutelage at home or had no schooling. Some families thought educating a daughter was a waste of time. Thankfully, Pandora's parents were not among them. The girls removed their tunics and slid into the clear water, each shivering against the chill.

"This is the lucky Pandora," Daphne said to Larissa. She lathered up her arms with the soap. "She wrote the winning letter and won the honor of marrying Epimetheus."

No scorn tinged the words, for which Pandora was grateful. These girls thought her fortunate and she would play to part, lest she disappoint her family or anger the gods.

After passing the soap to Melete, Daphne dunked her head under the water. When she broke the surface, she wiped water from her face. Galena yelled, and their four heads swiveled in the woman's direction. They watched her shoo away two men who had wandered over, whether by accident or not, Pandora did not know.

"I am bound for the temple of Aphrodite," Larissa said.

"How honorable, choosing to dedicate your life to the goddess," Pandora remarked.

"It was hardly a choice," the girl confided in a whisper. "I am the youngest of four daughters. With such a small population, there are few eligible men on Lemnos. Only

71

my eldest sister married someone from the island. My father made matches for my other two sisters in other lands, but did not have enough dowry money left for me. He decided I would be a temple maiden."

Melete waded over and handed Larissa the soap. "She is lucky. Her father let her choose which temple to serve. Ours decided we were to be servants of Hestia when we were born."

"He truly gave you no say?" Pandora asked, shocked at the statement. Maidens of the Hearth Goddess maintained an eternal flame—under penalty of death, should it go out.

"No. He arranged a marriage for our older sister in far off Corinth," Daphne added. "She cried for days."

"That's awful." Pandora never thought about the lack of suitors on the island.

"Our brothers, however, got to pick from a number of eligible ladies on Lemnos." Pandora now heard the derision in Daphne's voice.

Pandora took the soap from Larissa. While she washed, something akin to guilt filled her. As the only daughter of a wealthy family, Lycus could have arranged a marriage to a well-off husband. Furthermore, she knew he would have taken her wishes into account. She had never thought much about the circumstances of other girls. How little say they had in their lives. Of course, they would see her situation with Epimetheus as fortuitous. Danae's words to use this honor to help other women gained new meaning.

A wave of water hit Pandora in the face. The young ladies splashed each other, their enthusiastic giggles resounding across the air. Pandora joined them, frolicking with a sudden sense of lightness. Soon the others would be sworn temple maidens and she a wife, but for a few moments, the liveliness of youth reigned. Galena let them have their fun, but eventually, nudged them out with a reminder of the time and they rejoined their party. That evening, they stopped at an inn. Though less grand than the one in Araphen, the company still went to sleep in comfortable beds with full stomachs all the same.

The next three days continued much the same, the days covering ground and the nights at local inns. On the fifth morning, they woke to a raging thunderstorm. Rain poured in sheets off the eaves in front of the window of their room, prompting Galena to speculate, "I think it will be a late start today."

They breakfasted in a private room, waited on by the innkeeper and his wife. Thunder pealed across the sky, eliciting shrieks from the twins. Pandora picked at her food, her nervousness increasing each day. What would happen on Mount Olympus? Where did Epimetheus live? Did he even want a wife? Doubt and dread plagued her, both awake and asleep.

By mid-morning, the rain tapered to drizzle and Bastian deemed it safe to head out. Muddied ruts in the road slowed their pace. They pressed onward as dusk fell, still several hours away from the next village. Dark clouds clutched the moon with skeletal fingers, shedding little light on the road and the scrubby forest on either side. Pandora longed to be out of the chilly litter and next to a warm fire in a friendly dining room.

Horses' hooves rang out from the left side of the road and their caravan ground to a halt. Pandora parted the curtains to see a group of men ring their entire entourage. Galena grabbed her arm away, fear etched on her face.

"What do we have here?" a raspy voice snarled.

"Gods save us," Galena whispered. "Bandits."

SIXTEEN

"I am Bastian, High Priest of Lemnos. We are escorting maidens to temples in Thessaly. You would be wise to let us be on our way."

If the thieves scared Bastian, his voice held no trace of anything but confidence and annoyance despite being outnumbered. The horses pulling the litter skittered with nervous whinnies as the bandits tightened around them, each with a sword pointed at the guards. Galena, shaking with fright, lost her grip on Pandora's arm.

"Is that so?" the leader scoffed. "I think we would be wise to see what treasures you carry with you. Don't you agree, boys?"

A rumble of assent ran through the other gang members before springing into action. They ripped the curtains of the litter open. Rough hands seized Pandora, pulling her out into the murky night air. Thick arms dropped her on the ground, a shower of pebbles spraying around her. Galena landed next to her, too frightened to make a sound. The girls in the other litter screamed while the men herded them next to Pandora, who stood and helped Galena up. Three men them with scruffy beards and shabby attire stood guard over the women, each with a long knife in hand. The smell of their unwashed bodies was nearly unbearable, and the girls drew veils across their faces, earning them a lewd wink from one of their captors.

About a dozen other men ransacked the saddlebags, while the priests and servants stood by helplessly. One bandit hooted upon discovering a sack of gold drachmas, another held up a golden statue meant to be an offering to the sun god Apollo, greed filling his eyes. The leader, by far the largest man, unrolled the ceremonial robe of the high priest, the finely woven golden threading mirroring the ugly scars on his arms.

"Ain't this fancy," he chuckled, wrapping the garment around his shoulders.

"Unhand that at once, you cretin," Bastian demanded, his eyes bulging with anger at the sight of his treasured robe mishandled by these thieves.

The man walked over to the high priest and poked him in the chest. "You think you are in charge here? We will see about that." He turned to his men. "I say we take the money, treasures, and the horses."

"What about the girls?" a stocky man with a long scar across his cheek asked, gesturing to the women with a hungry glint in his eye.

"By all means, take the girls. We need some entertainment this evening. Kill the men."

The maidens shrieked collectively, huddling together in fear. Their guards moved toward the bandits, hoping to save them. Pandora heard the scrape of metal as they unsheathed their swords. An outlaw threw his knife, with sickening precision it lodged in the guard's chest. He dropped like a stone.

"The gods will punish you for this! Your lives will be forever …"

Bastian's words ceased when the leader severed the high priest's head with one stroke of his sword. It skittered across the ground near the girls, before a captor kicked it farther away. It rolled to a stop in some high grass, eyes and mouth still open. The girls wailed, hiding their faces, but Pandora could not turn away. She had heard of bandits and violence, but in her sheltered life, they had been but a cautionary tale. Now, as these heinous acts unfolded right in front of her, she kept her eyes fixed on the action. The outlaws made quick work of the remaining men, pools of blood seeping into the ground around the bodies.

Their leader grabbed Bastian's robe off his shoulders and stuck it over his head. The elaborate garment draped around him. "I am the high priest now," he gloated. "The gods can rot for all I care."

No sooner had the words left his mouth when an arrow flew from the forest's edge sinking into his throat. He collapsed, grabbing desperately at the shaft while blood bubbled from his mouth. The rest of the bandits only had a moment to turn toward the trees before another volley of arrows swept across the landscape. Each man fell on the spot, a mortal wound to either chest or neck.

With the dead guards lying at their feet, the maidens crouched low and cried for mercy. Galena tried to pull Pandora down with her, but to no avail. She grabbed a sword out of a dead guard's hand and stood tall, her gaze on the tree line where several archers emerged. Pandora expected more men, but these warriors were women, all donning short tunics cinched with leather belts. Soft suede boots muted the footsteps of their all but silent approach. Catlike was the only word Pandora thought fit. As the group stopped in front of the victims, Pandora noted ornately carved quivers on every shoulder. Though willowy, the band exuded strength and athleticism. Sensing no danger, she lowered the weapon.

"We owe you a debt of gratitude," Pandora stated, far calmer than her companions. "May the gods bless and keep you."

A tall, slender woman stepped forward. "I am Theia. We are huntresses who patrol these woods for the mighty Artemis. You are fortunate we came along in time to hear your cries of distress."

"Fortunate indeed," Galena exclaimed.

The girls finally stood and stopped screaming long enough to thank their saviors. They clustered together in a weepy mass. Pandora admired the warriors' fluid movements and self-assured voices, the antithesis of the quailing maidens. Though her mother always had a strong demeanor, these huntresses radiated a formidable yet subtle power, one that equaled that of a man. The thought of it thrilled Pandora to the core, and she gripped the sword she held tighter. In that moment, she ached to join this band, who now surveyed the wreckage of their caravan and the carnage all around.

"I am to escort these young ladies to Thessaly, particularly this one," Galena explained and pulled Pandora forward. "This is Pandora. She is bound for Mount Olympus. Will you aid us?"

"Pandora," Theia repeated with a cryptic smile. "Yours will be an interesting fate. Come ladies, we will give you shelter for the night."

At their leader's command, the other huntresses gathered up the undamaged supplies and treasures. They left Bastian's golden threaded robe, now covered in blood, along with the weapons. Theia ordered another to tie the horses together and bring them to the nearest inn. With the work finished, they left the road. Pandora followed the huntresses into the woods. How did Theia know her name? What did she mean by an interesting fate? Foreboding coursed through Pandora as they disappeared into the tree line.

SEVENTEEN

"You showed great courage," Theia said.

Wind blew against the canvas where Pandora sat on the dirt floor near a fire. Galena, worn out from the attack, dozed on a pallet nearby. Though rudimentary, the hut provided decent coverage. A small fire lit the space and drove out some of the fear which lingered from the attack. Empty bowls sat on the hearth, the stew from them now warming the women's stomachs. The inns, though far grander in comfort, never instilled Pandora with as much content.

"Or sheer stupidity," Pandora remarked. Theia rubbed healing ointment on a gash in her arm. "I've never encountered any bandits in my life. Their boldness and cruelty made me angry, but my fate would have been different if you had not come along."

"Neither I nor my sisters would have gone down without a fight," the huntress declared, wrapping a bandage around her wound. "It pleases me to find such spirit in another. Were it not for your gods' chosen fate, I would ask you to join our band. Artemis prefers strong-willed maidens in her service."

Pandora's heart swelled; finally, someone saw worth in her character. Was she not promised to Epimetheus, a spot among the huntresses sounded ideal. Their small knot of huts hidden in the woods, their athletic bodies and their obvious bond appealed to her nature. Artemis—goddess of animals, the moon, and chastity would be an easy deity to pledge herself to. A multitude of questions filled her mind about the lives of these huntresses. But they could wait until later. First, she asked the most pressing one.

"You said my fate would be interesting. You know I am to marry Epimetheus?" Pandora asked, surprised this isolated group knew anything about her.

"Yes, rumors filter down even to the lowliest when the gods scheme. Most likely by Hermes. He loves to have his mischief with mortals." Theia's pleasant laugh filled the small space.

"How is my marriage to Epimetheus a *scheme*?" Dread returned to Pandora's stomach at the word.

The smile left the huntress's face. She grew silent and stared at the ground. Pandora thought no answer would come until Theia said, "I cannot disparage the gods. They know better than us on all matters. My only advice to you is to tread carefully. Gifts from the gods are often accompanied by hidden perils."

With these words, she stood and stretched. She put the ointment jar back in a sack and handed Pandora a blanket. "Now we must sleep."

Pandora curled up next to Galena, who snored lightly. Theia extinguished the fire before lying on another pallet on the opposite wall. For a long while, Pandora stared at the glowing embers, pondering Theia's words until sleep overcame her.

The neigh of a horse roused Pandora from her slumber. Galena stood over the pallet, folding her blanket. Pandora rose and smoothed out her tunic. While her chaperone continued making the bed, the girl stuck her head outside to find a wagon waiting. The huntresses who brought the horses to the nearest town informed the local priests what had transpired. They, in turn, had provided the wagon and six men armed to the teeth to accompany the group the rest of the journey. Theia stood talking to one of them, but Pandora saw none of the other huntresses.

Larissa, Daphne and Melete emerged from another hut. They huddled together as bereft as a flock of ducklings who lost their mother. A man directed them to climb into the cart and, with dubious faces, they complied. Galena came out behind Pandora, handing the girl her bag as she passed. Theia walked over and nodded at the words of gratitude from Galena. When the older woman boarded, the huntress came to Pandora.

"I am glad our paths crossed, even under such tragic circumstances. I wish you strength and good judgment in your future." She opened her arms and enfolded the girl in her muscular embrace.

"Thank you for your kindness … and your warning," Pandora whispered.

Galena extended a hand to help her into the wagon. Pandora settled at the escort's side and the wagon jerked to a roll. Not nearly as comfortable as the litters, the maidens happily sacrificed luxury for protection. With a crisp click of his tongue, the driver guided the vehicle out of the woods and back onto the main road. Pandora gazed back at Theia, who raised her arm in farewell, and the myriad of questions Pandora had about the lives of the huntresses remained unanswered.

A subdued mood overhung the passengers, the initial excitement of the maidens snuffed by the events of the previous evening. They exchanged little chatter and not one giggle escaped their lips while the wagon bumped and jolted them along. Happy for the silence, Pandora contemplated her impending marriage. If hidden perils awaited, as Theia warned, she needed a clear mind to avoid walking blindly into any tricks. Was it possible to outwit a god? Prometheus had, but she was no Titan. Still, she resolved not to trust anything at face value.

A mottled sun shone weakly through wispy, gray clouds, which streaked across the sky as though fire chased at their heels. A few times, a fat drop of rain fell with a large splash, but they never converged into any actual storm. The seasoned horses made far better time pulling the wagon than they ever could have made in the unwieldy litters. As the sun set, the walls of Thessaly came into view. Mount Olympus loomed over the city, its peak eternally shrouded in mist.

All the maidens pointed at the peak, finally finding their tongues again. The group gaped up in awe as they passed through the imposing main city gate, where stone blocks soared high above. A guard directed them down a few roads to a small courtyard outside the stables. Moments later, two priests arrived to greet them, emerging as though specters from the gathering dusk. The driver helped Galena dismount, and she strode over to them while the remaining passengers disembarked.

"Welcome back to Thessaly, Galena," said a dark-skinned priest, his voice a rich baritone. He stood a few heads taller than his colleague. "We are honored you bring these maidens from the blessed isle of Lemnos, and we are sorry to hear of the misfortune you encountered on the journey. The road becomes ever more dangerous."

"It was worse than ever this time, Hesiod. Bastian is dead, beheaded right in front of the delicate ladies," Galena said. "And with one being such an important …"

The shorter priest put an arm around her shoulder and they led her away with sympathetic nods, the rest of her words too soft to make out. Pandora turned back when she heard a large grinding noise. Men worked a series of ropes and pulleys to shut the main city gate. Once closed, they dropped thick iron bars across it. As each thundered into place, Pandora sensed her charmed life on Lemnos was irretrievably lost.

EIGHTEEN

Dusk settled over the courtyard. Pandora's group stayed near the wagon. All around them stood other groups with their chaperones. Pandora counted about thirty girls, travel-stained and weary, anxious about what the future held. It took some time to divide up the maidens. The priests spoke to them individually. They sorted the maidens into groups of two or three based on whether they would serve a life dedicated to Apollo, Athena, Hestia, or another deity. Pandora wondered how many chose this path voluntarily instead of having it thrust upon them. One or two wore a countenance of self-assurance, but uncertainty clouded more eyes than not.

The rest of the girls went with the shorter priest, who led them out of the courtyard. Hesiod walked over to where Pandora waited with Galena. He held a regal air about his large frame, but without the condescension of Bastian. He smiled down at her, the skin around his dark eyes crinkling.

"I will take you to a temple halfway up the mountain," he said, every word dripping with the serenity a dedicated priest possesses. "Galena, it was lovely to see you again. May the gods bless you this evening."

"You're not coming?" Pandora exclaimed to her chaperone.

"No." She embraced the girl. "The temples on Mount Olympus are only for those requested. I am headed to the inn. I will wait there for your return."

Pandora fought back tears while the three walked out of the courtyard. Galena hurried to catch up with the others while the priest guided Pandora in the opposite direction. Though nearly dark, citizens milled about the main street.

A distracted man leading a horse, a woman carrying a burlap bundle, and a group of raucous young men all moved deferentially out of the priest's path. Pandora clutched her small bag of belongings to her chest. Realizing how disoriented she must appear, she straightened her shoulders and walked taller.

"I am Pandora. May I ask who you are?" Words finding her tongue at last.

"I am Hesiod, one of the high priests of Thessaly. I have been given the honor of escorting you. Come, we will walk a short way to the mountain's edge." Again, he smiled and Pandora, with the attack of the night before fresh in her mind, thanked the gods she had such an important person to guide her in the strange city.

She followed him to a street which circled the inner side of the city wall, a far quieter place than the main road. Pandora marveled at the enormous stones soaring high above her, a well-fortified barrier to protect the citizens inside. Lemnos, where the days passed in peace, had no such wall, such a defense unnecessary. Hephaestus' forge and presence were enough to deter any would be attackers. She placed her hand on the cool surface. How out of place this wall would be on her childhood island.

Small shops, shuttered for the night, lined this road. Lanes broke off it at even intervals like wheel spokes. In the twilight, Pandora discerned awnings whose colors must be cheerful and vibrant in the sun. While activity must abound here during the day, now she saw only a few children playing outside one door, a chunk of light from inside illuminating them. Their giggles rang down the empty streets.

Eventually, the road curved toward the mountain standing sentry over the city, its steep sides dwarfing even the largest edifices. Hesiod turned their course down a well-trodden path toward the foothills. Crickets serenaded from the grass, the air cool and crisp. A small hut materialized out of the shadows, a rudimentary edifice at the base of the mountain, a pen of donkeys behind it. The lone glow of a lantern shone from its only window until the circle of light bobbed down from its opening and reappeared with a man who emerged from the door.

"Greetings, Gregor," Hesiod called out. "This is the maiden who needs a ride up to the temple."

Gregor nodded. What Pandora mistook for his hood turned out to be his long, black hair, a complementary beard almost reached his knees. With a practiced hand, the unkempt man opened the paddock and saddled up an equally scruffy donkey. The creature flicked his ears, but moved with compliance over to them. Gregor gestured for Pandora to mount.

"Now I leave you," the priest informed her. "It is a short trip up. A temple servant will await you. I will see you at the wedding."

"Thank you," was the only answer Pandora uttered despite the number of questions which rose to mind. Apparently, escorts handing her off was the norm for the evening.

She swung her legs over the low, broad back of the donkey. With the lantern held high in the attendant's hand, they were off. A more than capable guide, Gregor led the animal, with various clicks of his tongue, up a steep path, knowing exactly where its hooves should step amid the rocky terrain. Besides the occasional cue to the donkey, he did not speak and Pandora decided against trying to make conversation. Darkness settled around them, the lantern illuminating a circle of land only a few feet ahead of them.

After a precipitous ascent, the ground leveled out and their pace increased. The faintest outlines of a structure emerged in the shadows ahead of them. Gradually it morphed into the shape of a temple, its modest configuration not at all the grand structure Pandora envisioned. As they drew closer, a figure holding a candle materialized from the doorway.

"I can take her from here, Gregor. Thank you," said a willowy girl with olive skin. Long black tresses blew across her face and she brushed them away.

Pandora dismounted, her bag held to her chest. Gregor proffered a quick bow before steering the donkey around. He left without ever uttering a word. She watched as the shadows enveloped him. How often had he made this trip? Did he have any other job? Was he able to talk, or was he a mute? Question piled on question until a hand touched Pandora's arm.

"I am Iliana, a maiden of the gods." A deep set of almond-shaped eyes lit with her smile. "Welcome to the temple of Mount Olympus."

She offered her hand, which laid soft and warm against Pandora's cold skin. First Galena, then Hesiod, then Gregor, she thought with a shiver. How long until this girl leaves me too? Light from the newly risen moon fought against the ever-present shroud of clouds hiding Olympus' peak. Pandora thought of Lemnos, her family, her bed, Rex. Despair pooled in her stomach by the time she crossed over the temple's threshold. Tears stung her eyes, but they did nothing to counter her fate.

NINETEEN

Brighter light filled the inside of the temple, the plain exterior giving way to the grandeur inside. Twelve marble columns carved in the likeness of each Olympian curved around the walls from the entrance. Gods on one side, goddess on the other, the representations of Zeus and Hera met in the center at the back of the temple, towering over a raised marble altar. Candles burned at the base of each column and on the altar's base, tendrils of smoke curling up toward the ceiling where it wafted out an oculus in the ceiling. The size and detail of each column humbled Pandora, who walked as though the weight of their Olympian eyes bore down on her.

"You must be hungry," Iliana said, her soft voice echoing in the high, hollow space.

The young temple maiden had a kind face, which still held a childlike fullness. She wore a fine silk tunic, drawn around her tiny waist with a golden rope. When she disappeared into a small chamber near the back, Pandora thought an older maiden would come out to greet her. Iliana returned alone, a cushion in each hand. After setting them on the ground, she brought out a wooden tray filled with bread, cheese, and fruit, along with a skin of watered wine. When the girls sat, dust surged up from the cushions, dancing clouds in the candlelight. Iliana brushed her hand across the air and they diffused. She motioned for Pandora to eat.

"Are you the only one here?" Pandora asked, selecting a slab of soft, dark bread from the tray.

"Yes. I serve at the temple of Apollo nearby." The girl broke off a hunk of cheese and took a bite. "Those priests maintain this one daily, but no one resides here. I only come up when there is need. It's not often the Olympians summon a mortal."

"No, I suppose not," Pandora sighed, fiddling with the bread in her hands.

"But when the gods summon one, they have no choice but to come," Iliana stated, popping an olive into her mouth. "The priests call upon me to assist if the mortal is a female."

While Iliana ate, nerves quelled Pandora's appetite. She gazed at the columns looming over them. The temple did not appear as tall from outside. Was it a trick of the eye? Or did she cower under the glare of the steely countenance on each statue? If the inanimate stone intimidated her, how would she endure their divine presence? The meager contents of her stomach soured.

"Have you seen them? The gods, I mean?" she blurted, her voice louder than intended.

"No," Iliana dipped her head at the columns in respect. "As you know, humans cannot survive the sight of their immortal forms. The last person summoned saw the guises they adopt for mortals, and proclaimed, even then, their presence is almost too glorious to bear."

"I come from Lemnos, where Hephaestus' forge is and I have never seen him at all," Pandora confided, the prospect of being in the company of even one deity a frightful prospect.

"Lemnos?" Iliana exclaimed, nearly dropping her goblet of wine. "Its beauty and tranquility are spoken of by all."

"Yes, I'm not surprised," Pandora sighed at the thought of her beloved home. The pristine beaches, the rolling meadows, the sense of community. "Where are you from?"

"I don't know. My parents died of a fever when I was a toddler. My grandmother, the only surviving relative, wanted to protect me. She traveled to Thessaly and took me to the temple of Apollo. The priestesses there raised me. It is the only home I've ever known."

A great sadness stirred in Pandora. Although she was mortal, her sheltered island insulated her from many of life's tragedies. Yet this temple maiden had already endured such horrible loss in her young life. On Lemnos, illness was rare. Its residents imagined sickness and premature death were curses placed on people who angered the gods. The thought of an orphaned little girl raised in a temple with no semblance of a normal life broke her heart. How could Iliana deserve such a fate? Surely the gods were not that cruel?

The maid busied herself dragging pallets across the floor and filling them with hay, the traumatic events of her childhood but a memory. Pandora tried to imagine a life with no family, no friends. At least she experienced that much before the gods upended her life. Tears rose unbidden yet again. She dabbed them away with her veil. Iliana smoothed out the straw with brisk strokes before laying the bed covers on top. Pandora noted the bedding, kept in a small cabinet, contained less dust than the dining cushions.

"You must be tired. Please go to sleep. We will leave early tomorrow and you will need to be well-rested."

Pandora laid on one pallet and pulled a light blanket across her body, noting the fineness of the material, even more luxurious than her sheets at home. Iliana stored the food and wine away in the back room. Before lying down, the maiden padded around the temple to extinguish all the candles except for one burning on the altar. It glowed dimly in the darkness, akin to the light of a faraway beacon. Pandora concentrated on the flame as though she was a ship on rough seas following the beam of a lighthouse. These last few days had tossed her life on ever-changing tides and she longed for the safe harbor of home. She drifted off with an ache in her heart.

Light swirled around her, snatches of visions playing across her mind. Desperately, she clung to something. A child, she realized. *Her child*? She did not know, but she needed to shield the girl from danger. Evil beasts hunted her, released by some force. She could not see where they came from, but they multiplied with each passing second. Their darkness grew until it blocked out the sun, leaving the earth dim and cold. With the small child clutched to her chest, Pandora ran, her heart a loud drumbeat in her head, her lungs gasping for air, her whole being in agony. A voice rang urgently in her head: *Shield the child. Shield the child.*

Her bare feet scraped on broken stones. She kept running, splotches of blood in her wake, wicked specters right behind her. Their malevolent breaths assailed her neck. Ahead of her lay a flat desert as far as the eye could see. Nowhere to hide, but she could not turn back. Her soles hit the searing hot sand and pain engulfed her. The child cried out in fear. She tried to run faster, but with each step, her legs sank deeper into the ground. Her progress slowed to a stop. The sand rose to chest level. She tried to keep it from engulfing the child. She would not make it, nor would the child. The malicious spirits sensed their moment. They merged into a thick, dark cloud and hurtled from the sky toward her. She clutched the child close as the specters enfolded her, racking her with pain. She floundered in their shadowy grip, praying to the gods for mercy.

TWENTY

"Pandora, wake up."

Iliana stood over her, a concern etched on her face. Pandora sat up in the still, dark temple, weak shafts of gray visible in the doorway, her blanket tangled around her like a mummy's wrappings. While she disengaged herself from the bedding, she tried to shake off the foreboding dream. Iliana's story about her childhood must have induced such a nightmare. Pandora's mind pinned the blame there, but her heart chilled at the thought of evil forces stalking her.

"Let's get you cleaned up and ready for the gods," the temple maiden said.

While she disappeared out a back door, Pandora noted an empty basin and towels laying on the floor. Iliana returned with a brimming bucket and emptied it into the basin. She reached into a sack around her waist to retrieve a handful of petals. They scattered across the water, buoyant as tiny, colorful boats. She beckoned Pandora, who dutifully joined her.

Iliana helped Pandora remove her travel-stained tunic. The maiden dipped a cloth into the basin and washed Pandora with cool, crisp water mixed with fragrant oil. Iliana poured more water over Pandora's hair, dust from her journey flowing into the basin. Once dry, Pandora pulled out her finest toga, and both girls arranged the folds across her shoulders, tying the garment with a gold-flecked leather belt. With practiced hands, Iliana braided Pandora's hair, looping it around itself on the top of her head, where she secured it with pins.

While the temple maiden cleaned the dust from Pandora's sandals, the girl studied at her wavy reflection in the basin. In all the times someone had helped her dress for a party or a festival, she never gave much thought to her appearance. Everyone always praised her beauty, but she never considered it important—until now. What if the gods did not find her pleasing? Could they rescind the offer? Could they send her into exile? She still found it hard to believe they had chosen her, especially given the content of her letter. The terror from the dream bore down on her.

"There. Now you are ready," Iliana said after securing Pandora's sandal ties.

Ready. But for what? the girl thought.

Iliana led them out of the temple and up a rock footpath. Along the way, they shared a small loaf of bread and some fat olives plucked right from the trees they passed. All morning they climbed. Iliana barely spoke, which was for the best, as Pandora needed all her energy to keep up. The cool morning faded to a pleasant midday. The ladies stopped at a stream where a small waterfall cascaded over a rock shelf. Pandora savored both the taste of the refreshing water and the revitalization it brought to her aching feet.

"See those flowers? They are called Jankea," Iliana said. "They only grow on Mount Olympus."

She pointed at small purple flowers which burst from fissures in the rocks, their petals cradled in a nest of green leaves. Pandora had read about them in school and even painted some. She saw now her artwork did little justice to the magnificent flowers.

"They are more beautiful than I imagined," Pandora admitted. "I've only read about them. A written description falls short of their splendor."

"Depictions of the sea must be the same," Iliana said. "I have seen many renderings, but am sure the sight of the real sea is far more majestic."

The girls moved on and spoke about more trivialities, with no mention of their important destination. Pandora pondered the conversation about the flowers and the sea. Laying eyes on the gods would be more awe-inspiring than words or pictures could evoke. Was she ready? Could anyone truly be ready for such a moment?

By late afternoon, they reached high up the mountain. The ground mercifully leveled out for at a flat expanse in front of them, the cloud covered peak of Olympus somewhere far above.

"We are almost there," Iliana said, stretching her hand out to Pandora, who lagged a few paces behind.

"Where exactly?" Pandora asked, taking her hand. She saw no temple, only grassland littered with rocks and a few stumpy trees.

"A meeting place where humans can see the gods, in their guises at least."

The maiden pointed to a spot ahead. Pandora squinted and could make out large shapes looming in the space before the ground sharply inclined again. With each step, the forms became more discernible. Towering stones ringed a circle of land as though ominous sentries stood watch. As they approached, Pandora noted the chipped, faded monoliths encircled one flat stone surrounded by a patch of dead grass. What kind of meeting place was this eerie ruin? Certainly not one fit for the gods. Wind whipped through the markers with a guttural howl.

"This is where I leave you." Iliana's voice made Pandora jump.

"Leave me?" she parroted, panic in her tone and her grip tightened on the girl.

"I am not invited to the meeting. I will wait here for you." She gestured for Pandora to enter the circle. "Good luck."

Pandora inhaled shakily and released Iliana's hand. She looked forward, then back at the maiden, who gave a nod of reassurance. With closed eyes, she stepped between two of the stones. The wind silenced, the air grew warm. Opening her eyes, Pandora faced soaring thrones of marble in a semi-circle in front of her. Six on one side, six on the other, the two in the middle a touch higher than the rest, exactly as the statues in the temple below. A carved symbol marked the top of each, a thunderbolt for Zeus, a diadem for Hera, and so on. Her eyes swept across the emblems taught to her since birth.

The grass no longer withered underfoot but grew lush except for where a marble altar stood in the center, bare of any decoration. When she peeked behind her, the area where she entered the stone pillars blurred in a gray haze, as though the meadow, the mountain, and Iliana ceased to exist. When she took a step back, pressure pushed against her. It was up to the gods to release her from this place now.

Pandora turned back to the empty seats, her heart filled with resolve. The gods may be able to command her and control her future, but she would meet them with dignity and courage. She straightened her shoulders and waited.

TWENTY-ONE

A radiant burst of light blinded Pandora and she staggered back, hands flying to shield her eyes. When the light receded, she peeked between her spread fingers. For the moment it took her pupils to adjust, large shapes floated in front of her. They transformed into figures seated in the chairs. Imposing yet ethereal, twelve countenances stared down at her. Six gods on one side, six goddesses on the other. Pandora adjusted her toga and stood tall.

"Welcome, Pandora, daughter of Lycus," the centrally seated goddess said. "You are one of the fortunate mortals to see us in our divine forms."

A false statement. Their divine forms were fatal to any human. Pandora knew this, knew she saw merely a diluted version of their beauty. Still, her breath caught at the sight of them. When asked in later days to describe them, she truthfully answered no words were adequate. The Olympians were both frightening and glorious to behold, filling Pandora with equal parts dread and awe. Her tongue eluded her, yet she managed to bow to the assemblage.

"My wife speaks rightly," the god in the center stated, taking Hera's hand. Though his lips moved, his voice sounded as though it sprung from the earth to Pandora's ears.

Zeus, King of the Gods, appeared both young and handsome, yet old and wise all at once. His brown beard, flecked with gray, did not diminish his regal air, but gave him the aura of a king. A blue and white robe threaded with gold flowed around his muscular physique. He held an enormous golden scepter capped with an eagle. No matter how hard Pandora tried, she could never get her eyes to bring him fully into focus.

In fact, the appearance of each divinity wavered among many traits, as though each moment showed another aspect of their character. Beauty, bravery, cleverness, and superiority played across their shifting faces. Each held her gaze when she met their eyes, a powerful yet specific energy emanating from all of them. Even their robes changed, images flashing across the stately fabric faster than Pandora could comprehend.

"You have been chosen for a special honor, Pandora. Selected from a multitude of girls," Hera said, her regal beauty pulsating across the room. A distinctive cylindrical crown rested on a head of light brown tresses. Her brilliant blue eyes dazzled against her milky white skin.

Pandora bowed her head. Until this point, she had not considered this forced marriage an honor. But now, a strange sense of pride and possibility filled her. Perhaps her life would change in positive ways, ways she had never considered. Her insides warmed with contentment at this thought. Why had she ever balked at this idea? How blessed was she to be this lucky?

"Of course, you and Epimetheus will have a grand wedding ceremony, befitting of his station," explained Hera. "But first, as the goddess of marriage, I suggested we grant you both gifts of our own. Hephaestus?"

The god rose from his seat out from behind the thrones, too imperfect to sit at the same level as the Olympians. He limped to the center of the room, an object in hand. Even through the everlasting blur, Pandora could see his crooked foot flash against his heavenly glow. His presence awed Pandora, who grew up on Lemnos without ever setting an eye on him. How the inhabitants would envy this privilege.

Hephaestus' large hands cradled an ornate pithos with intricate ears and a bright golden lid, his cudgel-like hands dwarfing the delicate vessel. In spite of his ogreish size and deformity, Hephaestus was renowned for his artistry and craftmanship. From the staff of the Greek king,

Agamemnon, to the armor of the mighty warrior Achilles, to Hermes' winged sandals, to the sun god Helios' chariot, Hephaestus' works for both mortals and gods were legendary. Countless more examples filled the homes and temples on Lemnos. That such a monstrous deity created objects of such splendor and renown was but one paradox of the gods.

The god set the jar down on the altar and hobbled back to his seat. Pandora hardly noticed. She could not take her eyes off the magnificent pithos in front of her. The body glowed an inky black, where golden images of gods and creatures swirled; ever changing, they created a hypnotic dance around its circumference. Bronze ears in the shape of grape vines extended from each side, fruit carved into delicate curves. The lid was a golden eagle, glorious wings outstretched, as if the lifelike bird would burst into flight at any moment.

Enraptured, Pandora had an urge to touch it, to keep it near, to protect it as though it were a living thing. Gratefulness surged through her being. Of all mortals, the gods chose her for the honor of marrying Epimetheus and now they gave her even more. The golden images transformed from an epic battle to a flowing stream where nymphs danced in the current. Flocks of deer ran across the surface, morphing into crashing waves on the shore of an island with a large volcano. Lemnos. Thoughts of her home warmed Pandora's heart. She could not wait to visit with her husband and, in time, her future children.

A flash of the nightmare from the previous evening struck Pandora like a thunderbolt. *The pithos.* She had seen the object in her terrible dream. The revelation sent her crashing back to the present. Her senses returned. The deities must have held her mind spellbound, conjuring gratitude and peace. Dread pooled in her stomach at such trickery. She needed to keep her wits about her. For the briefest moment, she tore her gaze from the jar and glanced at Zeus. His eyes narrowed, realizing the enchantment broke. Before Pandora could stop it, a mesmerizing fog

filled her mind once more. She turned back to the pithos
with calmness and tranquility, happy for her fate.

"Now we will confer our gifts to you," Zeus
announced.

TWENTY-TWO

Athena studied the girl who stood before them, impressed by her composure. Many humans cowered before the gods. Not Pandora. Though her frame trembled, she stood with back straight. After her initial riveted stare at the pithos, Athena noticed a flash of fear across her youthful face quickly replaced by a hypnotic calm.

The goddess of wisdom narrowed her eyes and stole a peek at her father. Zeus' gaze held a glint of victory, clearly up to his usual tricks. Bestowals from the gods never went fully in favor of the mortal. Did Pandora expect as much? A hint of this fear would explain her reaction before Zeus lulled her back into a state of enthrallment. Athena's keen perception piqued. She waited to see what Zeus and the rest of her fellow Olympians had up their sleeves.

"This pithos is our gift to you, your dowry," the King of the Gods said. "You can see the obvious beauty and magnificence of this container crafted by Hephaestus, but the rest of us are not stingy. All here will add a special endowment of their own to be carried inside."

Pandora nodded, her face a solemn canvas, while Zeus arose, his robes billowing around him along with puffy clouds, indicative of a good mood. He strode to the jar and, with a flourish of his hand, produced a key. Carved in the same gold as the eagle stopper, his giant hand nearly swallowed the tiny feather shape opener. Zeus inserted it into a lock on the back of the golden bird and with a twist, the stopper lifted from the jar.

"For a long and blessed marriage between you and Epimetheus, I give you vitality."

With a flick of his hand, he conjured a pile of silver dust, which sparkled as bright as the stars as he dropped it inside the jar. Pandora watched the trickling powder with awe. Only the keen eyes of a god could notice the shadowy powder of death mixed with the only a trace of vitality. Athena sat up straighter at the sight. She scanned the horseshoe of seats, yet saw no surprise on any face. *They know*, she thought, the words of Hermes falling into place.

Zeus returned to his throne, clouds settling in place around him. He motioned to his wife. With regal posture, she walked to the jar, the images on her chiton flickering. One moment a juicy pomegranate, the next a vibrant peacock.

"As the goddess of marriage, I bless you and Epimetheus with strength of partnership. May you ever be a source of comfort and support for one another."

She tapped her scepter against her other hand, creating a pile of bright blue dust. Athena watched the chief goddess drop in a tad of strength with a healthy dose of discord.

More evil than good from them both, Athena observed. She caught her father's eye and bristled at the triumph in them. Whatever he planned for Epimetheus would not end well. Sadness tugged at her psyche with the realization that a part of her had grown fond of the girl, now a pawn in a game she could never win. Perhaps she could still help Pandora somehow. Thoughts turned over in her mind while the gift giving continued.

Apollo followed. A nod of respect to Hera sent his sumptuous black curls bobbing against the golden laurels around his head. The goddess gave a terse smile to the son of one of Zeus' many mistresses. She likely wanted to hate him for his origins, but his beardless face, with the perpetual beauty of youth, charmed even Hera. He drew an arrow from the golden quiver strapped across his back. His hands gripped around the shaft, which he spun and dissolved into a pile of gold dust.

"As the god of prophecy and healing, I give you restorative capabilities to keep you both healthy and hale," his lyrical voice rang out.

This time, the meager proportion of healing mixed with an abundance of sickness did not surprise Athena. Outwardly, she tried to project composure, relaxed in her chair. Inside, her mind groped furiously for answers.

Aphrodite glided to the jar, her long, delicate neck craning across her fellow deities. Her golden hair shimmered like a waterfall, undulating in glossy waves down the back of her elegant, jewel-encrusted toga. Athena suppressed an eye roll at the usual ostentatious display of her sister-goddess. This deceptive game of Zeus' would be right up her alley.

"For you, Pandora, I give a beauty and grace from which your husband's eyes will never stray."

She fashioned a powder with the sparkle of diamonds, a gaudy touch. It slipped through her fingers into the jar. Athena watched a sampling of beauty and grace mingle with a generous amount of envy and cruel longings. Aphrodite's eyebrow arched wryly at Zeus on her way back to her seat.

Hermes flew on his winged shoes to alight center stage. Mischief was his very nature and Athena held no doubt her half-brother planted the seed of this plan in the mind of Zeus.

"To you both, I grant the gift of charm. May all be enchanted by your silver-tongued sagacity." With a twirl of his wrist, silver sand filled his palm. In a soft cascade, it swirled into the jar, a mix dominated by lies and craftiness.

Artemis followed, a matching bow and quiver of her twin, Apollo, secured across her back. Her tunic of mossy greens and wood browns hung short, emphasizing the muscular legs developed over a lifetime of hunting. After the gory death she delivered to the mortal Adonis, in the form of a giant boar, Athena knew her sibling would have no qualms helping their father with this scheme.

"To the happy couple, I give harmony. May your lives be balanced and no need ever befall you." With a smile at Pandora, she poured a bronze powder of harmony into the jar heavily laced with turmoil.

The remaining deities came in succession. Demeter, goddess of the harvest with her golden crown of wheat, added bounty spiked with famine. Ares, the god of war and Athena's bitter rival, gifted courage of spirit mixed with much strife. Hades, god of the underworld, lifted a hand to pour wealth diluted with poverty. Hestia, goddess of the hearth, her head ringed with a subtle flame, drizzled in serenity blended with abject madness.

Time ran short for Athena, only Poseidon remained between her and the jar. She racked her brain for some way to counter, or at least mitigate, the effects of this conspiracy on the life of this innocent young girl.

Meanwhile, the god of the sea rose, trident in hand. Dolphins, fish, and seahorses swam in and out of his robes, droplets of water raining to the floor, only to be sucked back up. With a bang of the trident on the stone, a ball of suspended blue liquid formed in his hand.

"My kingdom lies in the watery depths, a realm of comfort shielded from the cruel world. To you, Pandora, my gift is a fertile womb where your babies can develop in safety."

The fluid oozed into the jar in fat drops, tinged with scourge and barrenness. Poseidon roiled like a huge wave back to his seat, water drawing up behind him.

Once his brother settled, Zeus turned to Athena, who stewed at the wicked gleam of victory on his face. Though she had no love for either Epimetheus or his arrogant brother, Pandora's feisty spirit had won her over. The thought of the girl suffering for the misdoings of those two brutish Titans rankled her, the unfairness chafing at her sense of justice.

In the last second, as she stood, an idea formed in her mind. Though she could not undo what her fellow deities decreed, the perfect gift sprang to her mind.

TWENTY-THREE

Pandora stood captivated by the scene unfolding before her, a veneration for the gods swelling in her chest. Though, in truth, she could not hold her focus on any one deity, their fluid movements and animated attire never slowed enough for her to fully comprehend. She heard, or more precisely sensed, all they said, waves of words wafting through her mind.

The swirling images on the jar sped up and glowed each time one of the Olympians added to it. One generous gift after another streamed into the container, riveting Pandora's attention. The munificence of the gods left her humbled, honored to be chosen. Gratitude filled her mind, spreading over other thoughts. At some point, she realized she was on her knees, with no recollection of time or space, as though she floated in a peaceful cloud.

At last, only one goddess remained. Athena approached the jar with purposeful steps. The goddess fixed her gaze on the girl. Deep gray eyes filled with the acumen of timeless eons lifted the fog and Pandora saw clearly. Athena tried to communicate something in her stare. A secret? A warning? Pandora could not guess.

"To you, Pandora, I give the gift of wisdom. May you always be able to distinguish the true path from the deceitful one and may you never lose faith in yourself."

With a flash of her hand, Athena created dust of such pure whiteness, it glowed like the moon itself. Pandora watched it flow into the jar in a steady cascade. A trace of relief passed over Athena's face before her eyes shuttered all emotion. The deity returned to her seat, where she sat with her shoulders high. Pandora sensed disquiet amid the surrounding glory of the Olympians. A long silence followed, annoyance rippling from the other gods. Pandora lowered her head, unsure what caused the change in mood.

"Rise, Pandora, daughter of Lycus," boomed Zeus, and she stood with quaking knees. "These are our gifts to you and Epimetheus. May your marriage be blessed by them."

He sealed the jar with the eagle stopper, locking it with the key. The images on its side returned to their normal pace, dancers swayed, birds flew, men battled, an ever-changing collage of stories. Though still entrancing, the initial contentment of the gods diminished somehow, the entire atmosphere filled with brooding. Athena's gift fell in line with all the other blessings, yet inexplicably, her fellow deities chafed at it.

Zeus waved his hand, and something encircled Pandora's neck. She gazed down to see the feather-shaped key dangling on a delicate golden chain between her breasts. When her hand wrapped around it, the key vibrated with a soothing rhythm, warm against her fingers, as though a long-lost relic found its way home.

"But a warning," Zeus growled and Pandora's hair stood on end, "the jar must remain sealed or our gifts will scatter on the wind and disperse. Only you have the power to open it. Swear to protect its contents and guard the key for the good of yourself and your new husband."

"Y ... y ... yes, almighty Zeus," she managed, surprised her mouth worked.

A loud clap of thunder accompanied by a blinding light sent Pandora to the ground once more. When she sat up, broken rock pillars stood in place of the stately thrones. She was alone. The jar sat on the flat stone amid dead grass, pictures still awhirl, its grandeur not dampened by the humbler surroundings. She clasped the feather key and stared at it with wonder, unable to distinguish what had been real from what she may have imagined.

"Pandora?"

Iliana's voice made her jump. Whether five minutes or five years had passed, Pandora could not say. She turned to see the temple maid peering in from behind a column, the earlier blur eliminated. Rays of the setting sun framed Iliana's body, her face hidden in shadow. Pandora blinked, her mind too full of the power of the gods to fully concentrate on the mortal world. Words eluded her while she gathered her senses.

"Are you all right?" the maiden's soft voice echoed across the cavernous space.

"I'm fine," Pandora managed, her voice barely above a whisper. "The gods gave me this pithos as a wedding gift."

She rose, still trying to comprehend all she had heard and seen. Iliana came to her and helped straighten her tunic and tuck her hair back into place. The maiden's gaze flew around the empty circle until her eyes landed on the pithos. Pandora wanted to ask if Iliana saw the images moving too, but in the shadow of the gods' presence, her timid tongue remained silent. The maid regarded it for a moment, but without the fixation it evoked in Pandora.

"It's beautiful. I can help you carry it back to the temple," Iliana offered.

They each grabbed an ear of the splendid jar, but despite their combined strength, it did not budge. A look of confusion passed between them. Again, the pair heaved with all their might. Though it was the size of an average pithos, once the jar was an inch off the slab, they found it too heavy to hold. It clanged back onto the stone, the sound reverberating through the pillars.

"What on earth is in it?" Iliana exclaimed.

"That's enough girls!" The sharp voice made them jump. Hesiod stood before them, his normally affable face hard, his dark eyes sharp. Pandora wondered where he came from, but knew better than to ask. Both ladies bowed their heads in deference. "Away with you both. I will see to the conveyance of the pithos from here."

As they scurried out under his steely gaze, Pandora stole one last glance at her gift from the gods. Would she and Epimetheus be worthy of it? Would its gifts bring her all the wonderful blessing it promised? She touched the golden feather around her neck and its delicate contours filled her with tranquility. Zeus' only warning was not to open it. As long as she honored that request, no harm would come to them, as no one else possessed the power to unlock it. With a devoted hand around the key, she walked back down the hill with Iliana relieved the unprecedented meeting was behind her.

TWENTY-FOUR

The days that followed blurred together in a tumult of activity. Pandora's return to the temple was short-lived. Not two hours later, she bade Iliana goodbye, riding back down the mountain on Gregor's donkey. The stoic guide, who appeared younger in the light of day, uttered no words on their descent. At the foot of the mountain, Galena, brushing her windswept hair out of her eyes, awaited the girl along with a sizable traveling party.

"Welcome back," the woman said as Pandora folded into her embrace. "Back on the road for us."

Amid the entourage sat a curtained litter. At the insistence of Hesiod, Pandora rode in it with her chaperone, the sides tied shut against any nosy onlookers. Several other wagons joined the caravan, including one drawn by a dozen mules and guarded by twice as many soldiers. This vehicle carried the glorious pithos under a plain burlap tarp. *Twelve mules to pull it and Iliana and I thought we could carry it*, Pandora laughed to herself. A group of temple priests and priestesses, who made the journey on foot, rounded out the party.

For two days they lumbered across the countryside, the litter gently swaying, while Galena kept up a steady stream of conversation. Oddly, in privacy of their enclosure, she never once asked Pandora what happened on the mountain. Several times, the travelers halted when the pithos' wagon became stuck in a rut. It took all the manpower they had, with sweaty brows and taut muscles, to free the vehicle. Eventually, they sent scouts ahead to fill in any large holes in the road beforehand.

The weather cooperated, bright and mild, until the third day. Pandora peeked out a miniscule gap in the fabric. Wispy gray clouds fought with the sun, drizzle creating rainbows through meager rays in the sky. By afternoon, it rained in earnest. Their progress slowed, the party rode late into the night. When they finally stopped, men erected tents in the open meadow nearby, but Pandora and Galena chose to remain in the litter, where they snuggled next to each other, too comfortable to move.

Birdsong woke Pandora, a stream of pale light slanting through a slit in the curtains. She stretched and sat up. Her stiff body did not relish the thought of another day cramped in such small quarters. Perhaps she could walk today, at least for a little while, her constant confinement wearing her patience thin. She parted the curtains to a fine, cloudless morning and inhaled the refreshing air. Men scurried about the encampment, tending horses, and packing up gear. Pandora stepped down and circled the litter, hoping to find a small stream to wash up in. What she saw surprised her.

The caravan sat on the edge of the largest field Pandora ever saw in her life. Decorative flowers stood in large urns at the far end, encircling a large altar. Tables lined the perimeters, draped in fine silks, and set with delicate plates and glassware. Garlands festooned the outlining trees in grand swoops. Off to the right stood a large outdoor kitchen, chefs already bustling to and fro. The scent of roasting meat wafted across the air, and Pandora's mouth watered. Evidently, someone was planning a party.

"Good morning," greeted a familiar voice.

"Elara! What are you doing here?" Pandora exclaimed, leaping into the arms of her childhood maid.

"I'm here to prepare you for the wedding tonight," Elara said, her eyes crinkling at the words.

Pandora glimpsed back at the field, the decorations, the altar. This whole setup was for her? And the wedding was *tonight*? Not that she had asked when it was, but she assumed someone would tell her at some point. Her jaw gaped. How could she possibly be ready by tonight? Weddings took preparation, time to consider all the minutiae of the occasion.

"No one told you," Elara guessed at Pandora's bewildered expression. "Of course not. What else do we expect from men."

"Are my parents here?" she asked the importance of the day sinking in.

"Yes, they are camping with other guests over that hill." Elara pointed diagonally behind them. "We are near a temple on the outskirts of Thessaly, where the ceremony will take place."

Pandora squinted in the morning sun. When she shielded her eyes in a salute, she saw wisps of smoke over the top of a small rise where campers cooked their breakfasts. The happiness the thought of seeing her parents brought her did little to counter her rising anger at being the last one to know about her own wedding. Galena poked her head out of the litter, her eyes widening at her surroundings.

"Second to last, I guess," Pandora grumbled.

Her gaze fell on Hesiod, whose white teeth flashed in a bright smile against his dark skin while he directed a servant where to put another urnful of flowers. The entire trip he had known yet never told her, as though her presence would be some ancillary part of the event. Is this what married life had in store for her? Following the orders and whims of men? And the gods? She longed for her bedroom, her beloved Rex, and her simple life on Lemnos.

"Come," Elara said, hoisting a bag on her shoulder. "We will go to the river and bathe you. We can't have the bride looking like a soiled sack of flour."

Pandora took the hand Elara offered, the other raking through her matted hair. Together they strode past two guards into a small glade where willows tipped gracefully toward a rushing stream. The maid found a secluded pool ringed with their elegant branches. A warm breeze rustled the leaves, kissing the water's edge where they shimmered green and silver, the sound as soft and lyrical as the notes of Orpheus' harp. Pandora relaxed, inhaling the wintergreen scent of their bark.

The maid laid down her bag and dug inside. On a half-submerged rock, she lined up soaps, oils, and a sponge. Pandora undid her sandals, her ankles crisscrossed with light lines where the straps had kept off the dirt. Elara helped her out of her tunic and undergarments and Pandora slid into the water, cold at first, but soon refreshing. Elara scrubbed the grime off every inch of her charge, the pools of dust carried away by the current. When deemed officially clean, Pandora climbed onto a rock to towel off. She donned a robe and sat while her maid combed her long hair in a dark cascade down her back.

Elara returned all the toiletries to her bag and motioned to Pandora. "It's time to make you the most beautiful bride the world had ever seen."

These were the only words either one spoke. The maid was content to leave Pandora to her thoughts, which wavered between indignation and panic at the realization that at this time tomorrow she would be the wife of a stranger, alone in an unfamiliar land. The prestige that befell her in the presence of the Olympians for the honor of this marriage had long passed. Grand ideas of escape or outright refusal to marry played out in her mind, the preposterous musings of a petulant child. The time had come to put such notions aside and face her future. She could be a submissive observer or an active participant. The choice was hers. She rose with a new sense of resolve and followed Elara back to the camp.

TWENTY-FIVE

High in a tree limb, Athena watched the preparations. A warm breeze ruffled her owl feathers. On it came the clamor of mortals who quarreled below. One thought Zeus should receive the most tributes, the others argued, as goddess of marriage, they were Hera's due. Another spoke in favor of Hephaestus, since the bride came from his island. The din rose to a cacophony of Olympian names being shouted over one another.

Athena flew across the field to a quieter location, the squabbles of man tiresome to her ears. Ever they angled to be elevated by favor or sought the mercy of the gods for fear of retribution, only a few held any true honor in their hearts. Those rare breeds led lives of humble happiness, a trait scoffed at by most, who coveted glory and riches. But what could be done? In them, Prometheus created a rash creature.

Even Pandora, Athena mused. Though the goddess admired her spunk, her sardonic letter showed a certain impertinence toward the gods. Still, that trait in a man would be exalted as determination and grit. The deities usually welcomed these attributes when doling out blessings on a chosen hero, but frowned on them in a woman. Athena sensed a current of wisdom in the young Pandora, one that had drawn her interest, one that could blossom under the right circumstances. Whatever Zeus had planned with the pithos, Athena vowed to help the girl suffer as little as possible.

A loud thud jangled the branch, a mighty eagle landing next to her. Athena kept her gaze on the field where servants decorated tables and steeled herself for the anger which emanated off her new companion. She waited in silence while wrath washed over her in waves.

"What was the meaning of that?" the eagle demanded. A shout to her, yet unheard by human ears.

"Hello, Father," Athena cocked her tiny owl head. "The meaning of what?"

"You know exactly what I'm talking about. How dare you put that gift in the pithos!"

He jumped closer and his menacing beak ripped at her feathers. She tottered back, fully aware she should not antagonize him, but still angry at how little regard any of her fellow Olympians showed for the girl. The goddess made herself tall and hopped back toward Zeus, the limb shuddering beneath their talons. Some people lifted their heads to the tree line, but thought the noise only the rustling of a bird. They continued with their duties, unaware of the immortal spat.

"I see nothing wrong with what I added," she countered, standing high on her legs, though still nowhere near as tall as him. "Our plan was to give Epimetheus a bride, a partner, to imply he is the favored brother. When did that change?"

"It hasn't changed," Zeus blustered, his head dipping toward the field. "The wedding is imminent."

"But all the evils you put in the jar—the ones everyone knew about but me. What is the purpose of them if not to cause misery and suffering to an innocent girl?"

"Innocent girl?" he humphed. "You chose her for her brashness, her arrogance, and now you weep for her artlessness?"

Athena paused. Somehow, Zeus found out her secret. "Yes, I chose a strong-willed girl, the only kind who could get Epimetheus to listen to her over his brother. Is that not what you intended? To tip the scales in Epimetheus' favor as payback to Prometheus?"

"My intent is to *punish* Prometheus for his irreverence and to show what happens to those who intentionally trick the gods," Zeus replied, with a sharp bite on her wing.

"Why punish the girl?" Athena asked, shaking off a torn feather.

"Why do you care this much for this mere mortal? She has shown you no particular veneration. Or any of us, for that matter."

A fair statement. Athena rarely interceded on behalf of humans. Yes, she helped Hercules with his labors, Perseus with Medusa, and her favorite of all, Odysseus. Each of these heroes had possessed an innate wisdom which won her over. She saw a glimmer of this quality in the girl, though not fully developed, and it left her heart with the same impression, the same yearning to protect. Though she doubted any of this would matter to her father, she would still argue for Pandora.

"Because she does not deserve to be embroiled in this vengeance you seek. You asked for a clever way to get back at Prometheus and I provided you with one, only to have you go behind my back and devise this scheme."

"Be careful, daughter. I grow tired of your defiance. If you side against me, you will stand alone," he warned.

Athena sighed, ever this infighting. Zeus ruled over all, yet never found an ounce of contentment in his power. He only found satisfaction when pitting one Olympian against another, stoking strife among god and mortal alike. Was there no end to it? Weary of the argument, Athena conceded for the moment.

"By your command, the pithos is not to be opened. What does our difference of opinion matter?" she asked.

The silence that followed was answer enough and grim reality set in.

"You mean to force her to open it." She did not even phrase it as a question. "To bend her to your will as you have done to countless unsuspecting women. And this one not even a victim of your philandering, merely collateral damage in your power struggles with the Titans."

"Prometheus deserves to be punished," Zeus bellowed. "It is my will and I order you not to interfere."

With a clap of thunder, he vanished. Every mortal in the field dropped prostrate to the ground, whispering words of prayer to the King of the Gods for whatever transgression had upset him. Athena, from the safety of her leafy cover, shook her head. Her sharp owl eyes scanned for Pandora. She watched her enter a tent with a maid. The goddess vowed to keep a close eye on the soon to be couple. Though she did not hold sway over Zeus, perhaps there was a way to protect the girl from certain tragedy. With a flick, she spread her wings and flew off to begin her quest.

TWENTY-SIX

"There," Elara said, with more than a hint of pride.

The maid arranged one last lock of hair around Pandora's face and stepped away for the bride to see herself in the mirror. Pandora spent the last several hours of brushstrokes, hairpins, and makeup complaining, but the result was worth it. Never did she think she could attain such beauty. Danae, now reunited with her daughter, had collaborated with Elara on the hairstyle and the amount of makeup while Pandora's mind wandered. Was Epimetheus handsome or fearsome to behold? Would he be kind to her? What if he insisted on opening the pithos? Would the gods punish them?

"You're radiant," Danae proclaimed, wrapping her arms around her daughter.

"Isn't she?" Elara exclaimed, bouncing on the balls of her feet, eyes misty.

"Everything is beautiful," Pandora said and wound her finger around an unbound curl framing her face.

Next, they helped her into the dress. The exquisite material of lustrous silver, a gift from the gods which shimmered as sun on water with every movement. It clung subtly to her slender frame, both elegant and alluring. Beneath it, still between her breast, sat the golden key. At first, mother and maid wanted her to remove it, but when she explained it was from the gods who told her to keep it guarded, they relented. She had thought of wearing it on top of the dress, however, something told her to keep it hidden.

A golden diadem wrapped around a pile of curls on top of her head, interlaced with flowers from the meadow. Later, Elara would pin the final touch into place, the long veil. The material would drape across her shoulders before cascading to the ground like a shroud. At the ceremony, they would pull the front part over her face, hiding it behind the nearly opaque material. No one would see all the effort that went into her appearance, which made her question the value of this tedious process.

"You are as beautiful as a goddess," Danae declared.

"Mother, do not say such a thing!" Pandora reprimanded, her awe of the Olympians still fresh in her mind. "Surely, no mortal, no matter how attractive, can compete with the immortals. Not even Helen of Troy."

"Of course, you are right," her mother agreed. "Forgive me."

The three made a hand gesture in deference to the gods, lest a deity become angry by the comment. None of them wished to incur unnecessary wrath on this momentous day.

"Come, Elara," Danae said. "We must ready ourselves in the tent next door. Pandora, wait here and try to stay still."

The maid surveyed the bride-to-be one more time. Satisfied with her work, she left on the heels of her mistress. The flutter of the tent flap drew in the smell of roasting meat, but Pandora remained too nervous to think about food, her mind consumed with questions. How would life with an immortal be? Would the wedding night be as frightening as she imagined? Why had the gods chosen her? Or Epimetheus, for that matter? Why did they bestow such a generous gift?

As the Olympians flashed through her thoughts, Pandora heard a soft noise above. High on a pole that created one of the tent rafters sat a small, gray owl, its bright, yellow eyes fixed on her. Unease crept up from Pandora's toes. She knew the creature had not flown in when her mother and Elara stepped out nor had it been there before. Realization dawned.

"Mighty Athena." She dropped to her knee, head bowed. "Forgive us. My mother meant no harm by her remark. She is excited for me."

The bird flew down to perch on top of the mirror, where it continued to stare at the girl. Unnerved, Pandora peered up. Though small, there was a grandeur about the owl, a quiet dignity not normally found in animals, which unnerved Pandora. The creature cocked its head to the side while she gaped, as though it could see into her soul. After a moment of tense silence, Pandora sensed the goddess waited for her to speak.

"Are you mad at my mother?" she asked.

The owl stared down at her, a dismissive rustle of her wings. Relief filled Pandora. Her mother was not in the crosshairs of the gods. After more silence, she realized it was up to her to figure this out.

"Is it about the wedding?"

Again, an uninterested response.

"Is it about the meeting I had with the gods?"

The owl's gaze intensified. Knowing she was on the right track, she pondered the encounter. She remembered how Athena appeared to agitate her fellow deities when she added her gift to the jar.

"Is it about the pithos?" she asked.

The owl flew down to rest on the vanity at eye level with the girl, who grew frustrated at the one-sided conversation with the serene bird. Pandora recalled the warning from Zeus not to open the jar. Surely, she did not need an additional reminder. There was more going on here.

"Do you wish me to open it?" She asked, wondering why Athena would go against the King of the Gods, but infighting among the Olympians was legendary.

A shrill cry pierced the air as the owl opened its wings full span. Pandora cowered.

"You wish for me not to open it?"

The bird relaxed, but the keen stare remained. Pandora struggled to find exactly what Athena wanted her to know. She thought about the many stories of gods tricking humans into doing their bidding unwittingly. For Athena, she felt an inherent trust, but not for Zeus. The thought of him set off warning bells in her mind. Slowly, the pieces fell together.

"You wish for it never to be opened by anyone under any circumstances."

A solemn nod from the bird.

Athena had come to warn her. The pithos was not a gift, as the gods implied, but something incredibly dangerous. Memories of her dream, of evil chasing her, clawed at her heart. The despair. The pain. That is what the pithos contained. She sank to her knees under the weight of this insight.

"I swear to you, oh mighty Athena, I will not willingly open the jar nor let another do it in my stead. You have my word."

She bowed her head to touch her forehead to the floor. When she looked up, the owl was gone.

TWENTY-SEVEN

Epimetheus bent his arms to rest on the fence post, the sun nearing its apex in the sky as Helios guided his chariot on its daily path. The Titan reached into his pocket and pulled out a few apples. His horses ran to him, eager for their treat, Rosa and Hazel nudging their way to the front of the pack. Absently, he stroked one mane after another, soothed by the presence of these creatures who gave him such joy much yet asked for little in return.

"Shouldn't you be readying yourself?"

His brother's brash voice broke the tranquil silence. Several horses ran to the far end of the paddock, tails flicking while they cast wary eyes at Prometheus, whose visits usually led to alarming shouts. The steeds stopped under the shade of fig trees, branches laden with sweet treats, where they clustered together seeking consolation from the unwanted visitor. Their master shut his eyes with a sigh, wishing he could join them.

When Epimetheus failed to reply, Prometheus came to stand by his side. "Come now, Brother, surely you don't wish to be late for your own wedding."

The wedding. The exact thing he had come out here to forget. In the month since Hermes informed him of his prize, satisfaction at being chosen had given way to apprehension. What did he know of women? Of companionship? His animals kept him happy here in his secluded abode. He did not relish the idea of the constant presence of a mortal. He found comfort in his peaceful life. And ever, he ruminated on the warning of his brother, the smarter one, the one with foresight, not impetuous and senseless as he was. Could it all be a trick? Did the Olympians conspire to make him miserable? Whatever their motive, he had agreed, his word now an unbreakable pact.

"At least let's find you something better to wear than a tunic that reeks of manure."

Prometheus took his arm and pulled him toward the house. Epimetheus did not resist. In this matter, his brother was right. Earlier in the week, the temple priest had brought him a pristine white tunic and an ornately embroidered cloak of the finest linen he had ever seen. Not that he cared about such frivolous garments, sturdier clothes were the staple of someone around animals all day. But he supposed this day would be an exception in many ways.

"Since when do you care about my wedding?" Epimetheus snapped, happy to have a target for his frustrations. "The few times I've seen you since the announcement, all you've done is mock my stupidity."

Indeed, Prometheus tried to convince his sibling to back out of the deal several times with ideas on how to appease the gods, far more confident in the deities' conciliation than Epimetheus thought probable. But truly, pride played a bigger part in his compliance, the idea the gods may actually favor him over his brother too big a lure to ignore. Now, like a hooked fish, he wriggled on the line, helpless in the eventual outcome, for good or evil.

"Epimetheus, you are my brother," the silver-tongued Titan said, "if this marriage is what you desire, then I, as your brother, will be by your side."

At the words, Epimetheus glanced askance at Prometheus, who rarely professed any type of fraternal bond unless it benefited his own purposes. "Bah, you think I believe you after the constant barrage of insults you've hurled at me this month alone? Why do you really care?"

"Because I am smarter than you. Smart enough to pay attention to what transpires today for a clue to the Olympian's scheme."

"Do what you want," Epimetheus shrugged, annoyed his brother still would not concede that the bride was a gift to reward him.

They crossed the meadow to the main house, Prometheus with purposeful strides, next to his sulking sibling. When they crossed the threshold, the elder one stopped short.

"This will not do at all," he exclaimed, surveying the main room.

"What's wrong with it?" Epimetheus asked, his defenses raised.

"Women prefer order and cleanliness," Prometheus declared, chasing some chickens out the front door. He pointed to feathers and droppings left in the birds' wake. "Not this."

Epimetheus decided not to mention the goat who frequented the house. He imagined how his new bride would view his home. Probably more of a barn than a house, with its scant decor and animal smells. His failure to consider any of this may cause his marriage to begin on a poor foot.

"I guess I hadn't thought of that," he mumbled to his feet.

"Don't worry. I will have Hesiod send some women from the village to clean this place up before you bring her home tonight," Prometheus promised. "I'll also arrange for her handmaid. Now, let's get you washed up and dressed."

While Prometheus headed toward the bedroom, Epimetheus stood with a furrowed brow. Would a bride bring upheaval to his entire life? And not only her. Now a maid would live here as well? He shuddered, all thoughts of his peaceful existence vanishing before his eyes. A call from his brother roused him from his stupor and he rushed to the bedroom.

"What time did you tell your villagers to arrive at the temple?" Prometheus asked.

"Umm, I didn't tell them anything," Epimetheus muttered. "I didn't think it was important."

"Honestly, Brother, sometimes I wonder why I let you
have any humans. Do you ever communicate with them?
Do they even know about the wedding?" Prometheus
questioned, and his brother shrugged. "Now, it's too late.
Good thing there will be plenty of people from Lemnos
and more from Thessaly. The ceremony will be well
attended, regardless of your oversight."

Despite the animosity he sometimes held for his brother,
Prometheus' ability to take charge relieved Epimetheus.
Not only did his brother help him dress, but he would also
see to making the house respectable enough for Pandora.
Plus, he had the foresight to invite people to the wedding.
Epimetheus cursed his stupidity. Why had he not thought
of these matters?

When they left for the ceremony, both Titans had
donned resplendent tunics. Prometheus' constant chatter
allayed Epimetheus' nerves. Were it not for his sibling,
Epimetheus may still be leaning on the fence by his horses,
completely unprepared.

"Thank you for all your help, Brother. I know you don't
agree with my decision."

"Epimetheus, I wish you nothing but happiness. I am
here for you always, to have your back and alert you of
your blind spots. Let us put this quarrel behind us and
enjoy your wedding."

They embraced at the edge of the field and walked
down the hill to meet Hesiod, who would escort them to
the temple. For the first time in a long time, Epimetheus
felt optimistic about both his marriage and his future
relationship with his brother.

TWENTY-EIGHT

From her chair inside the tent, Pandora heard the rustle of garments mixed with the chatter of the guests, a low din occasionally pierced by a peal of laughter. The crowd quieted at the priest's intonation leading up to the sacrifice, the startled bellow of a cow abruptly cut short. Lilts of flute song commenced, interspersed with the clang of symbols, a melodious tune eliciting claps and cheers.

Pandora shifted in her seat, all attempts to calm her nerves proving unsuccessful, with her trip to the temple now imminent. Should she tell anyone about Athena's warning? What if Epimetheus demanded they open the jar? What if Epimetheus dismissed all her wishes? What if he was cruel and beat her? Questions went round and round her head that only time could answer. She remembered her mother's advice to be submissive and agreeable, two traits she did not think she could possess in infinite quantities. Her knee bobbed up and down of its own accord, tapping a dissonant rhythm from the outside music.

The tent flap parted, the music, smells, and sounds wafting in. A smartly dressed Elara entered with another smaller figure behind.

"Cyane!" Pandora exclaimed, off her feet at the sight of her friend.

"I came with a large contingent from Lemnos," she said, as they embraced. "Hephaestus wanted his people represented. It's the furthest I've ever been from home."

"I am glad you are here and how lovely you are," Pandora admired.

"*You* are the personification of beauty today, Pandora."

Elara pushed her way between them. "We are here with the veil."

The maid laid an oblong package on the bed, undoing the coarse burlap wrappings to reveal a length of magnificent silk. She motioned for Pandora to sit again while she fanned out the fabric. It wafted gracefully, a diaphanous cloud of fabric. Cyane pulled up another chair and took her friend's hand. Elara arranged the veil over the bride's head. After securing it with the poke of several pins, she stepped back.

"There," she said in her *I am pleased with the outcome* voice Pandora had known since childhood.

Pandora rose, her eyes only able to distinguish shadowy shapes beyond the semi opaque material, as though she viewed the world through a fog. The veil fell to her hands in the front, where her only clear view was her feet. Elara and Cyane straightened the veil around her shoulders, shaking out the back, which flowed behind her like a silken pool.

"I can hardly see," Pandora complained. "I'm likely to fall flat on my face."

"That is why Cyane is here to help guide you. Modesty must be upheld." Elara quipped.

"Modesty? Every other woman will have complete use of their eyes but I need to remain half blind?"

"Come now, Pandora, let's not be difficult," the maid chided in another tone all too familiar, one used prodigiously in her youth.

"Difficult? For wanting to see?" Pandora blurted, knowing this would win her no sympathy.

"You must be on your best behavior today, lest the groom finds you too much of a handful and backs out. Honestly, Pandora, you are to become a wife today. Stop acting as though you are a child." With a brusque motion, Elara shoved the tent flap out of her way. "Now, I'm going to see if the procession is ready."

"Don't worry," Cyane said, with a squeeze of her hand. "I won't let you fall."

"I know," Pandora sighed. "I feel like a piece of merchandise being sold to the highest bidder."

"Unless we want to pledge our chastity to the gods, all women meet this same fate," Cyane murmured.

The statement surprised Pandora, whose friend usually played the submissive female role convincingly. Pandora had never been one to hide her true thoughts, but it comforted her to know that Cyane, who divulged little on the subject, noticed the scales rarely tipped in the female's favor.

"I'm scared," Pandora admitted. "To have no idea what lies ahead and to have such little say in it."

"I will pray to the gods for you," Cyane took her other hand. "Especially to Hera, goddess of marriage. I will ask her to watch over you and protect you."

The dreadful images of her dream about the pithos crept into Pandora's mind, along with the warning of Athena. Though she stood a foot apart from Cyane, a chasm opened between them, one they could not bridge. Despite her friend's promises, Cyane would return to the sanctuary of Lemnos. There she would marry and reside with a husband, far from the eyes of the gods and their schemes. Pandora's girlhood dissolved in this moment, scattering into the depths of an abyss, separating her from the only world she had ever known, whose safety she took for granted. A certainty she would never set foot again in her beloved homeland filled her to the core.

Cyane took her trembling for wedding jitters. She whispered words of encouragement with continued promises to pray to the gods.

Perhaps Pandora should have prayed harder, taken the gods more seriously. Perhaps had she not ridiculed their letter writing assignment, someone else would stand here now, thankful and excited at the prospect of marrying a Titan. If only she could go back and warn herself. But sadly, regrets cannot turn back the clock. Her only path now was forward.

Elara eased back through the tent flap. Her face spread into a wide smile at the sight of the girls hand in hand.

"There now, isn't it better with Cyane here?"

Pandora managed a nod, happy the veil concealed the tears brimming in her eyes. The maid gave them each a once over. After a few tiny adjustments, she proclaimed them ready. She opened the flap and music sprung to life from the waiting entourage.

"Now, let's get you to your groom," Elara said, her excitement evident.

With a sigh, Pandora stepped through the yawning opening to her uncertain future.

TWENTY-NINE

A bright sky soared overhead, with puffy clouds resembling dollops of clotted cream. Tiny pebbles crunched underfoot on the well-worn path to the temple. True to her word, Cyane guided Pandora, a steadfast hand clamped on her elbow. In the daylight, Pandora could make out clearer outlines of people, though exact details remained fuzzy. Young men with flutes led the way, their celebratory notes punctured by an enthusiastic symbol player. Pandora and her friend came next with Danae and Lycus in their wake. The remaining guests trailed after, their voices a jubilant din. Ahead, the temple came into view, a modest yet elegant structure. At the top of the stairs, Hesiod waited, flanked by two men.

Thus, Pandora laid eyes on the infamous Titans Epimetheus and Prometheus. She tried to determine who was who. Even in their earthly forms, they stood a head taller than anyone—though their Titan forms would be much larger. Step by step, she drew closer. She gazed from one to the other through her gauzy veil, noting the similarities between them. Both were handsome and well-built. Though immortal, they held the appearance of men in their late twenties with thick, shoulder-length hair and chiseled jaws. Indeed, they appeared almost alike but for the expressions on their faces—one with pursed lips and calculating eyes, the other with a countenance edged with uneasiness. *Could that be him*, she wondered, *looking as nervous as I feel?*

"Welcome, Pandora, daughter of Lycus." Hesiod's deep voice resonated off the temple's stone pillars.

The priest motioned her forward. Cyane helped her friend to the top step and took a step back. Pandora tried to still her shaking knees, sorry to have lost the brace of her friend's arm. Between the eyes of the spectators buffeting into her back and the trio of men in front of her, her insides quailed. The altar visible inside the temple gate, laden with blood dripping sacrifices, did little to quell the tension in her chest.

"Epimetheus, join hands with your bride."

Lycus stepped forward. He took Pandora's left hand and held it out. A wave of relief flooded her when the man with the uneasy countenance came to stand next to her. When her father placed her tiny hand into his massive one, she snuck a glimpse up, but only saw the bottom of his chin. She leveled her eyes straight ahead, in line with his broad chest. While the priest rattled off his blessings and praises to the gods, Pandora lowered her eyes to the intricate belt around Epimetheus' stark white tunic. Three bands of soft brown leather wrapped around each other to form a thick coil. Each band etched with the dyed shapes of different animals. Rams, cows, horses, and some Pandora did not recognize. How extraordinary that he created such a variety of creatures.

She peeked up again at his clean-shaven chin. His head tipped down, and he flashed a quick smile, which Pandora returned, not sure he could see. She also noted how gently he held her hand with his large, calloused one, which gave her some measure of comfort. A sense of disquiet made her cast an eye at Prometheus, looming behind the groom. At his intense stare, Pandora's heart skipped a beat. Did her new brother-in-law already hold some type of grudge against her? She hoped not. One of the few things she knew of the brothers was their close bond. One small woman against two Titans? Not good odds at all.

The priest broke her thoughts when he put his hand atop the couple's clasped ones.

"Epimetheus, do you agree to take this woman, a generous gift from the gods, as your bride?" Hesiod's baritone voice rang rich and clear.

"Yes, I pledge to the gods my acceptance of their gift and take Pandora as my wife," Epimetheus declared.

The softness in his tone reassured Pandora, not at all the scary bellow she expected. Hopefully, he was this gentle of a soul away from the eyes of the public. *I have a lifetime to find out*, she thought ruefully. Hesiod asked Lycus if he approved of the marriage, which her father answered with enthusiasm. Pandora faced no questions. Brides had no say in these matters, apparently deemed not as capable as men in choosing a husband.

After bestowing some more blessings, he led the couple back down the stairs. A jubilant cheer broke from the crowd while the procession regrouped, this time with Epimetheus and Pandora leading the way to the meadow. She leaned heavily on his arm to keep her balance. Would he think she was weak? Or would he realize she could not see properly? Somehow, the difference mattered to her.

At the tables, they broke apart, with the men sitting on one side and the woman on the other, as was customary. Between the two main tables sat a large pedestal draped in a rich red brocade that pooled on the floor, reminiscent of the blood around the altar. In the center, amid decorative flowers and candles, sat the pithos. At the sight of it, the key around Pandora's neck vibrated, tingles running down her arms and legs. The tremors stopped as quickly as they started, leaving Pandora to decipher if the jar evoked gratitude or foreboding.

Cyane clasped her hand and guided her to the bride's designated seat at the women's table. Ladies filtered past one by one, each offering congratulations and blessings. A few Pandora recognized from Lemnos, but many were strangers, rich citizens who bought their way into this unusual wedding. The last to approach was her mother, arms stretched wide. Pandora fell into the embrace.

"Such a beautiful feast. No detail overlooked," she gushed, helping arrange Pandora's gown when she sat. "And a gift from the Olympians. You are fortunate indeed, Daughter."

Servants passed trays filled with fruits, bread, cheese, and the traditional cakes mixed with sesame seeds and honey for fertility. Wine flowed and lively conversation filled the table. Danae and Cyane, on either side of the bride, raved about the food, the music, the decorations, and above all, the pithos. Always their conversation returned to the object in deferential tones of adulation and the good fortune of Pandora.

Each time, while she nodded in agreement, her eyes turned warily to the infamous container. The dread from her dream crept into her throat. She glanced over to Epimetheus, where he sat quietly, showing more interest in the food on his plate than the pithos. Prometheus, however, kept peering over at it, eyes filled with cunning. She knew of Prometheus and his scheming. The last thing she needed was for the Titan to covet a pithos that needed to remain closed. Between her breasts, the key grew warm, as though in warning, and Pandora was grateful the opaque veil hid the dubious expression on her face.

THIRTY

Epimetheus sat rigidly next to his brother at the men's table laden with meats, breads, fruits, and copious amounts of wine. The priest, who graced his other side, showed little restraint when it came to either food or drink, refilling plate and cup with the zeal of a long-starved man. The Titan had little appetite. He snuck several glimpses at his wife, such a strange concept in his head. She appeared about as eager to be here as he was. Soon they would be home. Then what?

When he took her hand at the temple, he noticed her delicateness, akin to the smaller birds he created with their tenuous bodies and gossamer wings. A clumsy giant such as himself would need to take extra care with her. Her opaque veil flustered him. During the little experience he had with mortals, he had used their eyes to judge their character. Despite her frailness, perhaps she could turn mean as a Harpy if angered. Prometheus always laughed at this character trait he gave to women. *To keep men on their toes*, he had snickered.

He was curious about her hidden face. Perhaps she was as fair as Helen. A virtue which had not turned out pleasantly for most of those involved in the subsequent Trojan War. Perhaps his brother was right, and the gods played a trick by giving him a bride as ugly as a Gorgon. He shuddered at the thought of sharing his quiet home with such a creature and he ran his hand through his hair. What if his looks displeased her? He had never given his appearance much consideration, but now the thought of her disapproval quailed him. Thankfully, his brother made him dress for the occasion, or he would have shown up in a manure-stained tunic.

"Epimetheus." Prometheus elbowed him. "Pay attention. Hesiod asked you a question."

"Sorry," he stammered. "I was lost in thought."

"Not to worry, I would expect nothing less from a nervous groom." The priest enjoyed another long draft of wine and added, "I asked if you planned to live on your homestead on the hill. You're quite cut off from everything up there."

"Um ... I suppose I had not thought of it." He realized there were many things he had not considered about married life.

"Pandora may prefer to live in your village in the company of others," the priest stated. "After all, we want a happy bride, especially after the generosity of the gods."

Hesiod gestured at the pithos ensconced on its pedestal. Images swirled on the sides of the container, golden figures gleaming against the obsidian body. The eagle stopper on the top appeared ready to take flight. Its beautiful craftsmanship would normally evoke admiration in Epimetheus, yet the gift left him troubled for reasons he could not pinpoint. While the priest expounded on the blessings the pithos contained for a long and fruitful marriage, both Titans stared, one with unease and the other with greed.

"You are well on your way to a long and fruitful marriage," the priest declared.

At the word *fruitful*, Epimetheus choked on the bread he had in his mouth, yet another parameter he had not pondered. Prometheus thumped him on the back with more force than his brother thought necessary.

"Now if you will excuse me, I will see that the chariot is prepared and I will give my final blessing."

The priest rose on unsteady feet but still managed to drain his cup of wine before tottering off. Alone, the brothers sat in silence.

"The ceremony went well," Prometheus noted.

No reply.

"Dear gods, you are the picture of misery at your own wedding feast. What is wrong?"

"I don't know how to be a husband," Epimetheus muttered, pushing some grapes around on his plate.

"That's all? I would not worry if I were you. She is your property now. Just tell her what to do and how to behave. Simple as that. It's what I do with Hesione now that we are married and we have no issues." At his brother's blank stare, Prometheus said, "Now, if you will excuse me a moment. I need to relieve myself."

The elder Titan rose and stalked behind some bushes ringing the meadow. When he finished his business, he lingered by the edge of the grass, where the clamor of the party lulled to a quiet hum. The tables gushed with merry chatter, but for the bride and groom. Each sat silent amid the surrounding conviviality. Epimetheus sat with the expression of a trapped deer, and though a veil hid her face, Prometheus suspected Pandora expression matched. His gaze fell on the pithos, with its captivating imagery, and he tried to reason away the pang of jealousy in his heart. *Any gift from the gods comes with a catch*, he reminded himself in an effort to quell his resentment.

"Such a prize," a voice at his side lilted.

To any guest, the Titan appeared to be standing with a servant boy, who lolled against a tree, but the guise did not fool Prometheus.

"What are you doing here, Hermes?"

"It's a wedding. I came give blessings to the new couple," the deity replied, feigned hurt in his voice.

"Then the bride and groom are over there." Prometheus pointed across the field.

"Yes, yes, I will get to them. But the pithos truly is amazing, is it not?" Hermes baited. At the Titan's purposeful silence, he continued. "You should have seen all the marvelous gifts each Olympian placed inside. Shame it was so one-sided."

"One-sided?" Prometheus asked, annoyed to have let the trickster goad him.

"Yes," the god continued. "Only Pandora can open it to retrieve any of the gifts."

"So?"

"If Epimetheus, or by extension, *you* needed the favor of the gods stored inside, the matter would be entirely under that mortal girl's control."

Hermes sounded as though the issue upset him a great deal, but Prometheus knew his games by now.

"Are you not happy unless you are stirring up trouble?" the Titan asked pointedly.

"Me? Never! How could you say such things? I am offended."

With a snap of his finger, the god vanished, without bothering to congratulate the new couple.

Prometheus' eyes returned to the pithos and his brow furrowed. The hypnotic images on the surface whirled, the dancing movement seeming to creep across the meadow and up his toes, fixing him to the spot. His heart filled with a sudden sense of intense dread and desperation, he thought he would burst into pieces.

A clap on his back startled him back to reality.

"Come, the chariot awaits," Hesiod said. "Time to escort your brother and his bride home."

After one last hesitant glance at the jar, Prometheus fell into step with the priest.

THIRTY-ONE

Despite Pandora's wish for time to stop, the reception wound to a close. The moment she avoided thinking about had arrived—the wedding night. A chariot bedecked in flowers led by a horse with similar decoration pulled into the middle of the field amid the jubilant crowd. Her mother and Cyane each took an arm to guide her. With mechanical steps, she approached the vehicle, her mind in a stupor at the thought of leaving.

Cyane embraced her, words of encouragement whispered in her ear. Elara clasped her hand. Pandora saw a smile of reassurance from her longtime caretaker in the instant before their fingers slipped apart. Her father jostled his way through the chaos, and both parents helped her mount the chariot. Pandora took hold of the rail to brace her trembling legs.

Raucous laughter accompanied the men, the imposing Prometheus leading his brother at the front of the pack. The chariot groaned and shifted when Epimetheus stepped aboard. Cheers erupted from the crowd. Epimetheus took up the reins and with a flick of his wrist sent the horses on their way along a torch-lit path. The guests paraded ahead, full of song and dance, strewing the ground with coins and flower petals for prosperity and fertility. Pandora's stomach sank at that thought, but she forced herself to stand tall even if she blanched as white as her veil. At least the abominable thing would be off soon. Whoever decided brides should spend their wedding day nearly suffocating should rot in Tartarus.

She stole a glance at Epimetheus, whose massive frame dwarfed her. The Titan stared ahead with an unreadable face. His massive frame loomed next to her. The grind of wheels sounded behind them. Pandora peeked over her shoulder. Although she could only see its outline, she knew the wagon, pulled by twelve mules, carried the pithos. The key vibrated softly against her chest and she turned away, eager to forget the dread the object stirred in her. She did not relish the idea of living in the same house as it.

The flat roadway inclined steeply, slowing both the chariot and the revelers. An almost full moon hung in the sky, stars sprayed across the velvet blue, a tapestry of the ages with Orion, Cassiopeia, and others embedded forever above. She thought of these mortals, some who crossed the gods on purpose and others merely by chance, punished until another merciful god set them in the night sky. Again, apprehension filled her at the gift of the gods which followed benignly behind them. Would she watch the world from above forever frozen in the sky one day?

The road leveled out again, an edifice coming into view. Sconces flanked the front door, illuminating the entrance in dancing light. Though large, its outside was modest, no courtyards or grand staircases. Though she expected something grander, the simplicity of the home charmed her. The chariot pulled to a stop in front of the house. Epimetheus stepped down and, to Pandora's surprise, offered his hand for her to dismount. Prometheus broke away from the crowd and came over to her.

"Welcome to the family, Pandora," he said, one hand on her shoulder and one on his brother's. "May your marriage be blessed by the gods."

"Thank you, Brother," Epimetheus replied while Pandora bowed her head.

The exchange was simple enough, exactly the expected words, yet Pandora sensed an undercurrent of strife that only grew in the siblings' eyes before more guests stepped forward and broke the spell. With a hard squeeze on her shoulder, Prometheus gave way to Lycus, who stepped forward to perform the last symbolic act.

"Epimetheus," her father boomed, "I give you my greatest treasure. May the gods smile on you both."

He took Pandora's hand and gave it to the groom. Hesiod elbowed his way through the hovering crowd, his crimson robe cast an eerie blood red in the torchlight.

"Now Epimetheus," his wine-laden voice stuttered, "you may remove your bride's veil and officially become husband and wife."

Pandora held her breath, a thousand questions hurtling through her mind. What if he did not find her attractive enough? What if he preferred women more his own size? Were there women his size? If so, would it not have made more sense to marry one of them? What if that is what he wanted but had to concede to the gods? What if …

A surge of fresh air against her face broke the thoughts. She inhaled it in as a parched desert wanderer drinks his first sip of water. The invigoration cleared her mind and for the first time since donning the veil, she was alert. She would not cower in front of all these people, least of all Epimetheus. The gods selected her, deemed her a worthy spouse, and she would act accordingly. With head held high, she peered up at Epimetheus, finally able to focus fully on his face.

In his eyes, she saw the same fight between hesitancy and determination. Perhaps all brides and grooms shared these emotions. More importantly, she saw kindness, not the malice which glinted in his brother's eyes, who stood behind him. Epimetheus' shoulder-length black hair rustled in the wind. Without the encumbrance of the veil, she noted his muscular arms. Tales always spoke of Prometheus' handsomeness, but Pandora found Epimetheus quite pleasing to the eye. Her lips turned up into a shy smile, and he rewarded her with a broad grin.

Elara and Danae came forward and led Pandora into the house. They crossed a dimly lit room, its vastness soaring into darkness far above. Down a hallway, they came to a large door. A chamber bathed in candlelight opened before her, tiny tapers spread about at various heights. In the center stood a giant bed. Two maids strewed flower petals across the top. In the corner sat Pandora's two trunks, all the worldly belongings she had to her name condensed to their wooden insides.

While the maids scurried out, her mother opened one and produced a silken nightgown. With the help of Elara, they removed her dress and veil. While her mother unpinned her hair to put in a loose braid, Elara took a cloth dipped in rose water and rubbed Pandora's body, her skin bursting into tiny bumps. A shiver passed through her.

"Not to worry," Danae said as she slid the nightgown over her daughter's head. "All brides have wedding night jitters. You will be fine."

Dozens of questions about the impending deed rushed to the tip of her tongue. Ones she would rather not speak aloud, let alone participate in. Until now, she managed to push them to the far recesses of her mind, too terrified to examine them out in the open. Of course, she had a basic idea of what the act entailed, but somehow that made things worse. She and Cyane had danced around the topic as girls, always with the assumption they were madly in love with the groom. Lying with a total stranger did not induce the same giddy sensations those conversations imparted.

Danae helped her into a soft robe, adorned on cuffs and hem with elaborate embroidery. Pandora rubbed the raised stitching and tried to keep her mind from racing too far ahead. Elara patted her on the back, empathy in her eyes.

"Come," her mother said.

They led her back to the crowd at the front door, where Hesiod said a final blessing and congratulated the couple. After applause, the guests dispersed in a merry caravan back down the hill, the flute notes wafting back fainter and fainter, until all sound and movement melted into the night. The couple stood alone in the doorway, as stiffly as a wooden cake topper, eyes fixed on the spot where the partiers disappeared. Pandora wanted to say something, but what? Her mind, usually full of questions and observations, was as empty as a tree branch in winter, all her thoughts scattered in the wind.

After a moment of silence, Epimetheus said, "Let's go inside."

Still mute, Pandora followed him over the threshold into her new home.

THIRTY-TWO

Epimetheus led the way, fumbling to light sconces in the main room, self-conscious of his own house for the first time. He had never given the place much thought beyond its functionality, but the light revealed his delicate wife's incongruity with all his sizable belongings. Her beauty left him dumbstruck and, for a moment, he gazed at her in awe. Pandora stood in the center of the room purveying the chunky table and chairs, the only seating, which before served perfectly, yet now showed inadequacy.

"Have a seat," he offered, cursing himself for not noticing their uncomfortable design.

Pandora, who had yet to utter a word, hoisted herself into one chair, her feet dangling off the ground, in the fashion of a small child. The large wooden slab of the table stretched out before her with its worn, inhospitable top. Her eyes took in the cavernous space, stopping on the few cabinets, the fireplace, and a pile of old rags where a goat sometimes lounged in one corner. He watched her face for any sign of disdain, but found curiosity in her eyes.

If only she would speak. He racked his brain for something to say, anything that may sound commonplace. Animals were much easier to interact with. He could always sense what they wanted, but this girl remained an enigma. The silence pounded in his ears, a heavy presence in the room as though it squeezed out the air from his lungs. His tongue faltered for words no better than a large cotton wad in his mouth.

"What do you wish to do now?" he blurted, the reverberation of his loud voice making her jump.

Should he apologize for startling her? Make some suggestions of his own? Leave her be? Not even an hour in and he already found marriage a more complicated process than he imagined.

After some consideration, she finally spoke in a soft voice. "Some water would be nice and perhaps a snack. It was hard to eat with my veil on."

Epimetheus nodded at the manageable request. He took a wooden cup from the shelf and filled it with water. When he set it in front of her, she needed two hands to hold it. He laid an apple and a carrot down, not sure what her preference would be. She chose the apple and took a minuscule nip, which barely broke the peel. He normally ate one in two bites, core and all. Next, he brought over a block of cheese. When he realized it was bigger than her head, he got a knife and sliced off some smaller pieces.

"Thank you," she said, her eyes rose to meet his.

Epimetheus sat across from her with a new sense of purpose. She was his gift from the gods, he reminded himself, a reward for his loyalty, and he should find enjoyment in time spent with her. He should start a conversation and break all the tension. Except he did not know what to say. The only one he talked to on a regular basis was Prometheus, who usually dominated the exchange, leaving him to follow along. Now, the dialogue choice was his. Between his inconveniently blank mind and her expectant eyes, words came agonizingly slow.

"It was a lovely wedding." He cringed at how phony his voice sounded.

"Yes," she agreed, and maddeningly said no more.

"You looked very beautiful today, not that you still don't ... or usually don't," he stammered.

How did Zeus attract women with such ease? Certainly, the King of the Gods did not suffer from nerves such as this. Hermes painted married life as the picture of contentment, as though the gods were doing him a big favor. Maybe Prometheus was right. This whole interaction was punishingly hard, and he could not even ask her to leave. Would the rest of his existence be spent in this awkward silence?

Epimetheus rose abruptly and Pandora had to grab the cup to keep it from toppling over.

"Time for bed, I guess," he muttered.

Pandora hopped from her chair and trailed him down the short hallway, her soft steps drowned out by his clomps. At least in bed, he could feign sleep to cover up his lack of communication skills. Thoughts of a quiet bedroom bolstered him until he opened the door. The chamber glowed with candles, his newly made bed covered in flower petals by the devices of some maid.

The wedding bed.

His stomach dropped. Pandora clearly shared his dread, her footfalls stopping at the entrance. When he stared down at her, he saw his stricken expression mirrored in her face.

"How nice of them to decorate the room," he said.

He lumbered in and swept all the petals onto the floor with one stroke of his arm. Next, he set to work extinguishing most of the candlewicks with his fingers. Each taper emitted an angry swirl of smoke as though admonishing him.

Pandora had not moved, rooted to her spot, frightened eyes fixed on the bed. He needed no deep insight to know what images filled her mind. She probably feared he would force himself on her against her will. Come to think of it, that is how Zeus got most of his women. No wonder he never lacked company. Epimetheus had not given this moment much thought, but he knew he would do nothing to hurt Pandora. How Prometheus would laugh if he saw his brother right now. Maybe the gods laughed too. Maybe this whole marriage had been for their entertainment. Whatever the reason, he saw no need to consummate anything tonight. After all, she was his wife. She would be around, no need to rush.

"I'm pretty tired," he said, adding a yawn for effect. "I'm sure you are too."

Her head nodded woodenly.

"You can have the bed. I'll, um, go sleep in the barn or something."

Her eyes narrowed, a spectrum of emotions flashing across her face—confusion, realization, and finally relief.

"That is kind of you to offer," she said and walked into the room. "But I don't mind if you sleep in the bed too. It's quite large and I don't take up much room."

"Oh, um, all right."

He slid under the sheets on the far side, but cursed himself when she struggled to jump up on the other. Why did he not figure out she would need help? Some husband he was. She settled onto the mattress. With her light frame, he could barely tell she was next to him.

"Goodnight," she said.

"Goodnight."

Epimetheus blew out the last candle and laid back, careful not to let any part of him touch the fragile creature beside him. *Marriage*, he thought bewildered, and stared at the dark ceiling.

THIRTY-THREE

Pandora woke to birdsong that streamed in with the sunlight of morning. She sat up and rubbed her eyes. Epimetheus was gone, a large indentation in the mattress in his place. He had not disturbed her even once. For such a large man, he was a quiet sleeper. Considering it was her first night in an unfamiliar bed, with a stranger no less, she slept soundly and rose ready to meet the day.

Besides her trunks and the candles, the large room held only the giant bed and a single chest of drawers. No frescos or designs adorned the walls, no ornamental pillows dressed the bed, no personal objects sat atop the dresser. She thought of her bedroom on Lemnos and all its embellishments, somehow brash now when compared to this simple room. The idea of creating a space with her own touch appealed to her. The only thing missing was Rex. How she wished for his soft cat kisses to start her day.

She sprung down to the floor and went over to her trunks against the wall. She pulled out a plain tunic, her chitons too extravagant for the simplicity of the house. Two doors stood against the side wall. One went to an empty space, presumably a closet, the other was the bathroom. Bright and sparse, the clean room echoed the bedroom's decor. A tub filled one wall, large pots over unlit braziers right next to it. A rustic-looking sink stood across from it. The pump took a few good pushes before water spilled into a large basin.

Pandora rinsed, dressed, and rebraided her hair. She had to stand on tiptoes to see herself in the mirror, almost surprised to find her recognizable face staring back. Somehow, with all the changes to her life, she expected to look different, more like a wife. Her head still spun at the word. When she thought of the Titan's choice not to consummate anything last night, her reflection filled with relief. So far, he had been kind and acted as confused at this new situation as she was.

Back in the bedroom, she put on a plain pair of sandals and opened the door to a quiet house. She padded down the hall toward the main room, but stopped in her tracks. In a niche on the right side of the corridor stood her pithos on a marble pedestal, images still aswirl. Instinctively, her hand went to her chest, where the key rested on its chain. The jar looked garish in the modestly decorated home, but she supposed it deserved a place of prominence given its origin.

For the briefest moment, Pandora remembered the dread of her dream and the cries of desperation which surrounded her. Perhaps they could put it somewhere out of sight? But that could anger the gods. She needed to make peace with its presence.

At this thought, the merest hint of chanting rang in Pandora's head. The melody, which emanated from the jar, grew in intensity. Pandora took a step toward the pedestal, drawing the key from her tunic. Curiosity saturated her very being, a need to see the gifts in the jar. She would only open it for a moment.

A clopping noise in the main room brought her back to her senses, the spell broken. She tore her eyes from the pithos, her heart beating wildly at her near transgression. On her way to the main room, she cast a suspicious glance back at the niche. The jar had the power to enchant and allure. A dangerous combination. Pandora did not know what exactly that meant, but she must remain on her guard.

A white goat with a black diamond on its head stood inside the open front door of the main room. Girl and goat stared at each other in mutual surprise. The creature circled around the table, gave her one more wary glance, and left. Pandora climbed up into a chair, happy to discover fruit and bread on the table. She ate her fill, her eyes roaming around the room. Off the kitchen sat a small pantry with mostly bare shelves. *Small being relative*, she thought. Other than the table and chairs, no additional furniture graced the space. No couch or chair stood before the fireplace. No picture or other adornment hung on the wall. The simplicity she admired at first possessed an air of loneliness which outweighed any sense of hominess. She decided to pick some flowers for bouquets to liven up the room.

Outside the front door, a wide, flat expanse of land, which cut across the hill, stretched in front of her. A large barn lay at the far end of the property with several adjacent paddocks. Epimetheus stood, his back to her, by the fence of one enclosure filled with horses. On her walk over, she noted other pens and sties plus a chicken coop, its lofty roof and walls far more elaborate than the main house. Birds fluttered among multiple feeders and chickens ran around her feet, but left when she produced no food. Her goat visitor stopped mid-chew to watch her pass, a judgmental gleam in its eyes.

"Good morning," she said, coming up behind Epimetheus.

"Good morning," he replied and turned to her. "How did you sleep?"

"Fine, thank you."

"I apologize. I didn't think to have a maid here for you. I'm not used to this … marriage stuff," he said, and Pandora smiled inwardly at the nervousness in his voice. He was not the scary Titan she feared he would be. "I sent to the village for a girl to come."

"Thank you. That was kind of you."

A pleased grin filled his face, but silence filled the air. The horses, who had scattered at her arrival, inched back toward them, one finally bold enough to come over and nudge her master's hand.

"There you go, Rosa, that's a good girl. I told you she wasn't scary." Epimetheus stroked her side.

Pandora climbed the fence and sat with her legs dangling into the paddock. Shyly, Rosa crept in front of her. Pandora petted the silky, black mane and the horse nickered in content. With that show of approval, all the horses lined up to meet her.

"They were nervous about a new person," Epimetheus explained. "They are used to my brother visiting. He yells a lot."

"You can talk to them?" Pandora asked in awe.

"No, but I can sense their thoughts and they can sense mine."

"That's amazing," she exclaimed. "Only these horses or all animals?"

"All animals if I concentrate. The horses are easy because I am with them every day."

"What a wonderful gift. I would love to be able to communicate with animals," Pandora said.

"It's nothing," he muttered, redness rising in his cheeks. "I made them, I suppose that is why. Not a special gift compared with other deities."

"Well, I think it's wonderful," she said, happy to see his eyes light up. "By the way, there was a goat in the house before."

"White with a black diamond on her forehead?"

Pandora nodded, still stroking the horses who vied for her attention.

"That's Rhea. She comes inside sometimes." His face furrowed with worry. "Is that not all right? I can tell her not to."

"No, it's fine," Pandora assured. "She merely caught me off guard."

He nodded, but uncertainty lined his face. She could tell he wanted her to be happy and at ease, but did not quite know what to do. His life must have been largely solitary before she got here. She wanted him to be at ease with her and asked the names of the rest of the horses. Once talk turned the animals the animals, he perked back up.

"You truly made all the animals in the world?" she asked.

"Yes."

"That must have been hard. How did you decide which attributes to give each one? How did you come up with all the different ideas? I've heard there are animals that only live in faraway places. Is that true? What is your favorite one?"

Pandora paused for a breath to find an open-mouthed Epimetheus staring at her. She lowered her eyes to the ground and murmured, "I'm sorry for all the questions. They hated when I did it at home. Said I was too inquisitive."

Epimetheus put a finger under her chin and lifted. With a smile, he said, "Well, I think questions are wonderful and I would be happy to answer all of them."

THIRTY-FOUR

"I'm not sure I could name a favorite animal," Epimetheus said after some deliberation.

He answered all of Pandora's questions. Prometheus never showed much interest in his creatures, only ridiculed him for his mistakes, and the gods only cared when they needed an animal for something. To have someone ask about his thought process in their creation thrilled him. The sun swung high into the sky, a soft breeze lifting stray strands of hair off Pandora's pretty face.

"These horses are my closest companions."

He motioned toward the dozen or so steeds in the paddock. They crowded by the fence where Pandora fed them apples. She found a special marking, or eye color, or tail bushiness to tell them all apart with such care it impressed Epimetheus.

"I only keep them here because they are happy," he stated. "I could not keep any animal against its will."

"That is kind of you," she said, petting the nose of a tawny mare named Hazel, the smallest of the pack.

"Hazel here would not mind if you ever wanted to ride her. I could get you a saddle made."

"Really?" Pandora's eyes grew wide with delight. "I would love that."

Warmth filled Epimetheus, the misgivings of last night fading, the worry they had nothing in common unfounded. She loved animals more than anyone he ever met. Not that he met many people up here on his solitary hill. He enjoyed her company. Conversations where no one was yelling were actually quite nice. The horses agreed. He sensed their contentment, an issue he worried about since he told them a woman was coming.

"I can conjure the image of some faraway creatures if you want to see them," he offered.

"Could you? I would enjoy that," Pandora asserted.

"Let's move away from the paddock to keep the herd from getting spooked."

He helped her down from the fence rail. Pandora tucked errant strands of hair behind her ears while he admired her radiant smile. *Gods, she is pretty.* They walked a few yards away to a grassy area next to the barn. Epimetheus grabbed a hay bale for her to sit on. The chickens returned to swarm around her feet, still in search of food. He tossed out a pocketful of seeds to one side and they scurried over.

"Here is one of my favorites," he said.

In front of him, a patch of air swirled and shimmered before reconstructing itself into the shape of a large spotted animal with long legs and an even longer neck.

"I've heard such animals existed, but never believed it," the awestruck girl cried.

"It's a giraffe. They live in a hot land far south of here," he explained.

"How magnificent," she admired.

Next, he showed her an elephant, its trunk upraised, then a tiger, its black and orange stripes undulating with each movement and finally a bear with such white fur, it gleamed in the sunshine.

"That's a peacock," Pandora exclaimed when the shape morphed into a bird with colorful plumage. "Is it true Hera put the eyes on the tail?"

"Yes, she immortalized her faithful watchman, Argos, when Zeus tried to kill him. There are a few creatures the gods altered for their own purposes."

"They must have been impressed by the variety of animals you created."

The shimmering spot reverted to plain air, the peacock dissipating in a burst. Epimetheus hung his head.

"I think they were more impressed with my brother's humans."

"But humans are so ordinary, so alike in characteristics, whereas your animals are creative and diverse. You should be proud."

A strange mix of pride and embarrassment arose in him. Prometheus usually garnered all the praise and never failed to point out what an oaf Epimetheus was. Pandora sounded certain of her assessment. He wanted to believe her. He watched as she tried to explain to the chickens that she had no food. The birds settled around her like goslings with a mother goose. Now a new warmer sensation filled his heart at the thought she would be here from now on.

"I never asked you if you have a favorite animal," he said.

"I had a cat at home named Rex. He brought me a lot of love," she said, sadness clouding her face. "I miss him."

The shadow of loss in her eyes dismayed Epimetheus. He would miss his horses terribly if he had to leave them forever. Before he could respond, a man and girl walked around from the front of the house. Pandora rose, scattering the chickens, and the couple went to greet them.

"Hello, Epimetheus, sir," the man said, eyes downcast, "This is my daughter, Chloe. She will be your wife's new maid."

The stricken-looking girl bowed in deference. Unsure what to do, Epimetheus remained silent. To his relief, Pandora took a step forward.

"Thank you. I will take her to the house and show her what I need."

"I will pick her up tonight." The man nodded at them both and without gazing up, backed away and left. Chloe stood frozen, a small bag clutched to her chest.

"Come," Pandora instructed and led the girl away.

Epimetheus sighed and strode back to the paddock, the interactions with the humans more than he cared for. Except Pandora, of course. She was wonderful. He leaned on the fence rail, content to watch his horses. A sudden breeze shifted the air, and a figure appeared on the fence, a simple shepherd boy.

"Hermes," Epimetheus said, his nod of greeting not enough to hide the tone of annoyance.

"How's married life?" the sprightly deity asked.

"It's barely been a day," the Titan barked.

"No need to be surly. I want to make sure you are both happy. Please let me know if I can be of any service."

Epimetheus shook his head, dealing with a mercurial deity the last thing he needed. There was nothing he wanted from him. Or was there? He smiled at the thought.

"Actually, there is one thing you could do for me."

THIRTY-FIVE

Pandora walked with Chloe back to the house. If these new circumstances intimidate Pandora, the girl appeared downright terrified. She was nearly Pandora's height, but with a slighter frame. Where the young maidens of Lemnos shone as bright as jewels, Chloe, with her gaunt face and simple dress, was a muted stone. Her long auburn hair fell in a thick braid between her shoulders.

"How old are you?" Pandora asked, as Rhea stood up and trailed after them.

"Sixteen," came the meek response.

"I am happy to meet you. The house is not large, though the things inside are large, but it is only a main room, bedroom, and bath. There is not much to keep on top of. You shall come every morning and return home every evening for the time being." Pandora had no place to offer this young girl to sleep.

They stepped inside, the maid's eyes taking in the scale of everything from the table, to the chairs, to the cabinets, which dwarfed the two women. Rhea pushed past them and did a circuit around the table before plopping down on the rag pile in the corner. She munched on some hay with deliberate eyes on the trespassers.

"So ... the goat is allowed in?" Chloe's voice wavered.

"Yes, apparently," Pandora said. "I only arrived last night. You and I will have to learn all the idiosyncrasies of the house together."

After a brief turn around the main room, they headed down the hall. Chloe stopped at the sight of the pithos on its pedestal in the niche. She stared fixated, rooted to her spot. It took Pandora a moment to tear her eyes away, almost falling under the spell of the mesmerizing motions. She took Chloe's arm and moved her to the bedroom.

"I apologize for staring," the girl said. "We heard about the magnificent gift of the gods in the village. I wondered if, as many other things, it was exaggerated. I see that it was not."

"Yes, the gods were kind to bless us with such a beautiful gift," Pandora mumbled.

Off the bedroom stood a small closet, yet only dust and broken pieces of wood lay on the floor. Pandora explained she wanted to keep her belongings in it and Chloe went in search of a broom. She returned with one almost too big for her hands and went straight to sweeping. Pandora rummaged through her trunks for some paper and ink. Finding some, she spread it on the chest of drawers and wrote in small, precise letters.

"I will give you a list of items I shall need," Pandora instructed. "Can you go to the village for them?"

"Yes, my lady," Chloe stuck her head out of the closet, a wreath of dust around her head.

"I will speak with my husband about giving you money."

The words *my husband* sounded clumsy in her mouth. Of course, she had used them both before, but never together. *My husband.* Would she ever get used to saying it? She sighed.

"Are you all right, my lady?" Chloe asked, her voice echoing against the stones of the empty closet.

My lady. Two other words made different when spoken together. A phrase meant for her mother, not for her. Marriage had all together changed her vocabulary and would take some getting used to.

At Pandora's nod, the girl said, "Money won't be necessary today. Everyone knows who I am working for. The shopkeepers will work it out with your husband."

"Were you born in the village, Chloe?" Changing the subject from the still jarring word.

"Yes, my lady, I've been there every moment of my life until now ..." she trailed off.

Pandora went to stand at her side. The girl flinched, thinking she had displeased her new mistress, but found herself in a soft embrace.

"It is hard to leave everything you know. But you will be back tonight to sleep in your own bed."

"It must be hard for you to be here, to leave your life and family behind," Chloe ventured, her stance relaxing. "You are braver than I am."

"The decision to leave was not mine," Pandora told her, breaking apart. "Bravery was my only choice."

They pulled Pandora's trunks into the closet, Chloe protesting the entire time that Pandora need not exert herself. After that, they went into the bathroom. Pandora brought in her hair oils and soaps. The room shone, the marble sparkling in the sun. Since maids had been here yesterday, there was not much to do. The two headed back out into the main room, where the goat lolled contentedly. Pandora checked in the cabinets, surprised to find them almost bare of the most basic staples. She pushed a chair over to the counter and mounted it to examine the plates and glasses on the shelves, each carved of basic wood. Combined with the dearth of utensils and cookware, Chloe would be hard pressed to make anything other than roasted meat or porridge.

Pandora sat in the chair, legs dangling, goat snoring nearby, and shook her head. "It seems we are starting from scratch getting this place together. This list grows and grows. You will probably need a wagon to get it all back up here."

"My father will load up his wagon. I can find the scribe and have him help us." Chloe said.

"The scribe? What do you need him for?" Pandora asked.

"To read the list."

The statement was nonchalant, so commonplace, it took a moment to register with Pandora. "You can't read?"

"No, my lady, nor can most of the village."

"Is there no school for the children?" She asked, picturing Lemnos and Madame Tullia.

"No," the maid replied. "If you don't have anything more to add, I should probably get going if I want to be back by dinner."

"Yes. Of course."

Pandora jumped down and handed the paper to the girl, who dutifully tucked it into the pocket of her apron.

"I'll be back soon," she said with a warm smile and bounded off.

Pandora stood in the empty room perplexed. How was there no school? How did the villagers get by without knowing how to read? She could not imagine a life without the written word, all the stories, all the information she had learned and shared with others. The notion was unfathomable. A brush against her hand startled her back into the present. Rhea came over and pushed her head against Pandora's hand. She peered down at the creature, who nudged her again. Stroking its head, she walked outside, and the animal trailed behind her.

Epimetheus now fed the chickens in front of an impressive multi-storied coop. The birds clustered at his feet, pecking and bobbing. He glanced up, a smile lighting up his face at the sight of her. Something warmed in her, a comfort she had not experienced since leaving Lemnos. She smiled back, color rising in her cheeks.

"Where did your maid go?" he asked.

"Chloe went to the village to buy some necessities."

"Yes, I suppose I am not that good at keeping up with such things," he muttered.

"It's not a problem," she said. "That is what a wife is for."

His face dazed over at the word *wife*, the reaction much the same as hers to its counterpart. This arrangement would take them both some time to get used to.

"Chloe mentioned she does not know how to read, nor do most of the other villagers. If you don't mind me asking: Why is there no school?"

Epimetheus' brow wrinkled while he pondered this. "I don't know. I guess I never thought about it."

"These villagers are loyal to you?" she asked.

"Yes. Prometheus gifted some people to serve me long ago. They bring me what little I need in exchange for the land they live on. I don't ask for any payment. Mostly, I keep to myself as they do."

"Perhaps we should think about doing more for them." Pandora suggested, hoping she did not push too far.

"Do you think?" he asked, eyes narrowing.

A cloud appeared out of the sky on a gust of wind, startling Pandora when it landed in front of her. She backed up behind Epimetheus. The whooshing sound abated, the air clearing to reveal a shepherd boy, who held a writhing bundle under one arm, a shrill cry emanating from it.

"Rex," Pandora cried, leaping forward.

The animal quieted at the sound of her voice. It leaped from the grasp of its keeper and ran to her where she waited on her knees, arms outstretched. She buried her face in his side, its soft fur a salve on her lonesome heart. The cat purred as it nestled in her arms.

"I thought you might appreciate something familiar from home," Epimetheus said.

"Yes, oh yes," she gushed.

So enrapt by her pet, Pandora barely heard Epimetheus say, "Thank you, Hermes."

At the god's name her head jerked up, but the deity had already vanished, the cloud, wafting away in the breeze. She turned from the empty spot back to Epimetheus and then to Rex. Special deliveries from the gods. Yes, this new life would certainly take some getting used to.

THIRTY-SIX

In the late afternoon, the silhouette of a wagon appeared at the crest of the hill. Chloe sat in the seat next to her weather-lined father, piles of merchandise teetering in haphazard stacks behind them. Freshly caught fish dangled like silver pennants off a string. While her father unloaded the cart, Chloe instructed him where to put each item with maturity beyond her years. In no time, she had the goods ordered and put away as though she set up a household every day. Her work impressed Pandora.

Epimetheus came to greet the man, who bowed low in the Titan's presence, hat clutched tightly in hand. The Titan assured her father, Kostas, that Chloe would return home that night, and every night hereafter, on the back of one of his precious ponies. No harm would come to her and he need not worry about his daughter's safety after dark. The man thanked him profusely, and never daring to cast his eyes up, somehow made his way back onto the wagon to set off for home. Pandora watched the scene unfold.

"Is there a reason he is scared of you?" she asked.

"Scared of me?" Epimetheus said with genuine confusion.

"He never met your eyes. His hands trembled, and he didn't relax his posture until he was out of the gate."

"You are quite observant," her husband said.

Pandora hung her head, sure she had offended him. Her mother had warned her about bluntness and speaking her mind. *Submissive* was the word Danae used, yet another foreign term to go along with *husband* and *wife*. But to her surprise, far from being angry, her words puzzled Epimetheus.

"Do you think he was truly afraid of me?"

"His body language was not that of a relaxed man," she informed.

"Body language?" the Titan repeated.

"It's a way to tell how someone feels inside based on how they comport themselves on the outside," she explained.

"Oh." He stared at the ground. "You must think I'm stupid and unworldly."

The comment took Pandora aback. She did not know how she would describe him, but not with those two words. Earlier, when describing the animals, he had been informative and sociable. Now, he stared at his shoes with dejection. Rhea came over and gently butted his hand as if to comfort him. He stroked the goat, her head disappearing in his palm.

"I don't think you're either of those. I think you are simply more at ease around animals than people. Unless you have done something in the past that scared the villagers?"

"Not that I can think of. I've only been down there once or twice. I don't have many dealings with them." He thought for a moment and added, "But Prometheus comes through there whenever he visits. My brother does a lot of yelling here, maybe that frightens them. He can be intimidating."

"Then the answer is quite simple," Pandora said, silently agreeing with his assessment of his brother. "We will have to go down there and properly introduce ourselves. Show them you don't have your brother's surly disposition."

Epimetheus blanched. Without thinking, Pandora took his hand and told him it would be fine. Chloe called out from the house that dinner was ready. The couple walked back toward the house, with goat in tow, hands still intertwined. Inside, Chloe put new dishes on the table, with the aid of a stepladder. Steam rose in delectable tendrils. Pandora hopped up into her chair while Epimetheus took his place across from her. Despite the forks set out, he took a portion off his plate and ate it with his hands. He stopped mid-bite when he saw both ladies watching him. He wiped his hand on his pants, picked up the utensil, which was comically small in his hand, and attempted to eat with it.

"Chloe, maybe give my husband the serving fork." Pandora said.

The maid produced the larger version from the counter and handed it to her master. Epimetheus held the two forks up, put the smaller one down and stabbed some fish with the remaining one.

"Much better. Thank you," he said.

Pandora filled her stomach with fish, olives, cheese, and bread, happy to know Chloe could put a proper meal together. On Lemnos, she had many servants, but only spoke with Elara. Having someone closer to her age would be a refreshing change. She filled her fork with the flaky white fish. When she gazed up from her plate, Epimetheus examined his utensil.

"This is new," he observed.

"Yes, I took the liberty of purchasing some new items for the house. I hope that is all right with you."

Pandora's heart skipped at the thought she should have asked him first. Is that what wives were supposed to do? At home, she merely told her mother what she needed and it appeared, but perhaps her mother always consulted with her father on such matters. She hoped this walking on eggshells phase of marriage would pass quickly. Once she got a measure of Epimetheus, she would know how far she could push the boundaries. For now, the concern of angering him weighed down her stomach.

"They are nice," Epimetheus said, scanning the surrounding room. "I know my house is simple, maybe crude in your eyes. And not exactly the right scale for you, either."

"If you can build such a beautiful chicken coop, I am sure we can fix this place up in a way that works for both of us."

"Yes," he said with a bright smile. "I think that is a wonderful idea. What do you want?"

"Some furniture scaled for me to go along with yours, a dressing room and a room for Chloe where she can stay here all the time." Pandora proposed. "If that is all right with you."

At his enthusiastic nod, she turned to Chloe. "Bring me some paper, quill, and ink."

When the maid came back, Pandora tried to sketch out some ideas of where to add on to the structure. The rudimentary result made them both laugh.

"I'm used to drawing bowls of fruit," she said, "which apparently does not come in handy for blueprints."

"I understand exactly what you mean and I think it's perfect," Epimetheus said, and his smile made her stomach somersault with a delightful sensation.

They spent the next hour discussing various options, Pandora thrilled to discover they were incredibly like-minded. He had some suggestions that filled in the gaps in her plan. They even asked a startled Chloe for her opinion, who after some hesitation, contributed some good points. When they settled on a design, Chloe cleared the plates and set out some figs and grapes with honey. Pandora popped a fig in her mouth, savoring the juice even as it ran down her chin. Rhea came over to the table expectantly and, with a shrug, Epimetheus gave her a fig. Again, Pandora shared a laugh with her husband, who joked over his spoiled animal while the contented goat lay back in her spot.

After dinner, Chloe lit a small fire in the giant fireplace. Pandora sat on some large pillows in front of it. Rex crept out from the bedroom, where he had sought refuge in the unfamiliar home, and curled in her lap. The cat and the goat eyed each other warily. While the maid brought Pandora a blanket and a glass of diluted wine, Epimetheus said he was going out to tend to the horses one last time.

"Chloe, you may go. Epimetheus will send you home on a horse. Thank you for all your help today."

"Yes, my lady. I will be back at dawn to prepare breakfast."

Chloe crept out the front door, the darkening sky framing her small form. Pandora picked up the drawing, imagining the renovated home. As rendered in the drawing, it would have elements recommended by both her and her husband. They made a good team. Pandora thought of their easy conversation, their joking, not a moment spent as though walking on eggshells. In fact, she took every chance to brush fingers with him or put a hand on his arm, thrilled by the tingling sensation which coursed through her. A handsome, kind husband. The thought brought a smile to her lips.

Her wine finished, she padded down to the hall. In the niche, the images on the pithos swirled, but such contentment filled Pandora, she did not even spare it a glance. In the bedroom, she donned her linen nightgown. Rex zigzagged through her legs, his nails resounding off the stone floor. She scooped him up and dropped him on the bed, where he waited for her to get settled. Once under the blankets, Rex curled up by her feet. Content filled Pandora as she drifted to sleep, with a silent prayer of thanks to the gods.

THIRTY-SEVEN

Epimetheus waited, arms crossed over the fence post. A cool breeze lifted his hair from his brow. Chloe had ridden out on Hazel about a half hour ago, her expression daunted, whether over the pony or him, he was not sure. Pandora's words played out in his head. He did not want the villagers to fear him and though he had never given them a reason to; he guessed he had never given them a reason not to. In fact, he had not given them much thought at all since his brother sent them all those years ago. Prometheus said they were a gift for letting his humans interact with Epimetheus' animals. The younger brother made some of his horses, cows, and other farm animals tamable, which helped the humans in farming and transportation. When a handful of people had shown up, he figured they could take care of themselves and did not bother with them much.

He heard the trotting hoof steps of Hazel, a steady beat up the hill. She ran right to him and he gave her an apple for a job well done. Once she joined her fellow horses in the stable, Epimetheus walked back to the house. The lingering aroma of dinner made him pause in the doorway, the meal quite different from his usual solitary repasts. A smile filled his face when he noticed the blueprints laid out on the table, eager to improve the house for his new wife. In the hallway, he stopped by the pithos, its images glowing slightly even in the darkness. He said a silent thank you to the gods for Pandora, thinking how wrong Prometheus was. Pandora was a reward, not a curse.

His smile faded the more he stared at the pithos. From the moment the object entered his house, Epimetheus had a strong aversion to it. To the eye it appeared harmless enough, the moving images a gaudy touch he expected from the Olympians. However, if he watched it for too long, it filled him with a strange desire to discover what lay inside. Perhaps that was the test Zeus tethered to it, a warning not to open it mixed with an unconscious desire to disobey. The King of the Gods would fail if this endeavor. Epimetheus valued Pandora far more than whatever the jar held. A loud clap of thunder broke his thoughts, and he walked further down the hall.

Once in the bedroom, he took off his tunic and climbed into bed. The mattress sagged under his weight. Rex stood up, cast a momentary glance of disapproval for waking him, and repositioned himself by Pandora's feet. Epimetheus stared at Pandora, her slumbering face even more lovely in the slanted moonlight. His heart warmed, glad that he asked Hermes to get the cat, the gesture bringing her such happiness. Pandora turned in her sleep, her back pressing against his side. At first, he froze, terrified by the contact, but after a moment, he decided he enjoyed the warmth of her. A beautiful and smart wife, to be sure. He fell to sleep with a smile to match hers.

In the morning, he woke as the rosy fingers of dawn reached across the sky. Afraid to disturb her, he took extra pains to ease out of bed, the cat quick to jump into the still warm depression he left. Rex even allowed Epimetheus to stroke his head a few times, perhaps a sign of the ice breaking between them. At the doorway, he glanced back one more time to admire Pandora before heading to the kitchen with a warm awareness in his chest.

To his surprise, the room buzzed with activity. A small fire burned in the hearth, a bowl of porridge hanging above it. Rhea sat on a pillow, a carrot half-finished on the floor in front of her. Chloe, apron on, rolled out dough into a flat, malleable oval. Upon his entrance, she took in his astonished face.

"Good morning, sir," she welcomed, a circle of white powder on the tip of her nose.

"How did you get here?" he asked. By the way she cowered, it came out harsher than intended. He added with as gentle a voice as he could muster, "I mean, I was going to send the horse for you."

"I'm an early riser and the walk is pleasant enough in the morning. Would you care for some porridge, sir?" she answered.

Epimetheus considered the words *porridge* and *sir*, terms he never heard at breakfast before. Again, she watched him with trepidation and he concentrated on the tone of his reply. "No, thank you. I'll just take some dried meat with me outside while I tend to the animals."

She nodded and, in a flash, pulled some jerky from a cabinet and wrapped it in a cloth for him. He accepted the meal from her tiny hands. Though neither spoke, she smiled at him. *Progress*, he thought. Outside, the warm air spoke of an even warmer day, drops of dew sparkling like jewels on each blade of grass. Rhea trailed out after him with the rest of her carrot. Together they did the normal rounds, tending to the horses, pigs, and chickens. Once finished, he stood by the fence rail, working the jerky in his mouth.

"Now I suppose we should get some supplies for the house," he said to Rosa, who came to stand by him. "I guess a trip to the village is in order."

He hooked Rosa and Hazel up to his supply wagon and led them down the hill. The rising sun cast peek-a-boo rays through some swiftly moving clouds. Down the rocky path they rode, past an orchard filled with fig and olive trees. Several small children roamed among the trunks, their baskets momentarily forgotten as they played a raucous game of tag. One little boy spotted Epimetheus and stiffened, the others followed the child's gaze. As one, the smiles faded from their faces. The excitement of the game dispelled at the sight of the Titan.

Hoping to ease the tension, Epimetheus waved, but the group crept back to their baskets, where they whispered and pointed. Pandora's words rang in his head. How did it come to this? All the villagers frightened of him, even the children? Prometheus always told him what a fool he was. How could he not have noticed?

In town, he headed to Kostas, who helped him whenever he needed supplies. There had been scant interactions over the years, Epimetheus being mostly self-sufficient for his own needs. One main road made up the entirety of the village. For the first time, Epimetheus took the time to observe the people. Most bowed their heads and scurried away, doors latching behind them. No one greeted him. Eyes peering out windows were the most he saw of anyone. He stopped in front of Kostas' house where the man stood, eyes down, hands clasped in front of his body.

"I certainly hope that my Chloe is doing a good job for you. I can give her a talking to if needed," Kostas said, more to the ground than the Titan.

"No, she is an excellent maid." Epimetheus said, and the man's shoulders relaxed. "I am here because I need some supplies."

"Of course, you may have first pick of whatever you need," Kostas assured.

Epimetheus explained what his plans for the house were and the lumber, stone, and other materials the job necessitated. The Titan tried to keep his voice friendly, conscious now of how the people regarded him. Kostas listened intently, nodding, even adding a suggestion here and there. He called three other men over to discuss the situation, Epimetheus on constant alert about his mannerisms. The men, hesitant at first, provided answers and recommendations with less apprehension as each moment passed. After a productive conversation, the three newcomers left to gather the required goods.

"What you need will fill more than one wagon," Kostas said. "We will fill yours and some others and bring them up to you."

"That would be helpful," Epimetheus declared, happy the man acted at ease with him now.

"If you don't mind me saying, this sounds like quite the project you are undertaking. My friends and I could help you out if you wanted."

Epimetheus furrowed his brow. People to help him? That would make things go faster.

Kostas misread the expression and quickly added, "We wouldn't want no compensation or anything. We know you gave us this land and are surely grateful to you."

The Titan smoothed out his face into what he hoped was a friendly countenance. "I would appreciate the help. Anyone is welcome. And of course, I will pay you for the work."

"We will be up soon," the man said, extending his hand.

Epimetheus shook it, nodded, and headed back toward the hill. The street remained empty, but he heard doors crack open once he passed. At the orchard, he waved again at the children, this time more subdued, as they filled their baskets. A tiny girl with long braids lifted her hand, followed by a few more. It was not much, but it was headway. If only people were as easy to understand as animals. With a shrug, he continued the path home.

THIRTY-EIGHT

A wet, nudging nose woke Pandora, whose eyes opened to Rex. The other side of the bed was empty, the sheet still wrinkled. Pandora sat up and rubbed her eyes in the mid-morning sun that filtered across the room. She could hear her mother's voice in her head chiding her about wasting the day away. Epimetheus did not hold as strict a schedule as Danae, if any at all. *You need a purpose in life*, Danae always stated. Pandora remembered the renovation plans, purpose enough for now.

Chloe popped her head in the room. "Good morning, ma'am. Would you prefer to eat first or bathe?"

Pandora pondered the question, absently stroking Rex's supple back. On Lemnos, in the tightly run household, Elara never gave her such options. Wake, eat, school, dinner, study, bathe, bedtime—a well-oiled machine. Now, she planned her day. The cat meowed loudly and she made up her mind.

"As Rex suggests, I think today we will eat first."

The maid smiled, leading the way to the kitchen where a bowl of porridge and some fruit awaited the lady of the house. Pandora hopped up into the chair, her stomach grumbling. Chloe put down a bowl of water and some dried meat for Rex, who ate until Rhea came over to investigate. A slight standoff ensued, with the goat backing off after a swat. The women shared a laugh.

"Is Epimetheus outside?" Pandora asked.

"No, he took a wagon down to the village for supplies," Chloe reported from her stepstool by the sink.

"It will be nice to have some furniture in our size," Pandora commented.

"Yes," the maid agreed. "I feel like a toddler in here."

Again, they chuckled. A warm sensation filled Pandora when she thought of her conversation with Epimetheus the night before. He clearly wanted to please her. She needed to think of some things she could do for him. As his wife, she should try to make his life more pleasant. He lived such a solitary life up on this hill with no company but his animals. Remembering his genuine surprise about Chloe's father being afraid of him, Pandora thought maybe building better connections with the villagers might make his life less lonely.

As though the thought of him conjured the being, Epimetheus walked in the open front door. Rhea went over to get her head rubbed, while Rex regarded him with wariness.

"Good morning," Pandora said brightly. "How was your trip to the village?"

"Fine. Men are coming with supplies soon and we can get working." He waved the paper with their design in his hand. "But I'm afraid it will be loud and busy, and I don't want to make your day miserable."

"Not at all. Chloe was going to show me the village today. Isn't that right?"

The shocked maid only nodded, her eyes wide.

"That will be nice," Epimetheus said and walked back outside.

"I hope you don't mind showing me the village, Chloe."

"Not at all, ma'am, but there is not much to see. It's nowhere near as grand as Lemnos or Thessaly, from what I hear."

"I'm sure I will love it. Now help me dress. I need to make myself presentable to make a good impression."

The maid helped her into her everyday tunic, a plain linen and wool garment, yet luxurious next to Chloe's coarse one. After the maid set Pandora's hair in a braid looped around the back of her head, she deemed herself acceptable. Would they be happy to meet her? Should she bring anything with her? Would the villagers expect gifts? On Lemnos, the mayor and council always brought candies

for the children when they visited. She doubted
Epimetheus had any treats lying around. The usual barrage
of questions floated across her mind.

The ladies left the house. Rhea, who had trailed them
out, broke off and went to sit in a chunk of shade cast by
the barn. Rex stalked birds in the long grass at the edge of
the property, quite pleased with his lot. Pandora smiled,
happy her cat was here with her. At the gate, Epimetheus
stood by three wagonloads of supplies, accompanied by
eight men. Even with their burly figures, Epimetheus
towered over them. He gave instructions, pointing here and
there. She noticed his tone, softer, friendly even. Her heart
swelled, knowing he listened to her advice. He waved as
they passed and she waved back, butterflies rocketing
around her stomach.

Pandora and Chloe descended the hill with careful
footsteps on the rocky path, the sun at their backs. Scrubby
patches of grass sprouted out of the dirt like untamed tufts
of hair. In an overgrown orchard, olive and fig trees grew
as though scattered by a storm, unlike the orderly rows on
Lemnos. The air was dry in her nose, no tang of salt or
humidity. The foreignness of the landscape disquieted
Pandora, as though transported to another world.

"Is there any water nearby?" she asked, missing the
constant hum of the sea.

"There is a lake not far off. We use it, the villagers, I
mean," Chloe clarified. "It's full of excellent fish, too. Do
you want to see it? We can go that way."

"Yes, please," Pandora replied, happy to find she was
close to some water.

The lake sat in a depression ringed by hills, a large oval.
Several pools branched off it in irregular shapes. They
strode to the bank and Pandora touched the cool surface
with her fingertips. Chloe explained in which areas the
villagers fished, swam, and bathed, the latter areas
overhung with willow branches for privacy. Though
tranquil, the lake could not rival the majesty of the sea.

"What is that for?" Pandora inquired, pointing to a place marked off with wooden spikes. Several buckets lined the ground and a long rope hung with clothing stretched between two trees.

"That is where we wash and dry the clothes," Chloe noted.

Pandora nodded. She never thought about who washed her clothes on Lemnos or how they did it. Elara took the soiled garments away and returned with clean ones. How many other basic tasks had she taken for granted?

They made it to the village about a quarter of an hour later. *Village* turned out to be a generous word. Houses with small barns lined a single road dotted with a blacksmith, butcher, and lumber mill. The road terminated at a small temple. The steps, covered with new offerings and fresh flowers, belied its state of disrepair. Halfway down the street, Pandora scanned in front and behind her. This is it? Even the lowest class people on Lemnos lived in better conditions.

Curtains parted in windows, curious eyes taking in the stranger. A few doors cracked, figures stepping into the opening. Some wore clothing full of patches, while others had no shoes. Dilapidated buildings sagged on unkempt properties, the entire village, including its inhabitants, layered in a film of dust. The onlookers crept out when Pandora walked toward the temple. They huddled in the road, whispering to each other. Pandora's keen eyes took in what little else was there, and what was not there. She did not see a single pump.

"Chloe, that lake you showed me, where is the pump that runs from it?"

"Pump?" the confused maid said. "There is no pump."

"How on earth do you …" she did not need to finish the question, the answer now obvious. The line of buckets she saw earlier. "You carry water all the way from the lake to the village."

Chloe nodded.

"That must take forever, especially if you want to take a bath."

"We bathe in the lake, ma'am. Remember, I showed you where, one section for ladies and one for men," the maid reminded.

For a moment, words eluded Pandora, astonished at the revelation. So many questions formed in her head at once, they created a logjam. These villages lived in squalor. But why? Had it ever been nice? Why were there so few people? Why did they settle for these derelict conditions?

"How long has this village been here?" Somehow, this question sifted itself to the top.

"Quite some time. I don't know how long exactly. Paz," she called to a gnarled old woman, who watched them from her perch on a barrel.

Paz walked over and bowed to Pandora. "You honor us with your presence."

"She wishes to know how long the village has been here," Chloe said.

"Several generations. I was born here same as my mother and grandmother before me," she informed, her brow a stack of wavy wrinkles. "I think maybe another generation back is when Prometheus sent us."

"Prometheus only sent some people with nothing else?"

"Yes. He wanted to use some of Epimetheus' animals and gave his brother this land and the villagers in return."

"I see," Pandora said. "And you never spoke with Epimetheus about any improvements?"

"No, ma'am. We did not want to bother him. We all made many offerings at the temple for you and Epimetheus, for your marriage," Paz stated and gestured at the rundown steps ahead of them.

"Thank you. That was kind."

Pandora spent over an hour talking to villagers, asking them about their life and routines. At first, many were reluctant to speak, but gradually, they became brave enough to address her. She encouraged them to be candid in specifying what changes would enhance their lives.

Everyone agreed a pump would make life easier. Pandora promised to speak with Epimetheus about it. The profuse thanks they gave over such a minor fix left her unfulfilled. Certainly, she could do much more to help these people.

"Are you ready to go back?" Chloe asked.

"Yes. Thank you for bringing me."

All the way back up the hill, Pandora mulled over the dilapidated village. Her mother's words about purpose rang in her head. Improving her own home would be an easy matter, but developing the town would be a loftier objective, one she planned to attain.

THIRTY-NINE

Pandora and Chloe returned to a flurry of activity on the sunny hilltop. Outside, one group of men framed up the new addition. Hammers banged against wooden poles set out in a rectangle under the direction of one man, while others stacked mud bricks to form the walls. One wall stood completed, a square window gaping in its middle. The wind carried the smell of fresh cut wood and sweat to the women, who stood to admire the progress.

They stepped inside to find more men at work. The rudimentary blueprint sat atop the kitchen table, a much larger sheet of parchment alongside filled with a more skilled rendering. Kostas, standing on a crate, discussed measurements with Epimetheus and relayed them to the workers. When the ladies entered, the Titan motioned the ladies over.

"Pandora," Epimetheus said, excitement in his eyes, "see how our plan is coming together."

Kostas hopped down from the crate, and after a quick hug with Chloe, helped tear out the old kitchen cabinets. Pandora stood on his vacated perch to examine the more detailed plan. Epimetheus pushed it in front of her. This version contained specific dimensions in the precise ink of a practiced hand. Epimetheus pointed at the design for a larger main room, the two added bedrooms, and the spot with Pandora's larger closet.

"It will be wonderful when it is done," Pandora said, pleased with how suitably their ideas translated into reality.

"Yes, but I'm afraid it will take a few weeks of dealing with this." He wiped his finger across the sawdust on the table, a river-like trail in its wake. "Kostas will bring a few more men with him to speed things along, but I'm afraid construction is a messy business."

"That will be no problem, sir," Chloe assured. "I will clean up after them every evening."

Kostas beamed with pride at his daughter, an old cabinet balanced on his shoulder. Pandora counted the workers already there, at least ten outside and six more inside. And more may come?

"The workers will need easy access to drink and at least one meal throughout the day," she stated.

"You're right. I forgot," Epimetheus said.

"Don't worry. Chloe and I will make a midday meal for all of you," Pandora offered, though she had no idea how to feed a group of hungry men.

"No, ma'am, I will take care of it. You do not need to do any work," Chloe said, but the trepidation in her eyes belied the confident remark.

"Nonsense, this is my home and I will see to these men being fed," Pandora insisted. "Come, let's get to it."

She turned to the pantry, but the men had already torn it out. Kostas motioned out the open side door to a pile of goods. Pandora took the maid's hand and led her out, yet they had little selection for feeding a bunch of ravenous men. There were barrels of watered wine and a cistern of water, which was a start. The girls rolled one of them across the grass near the front door, setting wooden cups on top for the men to serve themselves. Several men came over wiping their brows and, after a drink, offered thanks.

"Now for something to eat," Pandora said.

On the side of the house stood the cooking pit with an iron spit over it. Logs in orderly stacks lay next to it. All they needed now was meat. Chloe saw where Pandora's gaze fell.

"There are cattle down the mountain a bit. We could slaughter one for dinner."

"Slaughter one?" Pandora echoed, her mind unable to grasp the concept.

"Yes, ma'am," the maid assured. "They are not hard to kill."

Pandora gave a dubious glance at the tiny woman in front of her. In Lemnos, meat appeared on her plate devoid of any hint of what it had previously been attached to. But if Chloe could kill a cow, certainly Pandora could. This hilltop ranch was her home now; she needed to learn how to do the perform the required responsibilities. Chloe went to the barn and returned with a piece of rope.

"Ready?"

With a nod of assent, she followed Chloe down a worn path behind the house. She had to watch her feet, navigating the rocks and scrubby bushes with care. By the time they walked a few yards, sweat covered her brow. She pushed damp hair from her eyes. Chloe traversed the path on steady feet. Pandora noted the well-formed muscles in the girl's legs, whereas her thighs already burned. *And this is only the climb down*, she thought.

A flat shelf of land butted out from the side of the mountain, a meadow filled with long grass and flowers. Here, they found a handful of cows. Chloe led the way over and inspected each animal. The cows, unbothered by their presence, chewed their cuds, the strong rays of the sun beating down on them. Pandora knew meat came from cows, pigs, and other animals, but she never played executioner before. Sadness pitted in her stomach at these trusting bovines, who did not know the fate awaiting one of them.

"I think this one," Chloe stated. "Not too young, but not old enough that her meat won't be tender."

"Um … all right." Pandora's voice quivered.

"You've never done this, have you, ma'am," Chloe stated the incredibly obvious.

"No, but I suppose I need to learn." Her eyes fixated on the rope in the girl's hand. "Are you going to strangle it now?"

"We can't kill it here," the maid explained. "How would we ever get it back up the hill? The rope is to lead it."

"Oh, yes, that makes sense." Pandora flushed at her ignorance.

The chosen cow allowed Chloe to tie the rope around its neck and walked back up the hill behind them. Half of Pandora wanted to untie the animal and tell it to run, but the other half knew people needed to eat. She peeked back at the gentle eyes and tears pricked her own. She fought them back, lest the maid think she was crazy, but all she could think of was the copious amount of blood in the temple on her wedding day.

"You need not worry, ma'am," Chloe said, with a gentle rub on Pandora's arm. "One of the men will kill it out by the altar and leave the offerings. They will bring us the carcass for the spit. Our only task is cooking it."

Pandora's knees nearly gave out at this information. At least she did not need to watch the death. With a deep breath, she composed herself, and her mind flooded with her usual barrage of questions. The rest of the walk back, the maid fielded a range of inquiries from where the altar was, to how to season beef, to what other food they could serve with it.

"I apologize for asking this much at once," Pandora said after the deluge poured forth.

"I am here to help you, ma'am, and besides, asking questions is the best way to learn about the world. At least that is what my pa says."

"Your Pa is a wise man."

They crested the hill, their oblivious victim plodding behind. Kostas, now outside supervising framing, motioned a worker to assist them. The young man trotted over and took the rope from Chloe's hand. Pandora noted the shy smile that passed between the two. While he led the cow away, she helped Chloe fill the pit with the logs and collected some greener branches for kindling. The maid picked up a hunk of flint and whacked it against a stone. A shower of sparks fell, one landing on a green leaf which caught fire. It furled up before disappearing in flame. Chloe tended the fire until it sprang to life, Pandora watching in awe.

They walked to an unkempt garden behind the chicken coop, where Rhea and another goat begrudgingly moved out of their way. Chloe found a patch of leeks and pulled them up, dirt clinging to the fragrant white ends. Pandora stumbled upon some cucumbers and proudly added them to her basket. When they returned to the hilltop, the spit already held the cow's carcass, the scent of meat tinging the air.

"I will stay here and turn the spit," Chloe said, putting the vegetables to soften in a small pot over the fire's edge. "If you don't mind, maybe you could pick some olives and dates from the groves over there."

Chloe pointed beyond the barn. Picking fruit should be easy. Pandora grabbed a basket and headed over. Rex, who sat in the barn's shade, ran after her. Rhea left the garden to join them. The sun bore down on her already damp brow and she was happy when she made it to the shade of the trees. First, she gathered olives, plump perfect orbs. She took a moment to savor one, spitting the pit on the ground. Rex came over to smell it, but was unimpressed. Next, she leveled off the basket with figs, juicy and purple. Rhea munched on a fallen one, a reluctant follower, when Pandora headed back.

She sat with Chloe in the shade of the house while the meat cooked, the girl turning the heavy spit every once in a while with impressive strength. They discussed the possibility of making bread for the men tomorrow.

"But we can't do it inside the dusty house," Pandora worried.

"No, but we can do it at my house," Chloe said. "If you don't mind, ma'am."

"That's a wonderful idea," Pandora agreed.

When the meal was ready, they called over the men and heaped their plates. The workers sat in small clusters to eat, the savory smell of the roasted meat lingering in the air. Epimetheus sat with Kostas, who spoke while pointing at different spots on the house. Pandora watched her husband, the way he listened intently, the way his wavy hair framed his face, the way his eyes sparkled at the activity around him and warmth filled her. As though he could sense her gaze, he glanced over, a handsome smile lighting his face. Her heart sped up and warmth surged to her fingertips.

By day's end, the home improvements progressed nicely, the men had full stomachs, and the house was clean. Chloe drew Pandora a hot bath, and the mistress dismissed the weary-looking girl for the evening. Pandora sank into the tub, muscles aching, skin filthy, filled with a sense of satisfaction she never knew on Lemnos.

FORTY

Epimetheus woke with a sense of purpose, the sun not yet risen in the gray sky of dawn. Pandora laid with her back against his side, creating a column of warmth. He remained still to enjoy the sensation a moment longer. Rex walked across the pillow and smelled his head, the cat's tiny nose rummaging through his mounds of hair. He sensed the animal thanking him for reuniting him with Pandora, even if he had not approved of the means of travel. Over the last few weeks, the cat had slowly approved of him.

As carefully as his frame allowed, he slid out of bed. Pandora rolled over but did not wake, beautiful to him even in slumber. She would be up soon and head to the village with Chloe, where they made food for the crew every day. After a quick wash up, he donned a fresh tunic, immaculate in its whiteness. His wife purchased him some new clothing when she learned his entire wardrobe consisted of two well-worn tunics, only one of the many pleasant changes she brought into his life. The bathroom always had clean towels, newly cut flowers adorned the dresser, and freshly painted pictures awaited hanging when construction concluded. But most of all he enjoyed her company, the way she made him laugh, the energy she brought to the lonely house, and especially her questions, endless questions all of which he loved to answer.

He walked into the kitchen, where Chloe had a breakfast of dried meat and fruit waiting for him. She arrived early every morning with her father. When Epimetheus stepped out the door, Kostas spoke with the ever-growing group of workers about the projects of the day. The addition was nearly complete, with only the roof left to finish on the outside. Inside, the new maid's quarters needed a door and cabinets needed to be hung in the kitchen. Furniture building took up most of the day now, specifically designed for the dual sized couple.

The men stopped to greet Epimetheus with friendly smiles. He had listened to Pandora's advice on how to be more approachable. Now, instead of cowering, the villagers eagerly shared their ideas and stories with him. He discovered one knew a great deal about horse breeding and told Epimetheus if the Titan bred the animals he had, there would be an enormous market for selling them. Of course, Epimetheus consulted with the horses and found some of them open to the idea of going out into the world beyond, while others did not. He assured them he would always take their wishes into account.

"We have seven men who are going to install the addition's roof and replace the old roof today," Kostas told him. "Better to have it all done now, I think, then have parts of it need patching sometime soon."

"That sounds good," Epimetheus replied, always impressed with the carpenter's knowledge.

"These men will build some chairs and a dresser." Kostas gestured one way, then his finger pointed to the other side. "And those will install the doors and cabinets inside. Now, are there any other projects you can think of?"

"I'm not sure. Do you have any ideas?"

Kostas and his men made many solid suggestions during the renovation, ideas Epimetheus never would have thought of. After living alone for such a long time, he gave more thought to the welfare of his animals than his own needs. He planned the extensive chicken coop down to the last detail, wanting his animals to be happy, whereas these workers considered the comfort of people.

"I checked over the barn for any fixing but it's solid. I was going to work today on the fire pit, sprucing up the border and cleaning up the spit," Kostas said. "But I was wondering if you think Pandora could use a vanity table."

"A vanity table?" Epimetheus echoed.

"Yes, for her girly things, makeup, jewelry, that type of stuff. My wife sure loves the one I built her."

"That's a good idea," Epimetheus said. Of course, someone as stupid as him had not thought of it, whatever it was.

Kostas noticed his bewilderment. "It's kind of like a fancy desk, a place to sit with some drawers for perfumes and makeup and a mirror attached to the top, all with feminine detail. I bet Pandora would love one."

"I'm not sure I can build feminine detail," Epimetheus confessed.

"By the looks of that chicken coop, you know how to do detailed molding and embellishment. It'd be similar to that woodwork, but for a woman, not a hen. I'd be happy to give you some pointers."

"I think that is a fine idea. Thank you, Kostas. This whole renovation would never have come together without you."

The man blushed from his collar to his forehead, insisting it was nothing. "There is a pile of nice ebony over by the barn which would be perfect. Use Pandora's beauty as an inspiration for the piece and I'm sure it will turn out wonderfully."

The Titan, who was no stranger to woodworking, took the wood to a small shed near the barn. On a piece of scrap cedar, he drew a few ideas for the vanity, trying to come up with the perfect one for Pandora. Since she loved animals and particularly admired the peacock, he designed the legs in the shape of their graceful necks. The back he shaped into a fanned-out tail with an inset for a mirror.

When he needed an extra set of hands, he went outside and asked a young worker, Demetri, for assistance. The young man turned the wood in the lathe frame while Epimetheus shaped it with a sharp tool. The intricate carving would come later. They made excellent progress with the tabletop finished and the legs ready to carve the next day. Demetri asked a lot of questions about the lathe machine and speculated on how to improve it with some clever ideas. The more time Epimetheus spent with the villagers, the more he respected them.

The next few days passed in the same fashion, workers finishing up the final projects. Epimetheus spent countless hours carving the vanity. Each leg, a slim peacock neck, with its head in a unique position. The tabletop edges sculpted into elegant curves and the back piece carved into exquisite tail feathers. Kostas bought a mirror from a traveling caravan and transported it up one day, wrapped in several blankets on a cart. Epimetheus held his breath when they set it into position, a fulfilled sigh when it slipped in perfectly. Next, he painted it with the help of Demetri, who mixed the vibrant blues and greens needed to capture a peacock's splendor. Epimetheus found himself giddy at the thought of presenting the gift to Pandora when he completed it.

In the evenings, he tended to the animals while Pandora bathed. Chloe prepared a light supper for the couple, who sat at the table long into the night. They talked about their respective days, Pandora with her thousand questions, but he never let slip about the vanity. Each night when they went to bed, Pandora slept closer to him, her presence a comfort he never knew he needed, and he praised the gods for their kindness.

FORTY-ONE

Pandora filled her days during construction with keeping the men fed. Every morning, she baked bread with Chloe in the village. They tried to vary between wheat bread, flat bread, and barley cakes. Pandora, who never baked in her life, was an eager student, finding tranquility in the routine task. At midday, the duo would return up the hill, gathering figs and olives when they passed the grove. Thankfully, the men brought a cow or pig up with them each day. Pandora did not have to serve any more animals with their death warrant, a duty she did not miss. After meals, she helped Chloe clean up, despite the maid's protest the task was beneath Pandora's station. Performing these daily duties filled her with a sense of accomplishment and pride she had never experienced on Lemnos.

"I think we should make sesame cakes today," Chloe announced while they walked to the village one morning, the sun peeking over the hilltop. "A traveler passed through yesterday and ma bought a whole sack of seeds. Besides, they are good for fertility."

She gave the blushing Pandora a good-natured nudge. A cluster of children waited for them at the village gate, a dilapidated crossing of beams, the writing on it long since faded. The youngsters loved Pandora and had taken to calling her *Prima Femina*, first lady. She always carried sugared dates in her pockets for them. The entourage followed them to Chloe's house, a modest structure in need of some work, but decorated in a homey fashion by her mother, Orianna, who opened the front door in welcome. Once Pandora handed out the dates, the young ones scattered like autumn leaves, happy squeals ringing in their wake.

The trio went to work on the sesame cakes, measuring out the ingredients with careful hands. Soon their sweet aroma filled the small home, reminding Pandora of days spent with her mother eating these cakes on the beach, with the warm sun countered by a soft sea breeze. She tried not to let her mind wander back to Lemnos, but sometimes an empty pang rose in her chest before she could help it. Yet today, for the first time, the pain did not cut as deep. Her life here had settled into a pleasant rhythm. Here she made decisions for herself. Here her questions were welcome. Would she even fit in on her childhood island anymore? Would she even want to?

When Orianna set out the last of the cakes to cool, the girls went outside to sit. The women of the village joined them and Pandora loved getting to know each one, learning their names and individual stories. The sun climbed higher in the sky, its warm rays cutting into the deepest patch of shade where the ladies gathered, plaited grass fans in hand. Pandora told them about Lemnos and the cooling sea breezes and most envisioned such a boon with longing eyes. Stories of her home island captured their attention, and they pulled every detail out of her about its landscape, the people and, of course, Hephaestus.

"I bet it was scary having him right on the mountain," Idalia said, a needle in hand for the tunics she mended. The garments sat in a basket at her feet.

"Actually, we never saw him. He kept to himself. Once or twice when he was angry, the volcano rumbled and the skies darkened, but other than that, it was easy to forget he was there," Pandora replied. For reasons she could not name, she did not bring up her encounter with all the Olympians.

"But he took good care of you. The island prospered, right?" Phaedra asked, a baby suckling her breast with hearty gulps.

"Yes. He treats the inhabitants of Lemnos well," Pandora confirmed, missing the salt-tinged air.

She noticed the mutual nods among the women, all with

dejection in their eyes. She scanned the group until her eyes fell on Paz, the old woman who had been there the longest. Paz studied Pandora as though she could see right into her very soul. Unnerved, Pandora shifted in her seat, but, as usual, a surge of questions leaped to mind, ones she thought the old woman may have some insight on.

"Paz, you told me once that your family has been here for generations. If the village has been here for such a long time, why are there not more residents?"

"Way back when the village was first settled, people were excited. Buildings and businesses sprung up around a beautiful temple. But alas, we had no notable statues or objects to fill it. With nothing to draw travelers and nothing important to trade, the city has been mostly forgotten by the rest of the world," Paz said, her frown emphasizing her wrinkles. "Many people born here leave to find more prosperous lives elsewhere."

The dejected group nodded at the old woman's assessment, and Pandora could hardly blame them. Even the buildings sagged as if dismayed to be stuck here. Overrun with weeds, the temple stood largely in disrepair, a shame since Pandora could imagine its original beauty. A gloomy atmosphere hung over the length of the street. The only source of joy around was the children, who rollicked and laughed in a nearby field, too innocent to realize the deficiencies of their home.

"The men have almost finished our house addition. Perhaps after that, they can work on the buildings here and we can plant flowers and paint, freshen up the town," Pandora suggested, remembering the sense of purpose her first visit instilled.

"That is a nice thought," Idalia said, her eyes brighter.

"Except with no significant temple idol or special item of trade, the village would still not provide a future that would make most wish to stay," Paz stated.

"What if we could figure something out?" Pandora asked, unwilling to be dissuaded.

"We would not want to anger Epimetheus with any notion that the town is not good enough," Phaedra said.

"Anger him?" Pandora asked, unable to reconcile her husband and anger.

"His brother's visits are not pleasant. His yelling reverberates all the way down here. The children hide when they see him coming," Orianna explained.

"Yes, I can imagine," Pandora said, the elder Titan's steely eyes flashing in her head.

"We don't want to cause trouble between you and your new spouse," Idalia remarked.

"Let me worry about Epimetheus," Pandora instructed. "If you could do anything to better the village, what would it be?"

After a long moment of silence by all, Phaedra declared. "I, for one, would like to see more businesses and even a school."

At the mention of a school, all tongues loosened about how much being able to read and write would help their children. Soon they all threw out thoughts to improve the town and elected Orianna to create a list full of their ideas to discuss with the men. Pandora now fielded a ton of questions, her opinion highly valued. Paz stayed quiet during the deliberations. A peal of thunder broke up the unofficial meeting, everyone gesturing piety to Zeus for whatever upset him.

"Time to get the food up to the men," Orianna announced.

She went into her house with Chloe to gather the sesame cakes and empty baskets. Pandora walked after them, but a tug on her arm stopped her.

"Do you think you can talk Epimetheus into revitalizing the town?" It was Paz who spoke, her gray eyes impossible to read. "And even if you can, we still need something of value to draw people to the village."

"I'm sure Epimetheus will be happy to help on all fronts," Pandora said, confident in her words. "By the way,

everyone keeps referring to this place as 'the village.'
What is its proper name?"

"If it had one, it was forgotten long ago with everything
else."

"Well, we are going to change that."

She squeezed the old woman's hand and Paz rewarded
her with a nearly toothless smile. On the way up the hill,
lightness now filled her heart. She had a mission and she
could not wait to put it into action.

FORTY-TWO

Pandora and Chloe stopped at the olive grove halfway up the hill to fill their baskets. The orchard, if it could be called one, rambled in every direction, clumps of trees scattered here and there, as though tossed by a storm. Fig trees grew in no particular arrangement, weaving in and out of the olive trees, the broad leaves of the former contrasting with the stubbier leaves of the latter. An undergrowth of weeds covered the ground, dotted with scruffy bushes in a labyrinthine pattern. *No wonder the children enjoy playing here*, she thought.

"Could the villagers not sell olive oil?" Pandora asked, swatting an errant branch out of her face.

"They could, but many villages sell it and there would be nothing special about ours worth anyone's trip," the maid explained. "It's nice that you want to help."

"I promise I will think of something," Pandora said, although no ideas presented themselves.

Once their baskets were full, they trekked up to the hilltop where the men labored in the hot midday sun. The wilting workers perked up once they ate, laughter ringing across the circle where they assembled, Epimetheus' head high above the others. Pandora took heart at the broad grin on his face. The Titan, solitary for untold decades, came to enjoy their company, and the villagers overcame their fears of their intimidating landlord. She excitedly awaited this evening when she could tell him her idea.

After the meal, the men scurried back to work. Pandora and Chloe doused the fire, left the bones in a pile for any animals to eat, and took the cups to the stream to wash. The first few days, Chloe insisted on washing all the cups herself and left Pandora in the shade to soak her feet in the cool water. On the fifth day, Pandora, never one to sit still, snuck up behind the maid and playfully splashed her. Since then, the two scampered into the water daily, much as Pandora did with Cyane in her youth. Probably not how most dignified mistresses acted, indeed Danae would likely faint at the prospect of behaving in such a fashion, but in these moments, Pandora felt more alive than she had in a long while.

When the women returned to the property, most of the men packed up their tools, an early ending to the day. Epimetheus stood on the far side of the property with three workers discussing a new paddock where buyers could inspect the horses who agreed to be sold. The rest of the crew bade them goodbye and headed off down the hill. Besides the paddock, no other work remained, the addition to the house completed.

Inside, a purposeful mix of large and small furnishings filled the space. Murals of the countryside decorated the walls of the main room, delightful scenes of people frolicking and picnicking with fauns and satyrs. A well-stocked pantry sat next to the kitchen. It held a new sink, which some inventive villager connected with pipes directly to the stream behind the house and produced water with the turn of a screw. The same technology ran to the sink and tub in the bathroom. The two ladies marveled at the device, amazed each time they turned it on and off. In the hallway niche, the pithos stood on the same marble pedestal, its hypnotic images in constant motion. Chloe always dipped her head in deference and rose her hands to the gods before quickly rushing past. Pandora gazed at the object for a moment, the depictions appearing to glow the longer she stared. She waited for the dread from the dream to overtake her, but today only a strange consternation filled her, as though it held an answer she needed.

Back in the kitchen, Chloe prepared a light supper, slicing dates and figs, which she arranged on a plate next to a platter of cheese and bread. She hummed softly to herself, a tune Elara used to sing, and a pang of homesickness threatened Pandora until her husband burst through the front door.

"I have a surprise for you," he bellowed, excitement etched on his face. "But you have to cover your eyes while I bring it inside."

"All right," Pandora agreed. His eagerness silencing all her questions.

She turned her back and brought her hands up over her eyes. Chloe came to stand beside her, wiping her hands on her apron. The sound of multiple footsteps filled the room and headed to the bedroom. Pandora peeked at Chloe and the maid's quizzical face mirrored her own. Rhea clomped in and settled on a new bed that replaced her old pile of rags.

"What's he up to?" Pandora asked the goat. "You look entirely complicit."

Chloe laughed, but the goat merely ignored the two of them and settled her head down for a nap. Rex crept over and curled up next to his friend, the two animals nearly inseparable now after their rocky beginning.

Two men returned to the main room with Epimetheus. They bowed to Pandora, who graced them with a smile. Chloe stiffened, her gaze fixed on the younger of the two. He stared back with an expression Pandora noticed passing between them on several other occasions. Young love, full of intensity and longing, was hard to hide.

"We are headed out for the night," said Demetri. "If Chloe is finished, we would be happy to escort her back home."

Pandora noticed the maid flush from her neck to stain her cheeks crimson while she waited for a reply.

"Yes, that will be fine," Pandora said. "Her room here is ready. Perhaps you could help her bring up her belongings tomorrow."

Demetri nodded heartily, his eyes never leaving Chloe, who smiled and took her leave.

Once the couple was alone, Epimetheus grabbed Pandora's hand and took her to the bedroom. Pandora gasped. Against the side wall stood a vanity, more intricate and vibrant than anything she had ever seen.

"What do you think?" Epimetheus asked, bouncing on the balls of his feet. "I made it for you."

"You made this? It's beautiful."

She walked over to admire the carved tail feathers that splayed from behind the mirror, each adorned with a striking eye. Her hands ran across the smooth marble top and down the blue-green head and neck that formed each leg. A tufted bench completed the set, topped with soft silk of the same hues. She turned to see his expectant eyes on her. Uncertainty flickered in them with the notion the gift would not satisfy her. With a warm heart, she ran to him and kissed him full on the mouth.

"Thank you, Epimetheus, I love it," she beamed.

Now she watched him turn seven shades of red.

"It was nothing, just a wedding present for you," he mumbled.

"It's the most exquisite gift I ever received," she gushed and gave him another kiss, one which he returned.

They broke apart and stood for a moment in awkward silence. Pandora had been here for a couple of months and he had never once mentioned consummating the marriage. Until now, that had been a source of relief to her, but the kiss was nice—more than nice, in truth. She would not mind kissing him again, but the thought of initiating another kiss suddenly terrified her, and judging by the trapped animal expression on his face, Epimetheus thought the same.

"I'm … glad … it made you happy," he stammered. "Should we have dinner?"

She nodded, and they strolled down the hallway. The couple stopped at the niche where the jar sat. Neither had ever mentioned their unease with the gift to the other, afraid to offend the Olympians. Epimetheus' brow furrowed as he studied it. Pandora, who had trained herself not to gaze directly at the pithos, watched the creases in her husband's forehead deepen. Usually, a wave of disquiet arose in the jar's presence. This time, however, clarity filled her, the answer she sought before now clear.

"Is the work here done?" she asked once they settled into their seats.

"Yes, except for some odds and ends on the paddock," he confirmed.

"I have something to ask you," she prefaced, and he nodded for her to continue. "I've been in the village. It's a little rundown, well, more than a little, and it doesn't even have a name. Did you know that?"

He shook his head, somewhat dumbfounded. "I never gave the village much thought. Not sure why? A mistake on my part, I see now that I've gotten to know some of them."

"I offered our help to make some improvements except the villagers worry there is nothing special to attract visitors. But I have an idea. It's about the pithos."

They spent the next few hours in deep discussion, Pandora growing more excited with each passing minute. Her spirit soared, her purpose further fortified.

FORTY-THREE

Epimetheus settled the large stone slab on top of the refurbished altar with gentle hands. Once lined up to satisfaction, he rubbed the top with a soft cloth, polishing the marble until it gleamed in the rays of sun slanting in from the oculus above. He stepped off the dais and surveyed the inside of the temple, a smile rising at the edges of his mouth at the beauty he saw. Kostas came to his side.

"It's wonderful," the man said with a clap on Epimetheus' back. "The altar is elegant yet plain enough not to take attention away from the pithos behind it. You have a smart wife, if you don't mind me saying."

"I don't mind at all because I wholeheartedly agree," the Titan remarked.

Over the course of the last two months, the entire village blossomed under the direction of Epimetheus and Pandora. New shops lined the street alongside freshly repaired houses. Demetri ran pipes to many of the buildings and upgraded the communal cistern to hold more water. Materials flowed in from neighboring towns—wood and stone for construction, fabrics for everything from awnings to chitons, plants, insects and snails for dyes, and livestock for labor and food.

The dusty road of dilapidated edifices transformed into a colorful boulevard with cheerful people all doing their part to enhance the village, now named Epideme, in honor of the Titan. Each day found the residents busy with construction, painting, and readying shops with new wares to sell. But the largest change occurred in the temple. On the outside, some workers scrubbed and patched the stone columns, while others fixed the crumbling staircase. Epimetheus hired a special designer who oversaw the restoration of sculptures and topped the pediments in gold. The surrounding grounds became a lush garden with tables for sacrifices.

In the interior centered around the cella, or inner shrine, sat the jar on a high gilded pedestal, exactly as Pandora suggested. She confided in Epimetheus the night she explained this plan how Athena warned her not to open it. This news set him on edge, a bane from the gods masquerading as a boon. Epimetheus had questioned the safety of public access to the pithos, but Pandora told him the only her hand could open the jar and had shown him the key. Comforted by this assurance, Epimetheus readily agreed.

The couple gifted the pithos to the city, where all could come and marvel at its majesty. Since the jar held gifts from each Olympian, the villagers dedicated the temple to them all. The main altar served for offerings to the twelve deities, but the sculptor carved a statue of each, should anyone wish to honor a specific one. The six males stood in one ante chamber and the six females in the other. However, the pithos was the principal attraction, its swirling images already legend among the villagers. Pandora knew people would come from far and wide to get a glimpse of it, thus driving commerce and notoriety to the forgotten town.

Loud footsteps echoed off the marble walls. Kostas turned, his smile fading along with the pallor of his skin. Prometheus strolled over to his brother and they greeted each other with kisses on both cheeks, while Kostas slunk away to a safer distance.

"I went up to the house for a visit, but was told you were down here," the elder brother said. "From the looks of things, both there and here, you have been up to a lot lately."

"Yes, I am helping the villagers renovate the town in order to draw more visitors."

"Why this sudden concern with them?" Prometheus asked. His condescending tone rankled Epimetheus.

"To improve the quality of their lives, Brother. Pandora had the smart idea to put our wedding gift in the temple," he gestured to where the pithos sat.

"Did she now? What a clever girl." His comment sounded unimpressed, but even as he uttered it, his gaze rose to the jar.

Prometheus' eyes fixed on the object, time and place melting out of them, supplanted with an unnerving hunger, an expression Epimetheus recognized. The pithos held sway over anyone who stared at it for too long. For some, marvel and tranquility saturated their mind, but for others a spark of avarice arose. Though the greed in his brother's eyes never consumed Epimetheus, the pithos made him uneasy, particularly after Pandora's tale. For this reason, he had been happy to remove it from the house. He grabbed his brother's arm and pulled him toward the door. The spell broke from Prometheus' face. He shook his head to recover his senses and walked outside with his younger sibling.

"And where is this brilliant wife of yours?"

Though asked with propriety, Epimetheus heard the derision laced in his voice. They descended the stairs, weaving around a few laborers. Epimetheus spotted Pandora with Orianna part way down the street. He led his brother over, unsurprised to see children scattering out of sight. In fact, most people avoided any eye contact with Prometheus. *They used to be afraid of me like this*, Epimetheus thought, thankful they no longer viewed him in such a light.

"Sister-in-law, how good to see you?" Prometheus declared.

Pandora stood over a vat of blue water where she dyed a swath of rough fabric. Orianna crept backward, head down, until she reached the safety of her door. She slipped in without a sound.

"It's nice to see you too, Prometheus. You must be proud of your brother and the interest he has taken in the people you entrusted to him. See how the town flourishes and when travelers come to see the pithos, Epideme will only expand in size and renown."

Prometheus peered down at her, boredom etched on his face, but Epimetheus knew his brother enough to see the underlying contempt.

"Are you not worried you will offend the gods by this choice to display their gift in public?" His rude tone did not affect Pandora.

"On the contrary, I should think they would be pleased to have their present, both grand and generous, admired by as many humans as possible."

She smiled at him, the picture of innocence. Epimetheus inwardly smiled, proud to see his wife get under his brother's skin. Prometheus barely nodded and walked away, his brother on his heels.

"Let us return to your house and have some wine together." Prometheus suggested.

They strolled up the hill, people skittering out of the way, with none of the pleasantries usually aimed at Epimetheus. He showed his brother the improvements to his property and the renovations to the house, including the vanity. While Prometheus complimented its craftsmanship, Rex took refuge under the bed. They sat at the table inside and Chloe, unfazed by the elder Titan, set out two glasses of wine before excusing herself. Prometheus studied the main room, his eyes stopping on every new piece of furniture and fresco.

"Things certainly are spruced up around here. A woman's touch, I suppose," he stated after downing his glass in one sip.

"Yes, Pandora helped me plan it all out. When we finished here, she suggested we help in the village."

"She sounds like quite the handful," Prometheus speculated, ever ready to stir up trouble. He poured himself another glass of wine.

"She certainly has a mind of her own, but I enjoy her company."

"Well, well," his brother said, wagging an eyebrow. "You will have little ones running around here in no time."

Epimetheus flushed at the comment, wanting to change the subject, but his brother missed nothing and used any opportunity to belittle his sibling.

"Have I embarrassed you? It's only natural for a husband and wife to have children," he said. At Epimetheus' silence, comprehension crossed his face. "You are coupling with her, are you not?"

"Umm …" an even redder Epimetheus said, "I don't want to hurt her. She is so tiny next to me."

Prometheus roared with such laughter, Rhea woke from her bed, and with a scornful stare, clopped outside. Meanwhile, Epimetheus wished the floor would swallow him whole even as thoughts of Pandora's lips on his rose to mind. His whole body warmed at the picture of her wrapped around him.

"Brother," Prometheus said, putting a hand on his arm, "there is a glamour you can adopt to make you mortal sized in order to be with her."

"There is?" How did he not know this already? He truly was the stupid one of the two of them. No wonder his brother never let him forget.

When Prometheus explained what to do, his words held no mockery or insults, for once pleased to convey needed information to his younger sibling. Epimetheus listened intently, amazed how this knowledge escaped him all this time.

"And that is how it's done," Prometheus finished. "How do you think Zeus can mate with all those mortal women?"

"I suppose I never gave it much thought." Humiliation stung at him and he cursed his idiocy. Pandora must think he did not find her attractive enough.

"I hope I have been of some help," Prometheus said, emptying the last of the wine bottle into his cup.

"You have, thank you," Epimetheus said. "Speaking of Zeus, is he still angry with you? You haven't done anything else to upset him, have you?"

"Is he still angry? Who knows? He's always angry at someone," Prometheus shrugged. "Besides, I still have a secret up my sleeve in case I ever need the leverage."

A shiver of fear raced through Epimetheus. Whatever the secret was, he was better off in the dark. The gods had blessed him with Pandora and he enjoyed a happiness he never thought possible. He intended to remain far out of the sight and thoughts of the Olympians if he could help it. Turning the conversation to a different subject, he asked about Hesione, Prometheus' wife and her pregnancy.

The brothers talked for the rest of the afternoon, Prometheus quite amiable after his initial brashness. When he took his leave, he embraced his younger brother fondly. Epimetheus watched his Prometheus' silhouette disappear down the hill. He returned inside, where Chloe prepared dinner. *Forgive me*, he thought, *but I hope my brother stays away for a while.*

On his trip home, Prometheus pondered the surprising developments in the village. With the improvements, Epideme would surely become a place of renown, further elevating the status of his brother and that wretched girl. His mind flashed to the jar, to the extraordinary gifts inside. What had Pandora done to deserve such a boon? And what good was it to possess a pithos full of blessings only to leave it sealed? Prometheus coveted the jar with every fiber of his being. Surely, he held more sway over his brother than Pandora. One way or another, he would convince Epimetheus to open it and take some of the blessing for himself. Perhaps he would take them all. A wry smile filled his face at this thought as ideas to carry out his plan formed in his mind.

FORTY-FOUR

Pandora returned from the village, her hands stained blue from her work. Chloe helped her bathe in the renovated tub with its intricate tile design in rich blues and greens. The colors reminded Pandora of the green hills of Lemnos and the surrounding sea. While the maid rubbed oils through her hair, Pandora lay submerged up to her neck. The warm water relaxed her muscles, which ached from turning the fabric in the tun and hanging it, heavy and wet, to dry. Never had such hard work been more gratifying.

"Ma'am, I was hoping I could ask a favor," the maid said. At Pandora's nod, she continued, "Demetri asked if he could have dinner with my father and I tonight. I have everything prepared for you and the master. Would it be all right if I left early? And I appreciate my beautiful room here, but would it be all right if I stayed at my father's tonight?"

"That would be fine and may I say, Demetri is rather handsome, is he not? Fine husband material." Pandora grinned from ear to ear.

The crimson maid stammered over a few unintelligible words. The idea of their love brought a smile to Pandora's face. Her mind wandered to Epimetheus, the crooked tilt of his smile, the tenderness in his eyes, the comfort of waking nestled against his side each morning. Their kisses grew longer, sweet and lingering. The recollection drew a sigh.

"Though I am not the only one with fine husband material," Chloe ventured.

After a startled look from Pandora, both women laughed. Despite their difference in station, Pandora truly considered Chloe her friend and confidant. When she dried off and the maid combed out her hair, they recounted details to each other about their emotions as only females can.

"I'm going to eat now. If you want, you can freshen up with my makeup before you see Demetri," Pandora said, slipping a clean tunic over her head. "And use some of my perfume, too."

The excited maid thanked her and Pandora went to the main room, stopping briefly in the hall where the niche stood empty. How nice it was to not have the pithos looming over her every move. Though she knew the gods honored her with the gift, its presence disquieted her. The idea of having it in the village for all to see solved that problem, after all, a divine object deserved a divine setting. At this thought, the key vibrated softly, but she paid no mind and entered the main room. Epimetheus sat at the table, several platters spread out before him. Rhea stood next to him, munching on a carrot.

"Did you start without me?" Pandora joked. "And with another woman."

Epimetheus chuckled. "It's hard to resist this one."

He patted the goat on the head and Pandora sat down across from him. Chloe came out of the bedroom with a pile of wet towels. She put them in a basket outside the door to her room. Pandora noted the soft stain of red on the girl's lips and cheeks, which complemented her newly braided hair. Another smile crept up her face.

"I'll be going now," Chloe announced.

"Have fun," Pandora called after her as she stepped out the door. Rhea tracked the unusual departure.

At her husband's quizzical face, Pandora explained, "Chloe went home for dinner. Demetri asked to dine with her and her father. She will return in the morning."

Epimetheus gave a slight nod until the realization dawned on him.

"They would make a fine couple. Demetri is a hard worker and a good fellow," he said.

"She is quite smitten with him. It's fun to see love blossom," Pandora replied.

"Chloe is a pretty thing, too," Epimetheus remarked. "Though not nearly as beautiful as you."

Their eyes met and held, as though a magic force fixed them. Everything around Pandora faded, but Epimetheus and a thousand butterflies burst into her stomach. All the times she and Cyane dreamed of love, they assumed it to be sheer bliss, and she was happy, but there was something more—a trust, a respect, and an emotion that transcended superficial delight to a deeper bond. She read the same feeling in his eyes. No need to even speak a word to describe the raw power between them. Epimetheus turned away and the break in connection pierced her heart as though an arrow struck it.

"Prometheus told me something," he muttered, "about a glamour I can adopt and how to use it for us …" he stuttered to stop, unable to meet her eyes again, "you know … to be together … as husband and wife … without my hurting you."

Epimetheus met her gaze, his eyes a study of vulnerability. Pandora had no love for her brother-in-law but silently thanked him for this input.

"I would like that," she said, heat rising in her body.

He stood, offered his hand, and led her to the bedroom. Utilizing the information from his brother, he pulled the glamour across himself and changed to the size of a human man. He laid her back on the bed, their bodies melding into one another. Caresses and kisses grew in urgency. Their skin charged as though lightning surged through their touch. Pandora recalled her fear on their wedding night. How wrong she had been. When she reached the pinnacle of pleasure, she cried out in both ecstasy and disbelief, the act more satisfying than she had ever imagined.

After, she lay with her head on her husband's chest, the steadiness of his breathing an anchor for her heart. He stroked her hair, wrapping coils around his large fingers and unfurling them as she drifted to sleep. In the morning, she woke to his touch, and they rekindled the flame from the night before. When the pinkish tones of dawn seeped in the window, he rose, their hands entwined. He kissed her palm, and they beamed at each other. He slipped on his tunic and left the room. Pandora laid back in the warm spot where he had been, reliving the intimate moments over and over in her mind.

She must have dozed because someone shook her shoulder to rouse her. When she opened her eyes, Chloe stood over her and the sun of late morning slanted into the room in rectangular chunks.

"Do you feel ill, ma'am?" the maid asked. "Do you want to remain in bed?"

She did, but not to sleep. Sitting up to stretch, she smiled again at the sensual memories. Chloe's expression changed from worry to comprehension. While Pandora dressed, the maid changed the sheets without a word, trying to contain her grin.

"How was your dinner with Demetri?"

"It was pleasant. Though not as pleasant as your evening, I daresay."

Normally, such a conversation with anyone would be awkward, but somehow her and Chloe's relationship differed. A genuine friendship existed between the two. Pandora confided all the events of the evening to her captivated maid, who squealed with happiness for the couple.

"It all sounds amazing," Chloe said with a wistful sigh.

"It was. Hopefully, you will experience it soon enough yourself," Pandora remarked.

"I will," she replied, elation in her tone. "Last night, Demetri asked Father for my hand and he agreed."

Pandora jumped up from her dressing table to embrace Chloe. They spent the rest of the morning discussing Chloe's wedding. When they went to the village in the afternoon, Pandora visited the temple. She kneeled before the pithos and praised the gods for their generosity and the gift of a love she had never expected. *How blessed I am,* she thought. When she rose to leave, the key vibrated wildly against her chest.

FORTY-FIVE

The village of Epideme blossomed over the next few months, word of mouth drawing visitors from far and wide. Once rundown buildings came to life along the new brick road, its forlorn dirt predecessor forgotten. Shops lined the main thoroughfare, adorned with colorful signs, bright against the mud brick facades. The village grew daily, spreading out along the flatlands at the base of the hill. The thrum of residents filled the air, wrapped in the scent of baked good, freshly cut lumber, and sticks of incense.

A newly elected council approved a design for side streets filled with new homes to accommodate the influx of residents. More families meant more children, and Pandora saw to the construction of a school, with an elegant portico across the front that reminded her of Lemnos and Madame Tullia. Gardens and flower boxes filled with lilies, amaranth and hyacinth dotted the town in bursts of vivid color.

In the center of all the beauty stood the temple, repaired to its original grandeur, the fresh gold leaf shining at the pediment's apex. A sacred grove of olive trees, next to the temple, gave worshippers an additional place to pray. The grounds were busy from sunrise to sunset, offerings heaped in front of every statue. Several temple maidens and a priest tended to the complex.

One day, a lone gray owl perched on a leafy branch, watching the comings and goings of the townsfolk. Since the wedding, Athena tended to other matters, crises caused by one of her fellow Olympians or the occasional arrogant human. She took in the village and its inhabitants, impressed by the development over a short period. Pandora certainly used her time productively and selflessly. The goddess had assessed the girl's character correctly. A whoosh of wings rushed toward her and the branch sank when a brown hawk settled next to her.

"What are you doing here, Hermes?" Annoyance laced her tone.

"I might ask you the same question, Sister." He ruffled his feathers and puffed out his chest.

"I was interested to see how the new couple fared," Athena replied. "I am happy to see all the progress they have made. The temple is lovely, don't you think?"

"Yes, and dedicated to us all," Hermes quipped, "so smart of Epimetheus to not play favorites."

"I think the girl is the wise one. Clever of her to put the pithos in the temple for all to admire." Athena appreciated this shrewd idea.

"And to keep it away from herself," he countered. "That is what you truly mean. I wonder what our father would think about that."

"Why do you always aspire to stir up trouble, Brother?" Athena asked, her wide yellow eyes firmly on him.

"What would become of these humans if we did not?" he disputed. "With no trouble in their lives, they may consider themselves as equal to us."

Athena sighed. Ever since Prometheus brought the mortals fire, they evolved into more and more sophisticated beings. Such advancement could never go unchecked by the gods.

"There are already countless examples of men who thought themselves as worthy as the gods," Athena contended. "We deal with them accordingly. But neither Epimetheus nor Pandora have offended any of us enough to merit what that pithos could release."

"Was it not *your* idea to marry the Titan to a mortal?" he replied with feigned confusion.

"To make Epimetheus appear favored over his brother. Not to cause unnecessary calamity," the goddess clarified. "I'm sure the popularity of the village is a thorn in Prometheus' side. Can't that be enough?"

"Sister, you grow too soft where this girl is concerned. You had no problem cursing Medusa with a headful of snakes for something not entirely her fault. What makes Pandora different?"

Athena turned away, no answer ready on her tongue. She did not understand why such a connection existed with this girl. Perhaps she saw a bit of herself in Pandora's spirit.

"Now, if you will excuse me," Hermes said. "I must go and turn an arrogant man into a statue. However, I do think Father would be most interested in learning what transpires here. I'll make sure to update him."

With a flick of his wings, the hawk took flight, climbing higher and higher into the air until only a tiny black spot was visible. Athena shook her head, doubtful Zeus would care much about one village. She scanned below and spotted Pandora and Epimetheus. They strolled down the street, hand in hand. The couple stopped to greet various people on their way to the temple. Once at its steps, they whispered, their heads close. When they parted, they embraced and kissed. Pandora continued up the temple stairs while Epimetheus walked further down to a lumberyard, where he conversed with several men.

Athena flew to the rafters of the temple. Pandora circled around to each statue, offering devotion to every deity. She ended in front of the pithos. Here she kneeled, clutching the key around her neck and whispered words of prayer. Once she rose, she stared at the jar for a long time. A temple maiden approached her, breaking the spell.

Athena observed Pandora for the rest of the afternoon. She left the temple and consulted with many women from the town. Some asked for advice on a personal matter, others asked for permission to further improve the village, a few even asked for her blessing, referring to her as *Prima Femina*. Pandora's attentiveness, patience, and willingness to help all who came to her impressed the goddess. More striking was the level of authority and autonomy granted to the women of Epideme.

Epimetheus' day went much the same, the villagers eager for his counsel and support. The day ended with the opening of a new inn. The couple presided over the ceremony, uncovering the newly painted sign, and making the appropriate offerings to the goddess Hestia for the gift of hospitality. After a celebratory meal, they left and headed up the hill.

Athena took flight to trail along. She watched the relaxed couple, chatting, laughing, and kissing, their interactions filled with love, an unexpected outcome. *Did it change anything*? Athena wondered, alighting on the barn's roof. Unfortunately, it probably did. Her father enjoyed nothing more than destroying happiness when he found it. Another reminder mortals were no equal to the gods. The couple went inside for the evening and Athena hoped Zeus would forget about them for a long while. She spread her wings and soared toward the heavens.

FORTY-SIX

"What do you mean, they moved it to a temple?" Zeus roared.

The sky stormed, dark, roiling clouds pierced by spitting bolts of lightning. The King of the Gods paced the throne room with eyes mirroring the angry tempest above. Ganymede cowered behind his master's chair. Artemis rose with a sigh, the tranquility of a moment ago shattered by the news Hermes delivered. The goddess of the hunt threw a knowing glance back at her twin on her way out, and Apollo quickly followed. Ares, the only other being in the room, chose to stay. He loved witnessing his father's infamous tantrums.

"Yes, I thought it was unusual," Hermes said from where he leaned against a pillar, ever the picture of calm. "After all, the pithos was our wedding gift to them."

Zeus made no reply, but the clouds churned with menace, their darkness punctuated by haphazard explosions of light. A gray owl burst through the gloom, morphing into Athena when she entered the room. She landed next to Hermes. He smirked in her direction and she stifled some choice words. If everyone resorted to shouts, she could not placate an angry Zeus. Instead, she sought her composure.

"Though it was a gift to the couple, they have displayed it with honor in a temple dedicated to us all," Athena pointed out.

Her father turned to her and spat out through clenched teeth, "I don't need that pithos *displayed*. I need it *opened*."

"Why?" his daughter challenged. "You wanted to punish Prometheus. I can assure you the fact that his brother has gained a beautiful wife, restored a town, and is now the celebrated Titan surely eats at Prometheus. You got what you wanted."

"You think a bruised ego will satisfy me after all that Titan has done?" Zeus bellowed. "I want him to suffer brutally for his insolence."

"You should let me torture him," Ares interjected, eager at the thought of bloodlust. "I'll make sure it is slow and painful. You can give me exact instructions."

"No. I can't punish him after he bound me to an agreement. I must keep my honor," Zeus proclaimed.

His children exchanged dubious glances. Their father was never a stickler for principles. Examples of him bending ethics to his favor could fill the Parthenon. Prometheus, however, was a fellow immortal and had been a great asset in the war against the Titans. If Zeus reneged on his word, it could cast a bad light on all the Olympians. The King of the Gods knew his reign must hold equal parts fear and respect. The former kept people in line, the latter gave them reason to revere.

"Why not simply cause an accident that opens the pithos?" Ares suggested. "I'll disguise myself as wind and knock it over."

"I don't want it to be an accident. I want that blasted girl to open it. How has she resisted its powers thus far?" Zeus shot an accusatory glare at Athena.

"What do you want me to say? She is a strong-willed girl," the goddess of wisdom replied.

"Too strong-willed it appears," Zeus mused, taking his seat. "Daughter, this whole idea was yours. Surely, I don't need to worry whether you are on my side, do I?"

Out of the corner of her eye, Athena watched Hermes' smile grow. How he loved to watch her squirm. Ganymede hurried to fill a goblet with nectar. Zeus drained the cup in one sip and motioned for a refill.

"With all due respect, Father, I only suggested elevating Epimetheus to vex his brother. I did not agree to unleashing misery on all of mankind."

"But Prometheus created mankind. They must suffer too. That is the point," the exasperated king yelled.

"Might I make a suggestion?" Hermes offered, flying to the center of the room. "Sooner or later Prometheus will cross you again. It's merely a matter of time and patience."

"I'm listening," Zeus said, his eyes narrowing. He took another long draft of nectar.

"Prometheus already covets the jar. He wants the blessings inside. Next time he angers you and he fears you will retaliate, I will convince him he needs those blessings and assist him in opening the pithos." Hermes hovered in front of the king's throne.

"How?"

"Do not trouble yourself with such trifling matters, Father. You know my proclivity for this type of work. I assure you, when the pithos unleashes its evil, your name will remain above reproof."

"Fine," Zeus relented. The King of the Gods rose to leave. He called back over his shoulder, "I will have patience for now. But remember, it is not limitless."

"Of course. Leave it to me," Hermes assured, with a deliberate grin at his sister.

A relieved Ganymede scuttled out in his master's wake. The sky cleared to a bright azure, fluffy clouds replacing the angry gale. Hermes took his seat, draping a leg over the armrest. Ares shook his head and rose, disappointed the spectacle ended already. The god of war hoisted his spear and regarded his siblings with a weary sigh.

"Whipping humans up into a battle frenzy is much easier than this intricate plotting," he declared and disappeared in a cloud of red smoke.

"I think that went well," Hermes declared from his place of repose.

"I'm sure you do," Athena countered, the bite in her tone unmistakable.

"Honestly, Sister, you are far too attached to this girl." At her silence, he continued, "There are thousands of other maidens out there. Again I ask, what makes this one special?”

“Because I chose her. The original plan was mine, and I selected her. Had I known Father’s true plan, I *would* have merely thrown the letters in the air and picked one at random, as you suggested.”

“Dear Sister, you may have chosen her letter anyway,” Hermes consoled in a rare moment of sympathy. “The Fates also have their say in all matters.”

The Fates. Three immortal beings who wove a human’s destiny. Clotho spun the thread out, Lachesis measured it out in years, and Atropus severed it at the moment of death. The trio of sisters indeed guided the course of life, but did that leave Athena inculpable? No. In Pandora’s case, Athena not only intervened, but she went directly against the express wishes of the innocent girl. The goddess played a large role as Pandora’s life hurtled toward destruction.

“This is why we don’t get attached to humans,” Hermes rebuked, handing his sister a goblet of nectar.

The thick liquid cloyed in Athena’s throat. Despite her gift of wisdom, she knew no effort to save Pandora would succeed. The scheme to open the pithos was inevitable, Zeus’ desire from the plan’s inception. Even had the goddess realized earlier, she could not redirect Pandora’s steps from this grave path.

FORTY-SEVEN

Life continued, the village flourishing into a small city, no longer a forsaken spot on the map. Over the next six months, businesses thrived and trade expanded. New materials arrived from the far edges of the world, foods and spices that delighted the tongue, and durable tools for even more construction which the ever-growing population demanded. Worshippers ribboned out of the temple daily, long lines of travel-weary people who longed to see the famous pithos. Their presence required the assignment of additional maidens to the temple, with Paz as their mistress.

Pandora's days were full. The *Prima Femina* administered to most of the town. With the help of Epimetheus, they established guilds, appointed emissaries, and oversaw the distribution of money from the temple. While her husband spent the bulk of his time with his animals on the hill, Pandora visited the town each day. Chloe acted as her assistant in town matters, the job befitting her station now that she was Dmitri's wife. Epimetheus met with Kostas on a weekly basis to review construction projects or infrastructure concerns. Prometheus visited on occasion with his wife and new son, Deucalion. Though he praised his younger brother for the rejuvenation of the village, Pandora always sensed his underlying current of annoyance at the success of Epimetheus. Despite this, the days left the couple filled with pride and purpose.

"Are you feeling all right, ma'am?" Iris asked Pandora one morning.

The recently hired maid stood over the bed, the hour well past dawn. Pandora sat and forced down another wave of nausea. The third morning in a row such an affliction overtook her, only to be gone by midday. Iris handed her a clay pot, and Pandora heaved the meager contents of her stomach into it.

"Shall I fetch a doctor?" Iris asked, holding Pandora's hair behind her neck.

"No," Pandora replied. "I think we both already know what the cause is."

Iris smiled, no stranger to the condition. The eldest of ten children, she had seen her mother suffer from morning sickness her fair share of times. "Does the master know?"

"Not yet. I wanted to be sure, but now I'm at eight weeks since my last monthly courses. Do you think that is enough to assume I'm pregnant?" She swung her legs over the side of the bed and the room spun.

"Mother always said her breasts got sore and her belly got hard," the girl informed, her youthful face full of concern.

Pandora poked at her chest and stomach. Sore and hard. Although she suspected this for days, the reality now engulfed her in emotions, which ran the gamut from fear to elation. How she longed for her own mother, for Elara, to ask the multitude of questions flooding her mind like a tidal wave. She paled and Iris held out the bowl again. Pandora shook her head.

"Help me bathe and dress," she instructed. "I will visit the midwife in town."

She left the house shortly after, declining the breakfast offered by the maid. With a wave to Epimetheus in the paddocks on her way past, she walked down the hill. Warm sunlight filtered in soft rays through fluffy white clouds. The boisterous children in the orchard greeted her, echoes of *Prima Femina* trailing after her. Chloe waited at the gate, a hand on her newly rounded belly. She and Demitri, married five months, wasted no time starting their family.

"Here is today's list." The assistant held out a piece of paper lined with various meetings and tasks, but dropped her hand at the sight of Pandora. "Are you ill?"

"No, and I think it's time for me to a visit the midwife."

Chloe's brow furrowed until the meaning of the words dawned on her. She grasped Pandora's shoulders. "Do you think so?"

At Pandora's nod, the woman embraced her. "We will be pregnant at the same time. Our children will grow up together."

In her excitement, Chloe practically dragged Pandora to Xenia's, a small house on the edge of the village near the lake. Her former maid held no misgivings about pregnancy, elated from the moment she realized. Pandora longed for such optimism, but a healthy dose of fear ran through her veins. A bell rang when Chloe pushed the door open and a rush of medicinal smells threatened Pandora's fragile stomach.

"One minute," a disembodied voice rang from the back room.

Dried herbs hung from every eave of the cottage like a floral headdress. An open book sat on a workbench strewn with bottles and a mortar filled with fragrant crushed leaves, the soiled pestle resting against it. One smudged window let only weak light into the cool space. A woman popped out of the only door in the wall, wisps of gray hair escaping from under a kerchief.

"Chloe, love, is everything all right?" Concern etched the wizened face of the speaker.

"Fear not, Xenia, I am fine," Chloe assured. "I'm here for you to check my friend."

She gestured to Pandora. The midwife took a step forward, wiping her hands on a stained apron. Her eyes widened at the sight of Pandora.

"*Prima Femina*, you honor me." She bowed her head.

"Thank you. I suspect I am with child and hope you can confirm this."

Xenia gestured to a small cot on the side of the room. Pandora studied the midwife during the brief exam, comforted not only by her kindly face and gentle touch, but also her practiced hand. The midwife prodded her stomach, checked her ankles, and took her pulse, fingertips stained green with herbs. While Pandora answered a series of questions, Chloe bounced on the balls of her feet in the corner. Once finished, Xenia motioned Pandora to sit.

"Two months along, I would say. Seven to go," came her prognosis. "I will give you a special tea with ginger, chamomile, and peppermint to help with your nausea."

Chloe squealed and grabbed Pandora's hands. The midwife rummaged through her workbench until she found the jar she sought. She placed some tea bags into a small burlap sack. When she turned to hand it to Pandora, she stopped. "You have some questions. I can see them in your eyes."

"Yes," Pandora admitted. After a few basic inquiries, she asked what concerned her the most. "Epimetheus is a Titan. Will the baby be … as large as he is?"

Xenia smiled. "That is a fair question, but I would not worry. Whatever glamour enables him to lie with you should result in a human sized baby. Have no fear. Come and see me every month or if there are any problems."

"Thank you," Pandora said, accepting the burlap bag.

She exited with Chloe into bright sunshine. Each girl shielded their eyes. Chloe practically burst with excitement.

"Please don't tell anyone yet," Pandora ordered. "I've yet to tell Epimetheus."

Chloe nodded, squeezing her friend's hand. When they came to the main thoroughfare, several villagers bombarded them with issues. Chloe promised to listen to them all in turn. They walked to a small edifice next to the temple where Pandora dealt with the day-to-day business of the town. Others already waited outside for her help.

"I need a moment of prayer," Pandora told her assistant.

While she headed to the back of the temple, Chloe herded the townsfolk into an organized line. Pandora climbed the steps and slipped a key into a hidden door. She entered a small hallway and ascended a spiral staircase which brought her onto a balcony overlooking the pithos.

Here she worshipped in private, an idea from Paz whom she could not thank enough.

She sank to her knees on a cushion and gave praise to the gods for their blessing her not only with Epimetheus, but now with a child. As she whispered her prayers, the key around her neck quivered, as it always did in the pithos's presence. For a moment, it felt as though the ground dropped out from underneath her and memories of the dream assaulted her, the dread so acute her heart throbbed in her ears. Pandora pressed her hands on the stone wall, her breath shallow pants, her head awhirl. The sensation dissipated, the hum of people below returning. Pandora rose on shaky legs and departed without a glance back.

FORTY-EIGHT

Pandora finished out her day. The unease from her temple visit faded, her nausea the likely cause of the disconcerting reaction earlier. The pithos was strong with immortal energy. Of course, it would affect her in her weakened state. Excitement now filled her. A baby. She knew what the result of lying with Epimetheus could be, but the actuality of it blew her away. Sometimes you never knew how much you wanted something until it was within reach.

When the last petitioner of the day left, Pandora stacked papers in neat piles, one for the priest, one for Paz, and the last for miscellaneous vendors in town. She made a few cursory notes and rose from her chair. Chloe swept dirt from the floor out the door in a puff and set the broom back in its closet. Pandora locked the door, and they walked out together.

"I am happy for you, Pandora," Chloe gushed. "I bet you can't wait to tell Epimetheus."

All day, thoughts loitered in the back of her mind. What would her husband say? Would he be happy? Mad? Indifferent? His love for animals certainly surpassed his love for people.

"Yes, I suppose I will tell him tonight," Pandora mused. "Hopefully, all goes well."

Chloe, misreading her concern, stopped and took her friend's hands. "You are scared of giving birth? I understand. I get anxious about it sometimes too. But Xenia is highly experienced. You could not be in better hands. Besides, I insist on my baby having a playmate, so all *will* go well. Besides, the gods chose you to marry Epimetheus. Surely, you will have their favor in this matter."

Pandora nodded, her fright at the temple now exchanged
for fresh worries about childbirth and motherhood she had
not considered. The women parted near the village gate.
Chloe headed home with a spring in her step. The setting
sun framed the hilltop, a semi-circle of orange rippling
away. Pandora thought of her mother, of the soft hands and
gentle voice which filled her childhood. While Elara would
be firm, Danae indulged her every whim, her every
question, with grace and love. Pandora now could be this
woman, this life-affirming source for her child.
Gratefulness overwhelmed her.

She wandered into the kitchen where Iris prepared
dinner, the aroma of olives, rosemary, and lamb heavy in
the air. Rex wound through her legs and she bent to stroke
his head. Epimetheus sat at the table, a pile of leather and
string in front of him while he repaired some farm
implements. An almost identical scene greeted her each
evening, yet tonight, she soaked it all in, her love for her
home and her husband magnified by her news.

"Did you have a chance to speak with Kostas about the
handle on the temple's pump? It keeps sticking,"
Epimetheus asked.

When she did not answer, he glanced up and saw tears
in her eyes. In a second, he jumped to her side, the picture
of concern, which made Pandora cry outright. Iris wiped
her hands on her apron and helped him lead Pandora to the
couch.

"I'm fine," Pandora reassured once she regained some
composure. "I'm crying because I'm happy."

Her husband's brow furrowed, unable to process the
contradiction, but a knowing gleam filled the eyes of the
maid.

"Epimetheus, I found out today that I am with child."

The creases in his forehead deepened, his expression a
study of bewilderment. His face changed from confusion to
shock, before landing on understanding. With a whoop, he
leaped up and embraced Pandora, spinning her around
while she half laughed and half cried. Iris bounced up and

down with glee. Rex ran to hide at the commotion, but Rhea clomped in from outside to see what all the noise was. Epimetheus put his wife down. He sank onto the couch, eyes filled with wonder.

"A child," he declared. "I guess I never realized how much I wanted one."

Warmth exploded in Pandora's heart and, if possible, she loved him even more at this shared sentiment.

They spent the rest of the evening discussing the pregnancy, the nursery, and even mulled over some names, though nothing fit quite yet. Iris turned out to be a great source of information for many matters first-time parents may have overlooked. Rex crept back out and sat on Pandora's lap, his head pressed gently on her budding belly. In bed that night, she said some extra prayers of thanks and promised even greater offerings at the temple. She dozed, amazed at how much happiness filled her heart.

Pregnancy was kind to her overall. After the morning sickness passed, she had few complaints. Xenia checked her regularly, happy with how the condition proceeded. Epimetheus bought some lustrous ebony in the market to build a cradle. Iris helped Pandora and Chloe sew blankets and diapers. Danae and Lycus sent a large trunk filled with even more clothing, a pomegranate seed filled rattle, and some carved blocks. Happiness spilled from the house like waves breaking on the shore.

Pandora sat in her small office one day in the heavy, humid air. She fanned herself with a makeshift piece of parchment. Loud footsteps approached, the door bursting open in front of Prometheus' giant frame.

"Sister-in-law, I visited the house. Epimetheus told me the wonderful news."

Pandora stood to greet him, the disquiet her brother-in-law evoked gnawing at her. To her surprise, he embraced her and stepped back to admire her bulging stomach.

"I am happy for you both," he proclaimed. "I have a son, you know. Deucalion. Now our children will either be brothers-in-arms or a lovely match to unite our families."

"Congratulations again," Pandora said. She and her husband sent a bronze statue of Demeter when they heard of their nephew's birth two years ago.

"And I see our children will have a friend," he gestured to Chloe, whose term neared its end. "How nice it will be."

Pandora nodded, words eluding her at this version of Prometheus. Normally, he scowled and paid scant attention to her. A friendly Prometheus almost scared her more, for she did not trust the man on an instinctual level. However, she could not accuse him of deceit with no proof but the tightness in her gut. He chatted amiably with the women for a while before taking his leave.

"That was … strange," Chloe remarked, never a fan of the elder Titan.

"Yes, but at least strange in a pleasant way," Pandora quipped.

They laughed until Chloe doubled over, hands clutched to her stomach. When the pains came regularly, Pandora helped her across the village to Xenia's cottage. The midwife performed a quick exam and declared the time had come. They escorted Chloe home, instructing someone to fetch Demetri on the way. The midwife barked instructions which Pandora and Chloe's maid jumped to follow. Demetri ran in, panting with exertion after his sprint back from the outskirts of town.

Pandora spent the next eighteen hours pacing the small living room, reassuring the expectant father. Xenia sent her assistant out every few hours with an update. According to the midwife, all was right on track, news belied by the growing screams of Chloe. Pandora tried to comfort Demetri, his face turning whiter with every cry of pain, but all the while, fear tickled at her mind. Soon she would be the one in labor, a disconcerting notion.

Near dawn, a fit of the loudest shouts Pandora ever heard filled the room, then all grew quiet. In the span of those few silent seconds, sheer terror engulfed Pandora, certain the worst had transpired. A singular cry pierced the air as newborn lungs gulped their first taste of air. Pandora's knees nearly gave out with relief. The door cracked open and a tired-eyed Xenia ushered them in. Chloe sat in bed, her face beaming, a tiny pink form cradled in her arms. Tears spilled on all sides. While Demetri held his son, determination filled Pandora. Whatever labor held in store, the end result was more than worth it.

FORTY-NINE

A nudge on his arm woke Epimetheus. Moonlight sliced across the bed, a slender shimmery stroke. His eyes wished to close again, to sink back into the peaceful valley of sleep, but Pandora leaned over him. She shook his shoulder with a firm hand.

"It's time," she said.

Her definitive tone jolted him awake. The sluggish mind of slumber replaced in an instant with a hundred questions.

"Are you sure? Should I get Iris? Should I get Xenia?"

He scrambled out of bed and startled Rex, who scowled at the disruption. Epimetheus had half a tunic over his head, his arm stuck as though he had never dressed himself. After a few frustrated tugs, he righted the garment. The strike of flint against steel sounded and the flame of the oil lamp ignited from Pandora's steady hand. Her expression of calm forbearance in this moment stuck in his mind for many years, the quiet strength behind her eyes.

"Wake Iris," she instructed.

He ran to the adjoining chamber and shook the girl, probably too roughly judging by the terror on her face. Pandora told the newly roused maid to run and get Xenia.

"No," Epimetheus interjected. "I will take a horse down and get her. It will be faster."

Pain gripped Pandora, and she clutched her belly. He went to comfort her, but she gestured for him to go.

"Take care of her," he bellowed at Iris, who sat on the bed's side with her arm around his wife.

His hurried steps flew out the front door. Cold night air engulfed him on the way to the stable. Rosa made no complaint at the saddle he strapped on, and despite the odd hour, happily trailed him out of the barn and down the hill on quickened hooves. Xenia's cottage formed from the mist in front of him and he pounded on the door. An eternity passed before the wood drew open.

"Epimetheus," the midwife spoke in the halo of candlelight, her eyes filled with comprehension. "How was Pandora when you left her?"

"She woke me and told me it was time to get you. She is having labor pains." The words tumbled from his mouth.

"I will get my things."

Another string of endless minutes passed with Epimetheus pacing under the stars. What could she be doing? Pandora needed her now. What if they were late and Iris had to deliver the baby? Frantic visions filled his head. At last, Xenia exited, a basket under one arm.

"Is that horse for me?" He heard the surprise in her voice.

"Yes, I thought it would be faster so we don't miss anything."

A peal of laughter rang through the still night.

"Faster? Oh, Epimetheus." She patted his arm. "Nothing about this process will be fast, I assure you. Now let's wake my assistant and we can be on our way."

The midwife spoke the truth. When they returned home, little had changed with Pandora's condition. Iris made breakfast for him in the blushing glow of dawn, but nerves smothered any appetite. Whatever childbirth consisted of for the women, for the men, it involved mostly pacing. As the hours passed, he ended up on a regular circuit through the house, around the table under the scrutiny of Rhea, out the front door, to the paddocks, where his horses rallied at the fence to console their upset master, and back to the house. The sun rose, wisps of gray clouds raced in at midday resulting in an afternoon sprinkle. Still, he paced. Iris made dinner and after a few bites, he rose, his feet already walking the familiar path. An occasional gasp of pain emanated from the bedroom and would stop him in his tracks until silence fell and his feet moved again of their own accord. Chloe arrived toward evening, a pat of comfort on his arm before disappearing into the bedroom. A perfect half-moon rose into the sky and still he paced.

His restless mind matched his steps. Would Pandora be all right? Would the baby? Why was it taking this long? Should he go into the bedroom and see? Or was that only the realm of women? He never fretted this much when one of his animals gave birth. *Because I trusted the gods*, he realized. Even the times when a mother or baby died, he trusted the Fates spun the threads correctly. But Pandora meant more to him than any creature. He fell to his knees halfway between the house and the paddock, beseeching every deity above to protect his wife. How could he live without her?

Memories of his brother's warning crept into his mind, notions that the gods only gave him Pandora as punishment. Epimetheus had not asked for a wife, nor had he meddled with the Olympians as Prometheus had. In truth, his only thoughts upon accepting the offer had been of himself, of the favoritism shown to him over his sibling for once. But now, a deluge of worry washed away that fleeting satisfaction. Was he merely a pawn in a grander game? Did the gods bless him with her only to rip her away? Pain and doubt lanced through him as screams of agony sailed from the house. He covered his ears and prayed harder.

"Epimetheus."

The shouting of his name lifted the fog. Chloe stood in the doorway and waved him over. He rose, crossing the gap in giant steps. Although he ran, the world moved in slow motion past Chloe, a sheen of sweat on her brow, past Iris with an armful of towels, down the darkened hallway, the niche where the pithos used to sit looming like the open maw of a beast, into the bedroom, full of foreign smells and sounds. His eye fell on Pandora, sitting up, a smile on her weary face, and time clicked back into place.

"Is everything all right?"

"Yes. Come meet at our daughter," she beamed.

Epimetheus' gaze fell to Pandora's chest, where she cradled a tiny form wrapped in a blanket. A shock of deep red hair was all he could see. He crept to the edge of the bed and eased down. Pandora turned the baby, who stared at her father with alert eyes. Warmth flooded his body, his heart full of love from the moment their eyes met. He stared in wonder at her tiny face and the perfect little hand she held by her cheek.

"Do you want to hold her?" Pandora held the bundle to him.

"Should I? I don't want to hurt her," he stammered, but his wife slid the baby into his arms.

"Epimetheus, I have seen you handle baby birds with the utmost care. You may be big, but your touch is gentle enough for our child," she said.

He gazed down at the infant, a gentle stroke to her cheek. His daughter rewarded him with a yawn, the most precious yawn he had ever beheld. She squirmed and her hand latched around his pinkie.

"There, you see? She loves you already," Pandora declared.

"And what about a name for this little one?" Xenia asked from the end of the bed where she stood with Iris and Chloe. "With such an exquisite head of hair."

Pandora and Epimetheus regarded each other, stumped by the question. They never had agreed on any names previously discussed. Not wanting to blurt a name out rashly, Epimetheus deliberated for several minutes.

"How about Pyrrha," he suggested. "It means fiery red. For her hair."

"That's perfect," Pandora said. "Welcome to the world, little Pyrrha."

Epimetheus kissed the top of the baby's head and handed her back to Pandora. Chloe and the assistant cleaned up the room while Xenia gave the new mother advice on nursing, which Pyrrha took to immediately. Iris brought in a light meal and set it on the dresser. With smiles and congratulations, the ladies left the small family to savor these first moments together. An hour later, Pandora dozed with Pyrrha fast asleep on her chest. Epimetheus thanked every god he could think of, promising bountiful offerings come morning. He watched them sleep for hours, certain Pandora had been no curse from the gods, but his greatest gift.

FIFTY

Villagers thronged the entrance to the temple on a fresh spring morning, excitement splayed across faces, which faltered only when they made way for Prometheus and his family. Once the Titan passed into the temple with his wife and son, smiles renewed and necks craned for a glimpse inside at little Pyrrha on her Naming Day. The entire town waited to celebrate after the official ceremony, the streets bedecked with bright streamers and fragrant flowers, but right now, all eyes were on their patrons and their daughter.

Epimetheus saw his brother enter and waved him over. "I'm glad you could come."

"Welcome to you and Hesione," Pandora said, striding over with Pyrrha on her hip, "and look how little Deucalion has grown to such a handsome boy."

The child's chest puffed out at the compliment, a miniature version of his father. Hesione greeted her sister-in-law with a kiss on each cheek before she fussed over her niece. While they fell into talk of motherhood, Epimetheus kneeled at his nephew's level.

"It seems only yesterday you turned one, and we had your naming ceremony. How old are you now?"

The boy held three fingers aloft.

"He will be four next month," Prometheus said. "But today is about you and your child, Epimetheus. How is the girl?"

"She is happy and inquisitive, like her mother," Epimetheus gushed. "She took her first steps on her own the other day and toddled right over to the paddock. She loves all the animals and they love her."

"How charming," Prometheus said, his contrived tone unnoticed by the proud father. "Hopefully she will make some young man a good and obedient wife someday."

The last words stung Epimetheus. His brother had never warmed to Pandora or her lively spirit, the opposite of Hesione's meek personality. Before he could think of a retort, Gaius, the temple priest, arrived in a crimson tunic draped about him in elegant folds. When he spoke, the thrum of the villagers hushed to hear the naming rites.

High in the temple, hidden in the shadow of the rafters, sat a gray owl, wise, amber eyes surveying the ritual. With a rush of air, a hawk flew through the oculus and sat beside it.

"And what brings you here this fine day, Sister?" asked the hawk.

"I am here to check on Pandora and her wellbeing," Athena answered. "I'm sure the same cannot be said of you."

"Me? Sister, you offend. I am only here with good wishes for the happy family."

"Spare me, Hermes. Where you go, trouble soon follows. Why can't you leave them alone?" She ruffled her feathers, annoyed by her brother's unwarranted meddling.

"Father is not happy with the way things have gone." Hermes tried to sound solemn, but Athena knew better. "You know he means for that jar to be open."

Athena glanced down at the pithos ensconced on a pedestal, the base overflowing with tributes and flowers from the thousands who traveled from far and wide to see it. She thought Zeus had forgotten about it, his mind and temper always occupied with other matters. Pandora and Epimetheus bothered no one. In fact, the pithos in this temple contributed to the worship of all the Olympians, increasing the number of sacrifices and gifts for each. If anything, her father should be grateful for the girl's idea to display it here.

"Pandora and Epimetheus have done nothing but bring additional praise and adulation to us," Athena insisted. "Why do you need to stir up trouble?"

"Because that is what I do best," Hermes bragged. "Fear not, Sister, if there is nothing of interest to tell Father, I will not bother with the matter right now. He is busy with many other concerns."

The hawk took off in a flash of brown wings, leaving the goddess to her thoughts. She watched the pure happiness on the couple's faces, the adoring villagers smattering the steps, and the bustling town created from a lonely dirt road. None of that would matter to Zeus if his attention ever turned his eye this way and she would be powerless to stop him. At least, for now, they remained out of his thoughts, though she could not deny the covetous gleam in Prometheus' eye. The pithos held the elder Titan transfixed during the ceremony. How long before he made a move to use it for his own purposes? With a heavy sigh, she flew off, the sound of the cheering crowd echoing behind her.

In a meadow near the edge of the lake, the party commenced, tents erected in long white strips along the soft green grass. Flowers erupted over the edges of every table, hyacinth, iris, and roses in opulent cascades. Smoke rose from spits where pigs, lambs, and cattle roasted, their drippings sending up fat sparks to the delight of the hovering children. Wine flowed from casks, pools of ruby red sloshing over the sides of filled mugs. At the center of it all, Epimetheus sat with his wife and child, an endless parade of well-wishers giving their blessings.

Prometheus watched the revelry from the corner of the tent, a surly expression on his face. He created humans and had never received such a heartfelt tribute. He had their respect and fear, but he would never have their love.

"Wine?" a peasant boy offered, only to be met with a gruff shake of the Titan's head. "I think you could use some."

Prometheus turned on the server, ready to explode at the insolence. When his eyes fell on the speaker's face, he sighed.

"Hermes, what a pleasure to see you," he grumbled.

"Isn't it? I do love a fun party, not as much as Dionysus I suppose, but his can get rather out of hand."

"Why are you here?" the Titan snapped.

"A question at the top of everyone's list for some reason," the god said. "Does no one think I came merely to bless this lovely girl on her Naming Day?"

The statement earned an icy stare from Prometheus.

"Fine," the god pouted. "I came to see how things were going for your brother and his wife. The pithos has certainly brought them great admiration and prosperity. Shame that Zeus did not choose you instead, but with all your naughty tricks, can you blame him?"

Prometheus eyes remained steely.

"Cat got your tongue?" Hermes mocked. "I'm off then. You are far too grumpy to be around. It is a party, after all."

Prometheus sensed him vanish, but the god's words hit home. Why did Epimetheus deserve this good fortune? Without Prometheus, Epimetheus never made any sensible decisions. The debacle with the animals proved that. Prometheus made the choices for them. They were not punished by the Olympians because of his quick wittedness during the war. His astute thinking saved him and his brother more than once. Epimetheus could not be left to his own devices. Until now …

Pandora changed that. Not only did Pandora treat Epimetheus as if he were capable of making decisions, but she also helped and supported him. Prometheus had worried about the god's offer, fearing they wanted to punish Epimetheus, but it was Prometheus who incurred the penalty. To have his place with his brother usurped by a mortal, a woman no less. The gods used his brother to get to him. *Let Zeus think he won*, Prometheus thought, spite coursing through him. His gaze went to Deucalion. In his son, he could mold a powerful man who would accomplish great things, one who would outshine Epimetheus in every way possible. The thought brought a smile to his face. His eyes fell back on his brother, who rose from his seat and approached.

"Prometheus," Epimetheus clapped him on the back. "I am happy you and your family are here to celebrate this special day with us."

"Indeed, I would not miss an occasion this important to you," he asserted, a hand on his brother's shoulder. "That is what family is for."

"I am glad to hear you say this. I know you worried the gods tried to trick me with Pandora, but you must admit, she has been nothing but a gift to me from the moment she arrived."

"True and she even brought that special pithos with her," Prometheus said. "Tell me, Brother, don't you want to know what blessings are inside?"

"It would not matter if I did. We were instructed not to open it," Epimetheus replied, noting the calculated gleam in his brother's eyes.

"You mean *she* was instructed, not you. Of course, the Olympians would not want a mere mortal dallying with their illustrious gifts. But you and I are Titans. I am sure we could find many altruistic uses for whatever lays inside."

Epimetheus' eyes narrowed at the use of the word *we*. "I'm sorry, Brother, but Pandora and I are of one mind on this matter. The gods granted us this gift and we will follow their bidding."

"Yes. How lucky you are to have their favor." Prometheus failed to hide the bite in his tone.

"You could have their favor too, if you only stopped meddling where they asked you not to," Epimetheus said, pulling his brother into an embrace. "You have a beautiful wife and son. Enjoy your family. Leave the Olympians to their own affairs and let us see to our own."

"Dear Brother, don't worry about me," Prometheus whispered. "I told you, I have a trump card to play, knowledge from Themis that will fetch a high price from Zeus someday."

"Please do not speak of such things. Especially today." Epimetheus drew back and gestured in supplication. He did not know what information Prometheus received from one of the original Titans goddesses, but it could only lead to trouble.

"You are right. Today is not for such heavy topics," his brother declared. "Let us celebrate with our families."

Prometheus threw his arm around Epimetheus' shoulder. They strode back to the table where they joined their wives and children for the celebratory meal. Prometheus lifted his niece and kissed her on both cheeks before handing her back to Pandora.

While the Titans enjoyed the party, the branches of a nearby tree rustled. A hawk lifted off on swift wings headed straight for Mount Olympus. When he flew over the throne room, Hermes did not see Zeus. After a long arc across the sky, he found the King of the Gods in the shade of a mighty oak near the side of a stream. A dozen Naiads fawned around him, enthralled with the attention. Zeus turned to his son, a hint of annoyance in his gaze at the interruption.

"It's about Prometheus," Hermes declared. "He deceives you again, Father. Time for the pithos to play its part."

Zeus waved the water nymphs away with a dismissive hand. They slipped back into the stream and swam away, half-moon ripples in their wake. The king of the god's aggravation changed first to anger and then to satisfaction. He rose, his full concentration on Hermes.

"Tell me everything, my son."

FIFTY-ONE

Pyrrha inherited her mother's precocious nature and required constant supervision. Pandora and Iris marveled at her predilection to find trouble—upsetting a hen's nest, yanking out herbs from the garden, pulling Rhea's tail. Pandora remembered Danae's constant presence, the way her mother never discouraged her natural curiosity. She tried to model that behavior with her own daughter, but found herself both exhausted and exasperated at the end of every day. Epimetheus always laughed when she related his daughter's adventures each night at dinner, happy to remind Pandora where the girl got it from, before stating how much he loved the trait in both.

"I think she got into that pile of dirt next to the toolshed," Pandora told Iris, her attempts to clean the squirming girl's hands proving unsuccessful.

Iris shook her head, the late afternoon light cutting across her face through the window over the sink. She put down the carrots she rinsed, wet a towel, and rubbed some soap across it.

"Here, try this." She handed it to Pandora.

"Dirt, dirt, dirt," Pyrrha squealed, her slippery hands difficult to keep still.

"Yes, dirt, but I need to wash it off so we can eat," Pandora explained. "Keep still."

"Still, still, still," the two-year-old parroted, her arms moving in all directions.

Pandora and Iris exchanged a glance of frustration, but in the end had to smile.

The door banged open, and the trio jumped. Prometheus barreled into the house as if fire were at his heels.

"Epimetheus!" he shouted.

"He's not in here. I think he is out by the barn," Pandora said, "but come in brother-in-law. It's been a long while since we had the pleasure of your company."

She rose to her feet, Pyrrha hiding behind her legs with a furtive peek out at her uncle. Though Prometheus watched Pandora speak, his maniacal eyes showed no sign of comprehension.

"Is everything all right? Perhaps you should sit down."

She pointed to a chair, and his frenzied gaze followed the gesture, but made no move to sit. Unnerved by behavior strange for even him, Pandora stepped forward to go find her husband, but Pyrrha's grip on her legs stopped her. Iris came over and picked the child up, cooing softly while the Titan stood frozen in place.

"Brother, welcome," Epimetheus said, walking through the open front door.

A clarity filled Prometheus' eyes at his brother's voice and he spun around.

"You! You told them, didn't you?" he snarled and lunged at his sibling.

"Told who what?" Epimetheus asked, confusion filling his face while his brother grabbed his shoulders.

"The Olympians, of course. You couldn't wait to tell them, I bet." Prometheus pinned his brother against the wall.

Pyrrha burst out crying. Pandora shot Iris an uneasy glance, and the maid disappeared down the hall with the child. Epimetheus tried to extricate himself from the vice-like grip of Prometheus.

"Brother, I assure you, I do not know what you are talking about. Please tell me what's wrong. Let me help."

Slowly, Prometheus' fists relaxed, enabling Epimetheus to move away from the wall. Pandora watched, her arms crossed over her chest, no fan of any interaction with the elder Titan. Epimetheus guided his brother to a chair, but Prometheus still had no interest in sitting.

"You told them about my secret," Prometheus accused.

"I did no such thing. As I told you, I have no interest in what games you want to play with the Olympians." Epimetheus retorted. "Nor do I even know what the secret is. You never told me, remember?"

"Well, someone told Zeus and now he is after me," a frantic Prometheus ranted. "If it wasn't you, it must have been her."

He pointed at Pandora, who remained too flabbergasted to respond.

"Pandora knows nothing of our conversation, Brother, I assure you. Leave her out of this," Epimetheus said, color rising in his neck.

"It had to have been one of you," Prometheus raged, wild-eyed. "I see right through your little plan. You couldn't be happy with their favor. You had to have more. You want to get me out of the picture and have all the praise and glory for yourselves."

"Brother, please calm down. I promise you we did no such thing, but please let us try to help you," Epimetheus pleaded.

"Liar," Prometheus spat. "You betrayed your own brother in order to win their favor. I will never forgive you."

"Enough," Pandora shouted, her shock finally succumbing to rage. "We have betrayed no one. We are not interested in your power plays and your games with the gods. Leave this house and don't come back. You are no longer welcome here."

Prometheus growled at her, like a cornered animal ready to attack, but when Epimetheus stood firmly at his wife's side, he turned and fled out the door.

"What in the name of the gods was that all about?" Pandora huffed.

"Prometheus confided in me he holds a secret told to him by our aunt, the Titan Themis, to use against Zeus. I don't know what it is, but somehow, the King of the Gods found out," Epimetheus explained. "I have to help him."

"Epimetheus, I know he is your brother, but are you willing to risk your life, mine, and Pyrrha's in your attempts to save him? How many times can he cross Zeus and expect to get away with it? It is madness to involve yourself."

Epimetheus hung his head. Thoughts of Pandora and Pyrrha filled his mind, their tranquil life together, the happiness he never expected to find. Pandora was right. Prometheus created his own problems with the gods, incited them even. To think the Olympians would allow him to continue was folly.

"I am sorry, dear wife," Epimetheus said and wrapped her in his arms. "The life we have is more important to me than all else. I would not risk it for anything."

Iris crept from the bedroom, Pyrrha asleep on her shoulder. Epimetheus held out his arms for her. The girl snuggled against her father's broad chest. He sank into a chair at the table. Pandora helped Iris finish dinner and set it out. She tried to eat, but each mouthful was a hard lump in her throat, dropping in her stomach as though she swallowed a rock. She had never cared for Prometheus and his arrogant ways, but tonight she saw a version she could only describe as unhinged. It scared her.

After dinner, she sat near the fire. Epimetheus settled next to her. She gazed up at him, with their daughter balanced on his shoulder, her tiny lips parted in sleep. A wave of panic filled her at the thought of harm coming to either. They had built a happy life together, one she never could have imagined. She grasped her husband's free hand.

"Don't worry, Pandora. Prometheus will have to work this out on his own. My responsibility is to you and her." He gently stroked Pyrrha's back. "We need not worry about this situation again."

Pandora forced a smile, even as dread crept up her toes and into her chest, a dread she had not experienced in a long while—the one attached to the pithos. The key vibrated against her chest and Pandora closed a hand around it, praying for safety from whatever lay ahead.

FIFTY-TWO

Prometheus stumbled out of his brother's home into the darkness. He ran down the hill, his steps as haphazard as the thoughts in his head. He wandered aimlessly for a long while until he stumbled and fell, his hand landing on a jagged rock. The pain jolted his senses back into place, and he sat on a boulder. Courting trouble with Zeus was not new terrain, but he needed to collect his thoughts if he were to have any chance of getting out of this unscathed. He inhaled deeply, the cool night air filling his lungs. Cicada song lilted across the breeze. The insects represented resurrection. *I have resurrected myself in the eyes of the Olympians many times*, he thought. *This time will be no different.*

But if Epimetheus refused to help him, who would? The thought vexed him. He assumed his brother would be at his side when he needed it, but now, Epimetheus chose his wife over blood. What he would give to send that blasted girl and her pithos back to where she came from.

The pithos.

The thought of it buoyed him. Plentiful blessings from the gods. He never got the chance to ask Epimetheus to open it for him, the entire reason for his visit. But how hard could it be to open it himself? He laughed aloud at the simplicity of it, startling an animal in the nearby brush. It scuttled away, the sound of crushed grass in its wake. All Prometheus needed was to open the jar, take out some goodwill from the gods, and close it back up. No one would be any wiser and he would be off the hook yet again. And if it would not open? Key or no key, nothing would stop him. He would smash it if he needed to and worry about the consequences after.

On spry feet, he bounced down to the village gate. Empty streets unfolded in front of him. The only activity he spied came from a taverna where light spilled out of the open doors to reveal a few drunk men passed out on the ground. Loud cheers and music rang from inside. He crossed to a quieter street and headed to the temple, sure to remain in the shadows. With a furtive glance around, he snuck up the steps and crept inside.

Moonlight streamed into the open atrium from the oculus, cool beams illuminating the pithos on its pedestal. Prometheus circled the stand, his eyes drawn to the swirling images. A voice, soft and insistent, beckoned him forward. The jar wanted to be opened. He reached out to trace the glowing pictures, and the voice grew louder. Transfixed, he reached for the stopper and yanked, ready to capture his measure of favor, but the plug held tight. A harder pull yielded no better result, but he kept at it, his Titanian strength never failing him before. Soon, sweat poured down his brow and his hands, wet with exertion, lost their grip.

Next, he wrested the pithos off the pedestal and threw it to the floor. It rolled a few feet away, undamaged. Furious, he snatched it and hurled it against the wall. The jar bounced off, landing again unharmed. He collapsed down on a bench, punching the seat, his yell of frustration echoing throughout the empty temple.

"Can't get it open?" a sprightly voice asked. "Such a shame."

Prometheus startled at the figure, who descended from the sky on winged shoes. The god fluttered through the oculus, staff in hand. He returned the pithos to its rightful place before he dropped on the bench next to the Titan.

"What do you want, Hermes?" Prometheus growled.

"Me? There is nothing I want. You, however, want to open this jar even though it does not belong to you." He wagged a finger at the Titan.

"I need something from it," Prometheus scowled.

"Whatever could you need?" Hermes questioned with contrived interest.

"You know exactly what I need. Your father is after me and I need to get some favor out of this pithos to avoid his wrath."

"Hmm, yes, I do remember Zeus being rather upset," Hermes mused, lifting off the bench to hover next to the pithos. "Something about an important name you withhold. Favor would certainly help you out right now."

"I know. So, if you can't help me, please go away," Prometheus snapped. "I'm short on time."

"Short indeed," the god agreed, zigzagging around the upper part of the temple. "I should not get involved, but ..."

"But what?" the Titan asked.

"I know how to open it," he said and landed next to the Titan with a triumphant flourish. "I shouldn't tell, but I hate to see you in such a bind."

"How do I open it?" Prometheus asked, his patience running thin.

"You can't."

"But you just said you knew how," he roared.

Hermes flew back up, a hand to his chest. "Dear Prometheus, do not yell at me. It is troubling for my constitution. I was getting to it. Only one person can open it. The one who has the key."

"Pandora." Prometheus' shoulders sagged.

"Yes." Hermes nodded. "She holds the key with her on a chain around her neck at all times."

"I'll figure out a way to steal it."

"I'm afraid that won't work. The pithos opens by her hand alone," Hermes informed him. "But I would not worry. I am sure your sister-in-law will open it for you gladly."

"We both know that is not true," Prometheus muttered.

"Hmm, what to do?" The god drummed his fingers on the side of a pillar.

Prometheus paced the floor, his large form moving between light and shadow. Hermes flew over to the statue of his likeness and examined the offerings piled at the bottom. Brushing aside flowers and candles, he found a tiny golden lyre, which he took with a smile.

"I need to bring Pandora down here and force her to open it," Prometheus stated.

"And you are sure Epimetheus will allow that treatment to his beloved wife?"

"No. I will have to restrain him somehow. I will think of something."

The Titan resumed his pacing. Hermes waited a moment to create the dramatic effect he loved.

"Again, I should not interfere, but we have always gotten along and I hate to see you in this mess. Here."

He waved his hand and two vials appeared. Prometheus walked over to him, hunger in his eyes, but Hermes held them out of reach.

"The blue one will make Epimetheus sleep. The red one will compel Pandora to obey your every command," the god informed, handing them over. "They each last no longer than an hour once ingested, use them wisely."

Prometheus snatched the vials and tucked them into his tunic.

"You have my thanks, Hermes," Prometheus said, racing for the door. "I will not forget your help."

"Yes, yes, I'm marvelous, you're welcome."

Hermes flew out of the temple into the clear night sky. His shoes carried him on swift wings to Mount Olympus, where he found Zeus brooding on his throne. The King of the Gods waited for his son to land in front of him.

"Well?" he asked.

"It is done," Hermes replied. "It should not be long now."

A satisfied smile filled Zeus' face, his revenge now within reach.

FIFTY-THREE

The setting sun skimmed the crest of the hilltop, the bright orange glow casting the front of the house in shadow. Pandora sat on the front steps, the soft scent of rosemary in the air. Epimetheus strode toward her from the paddocks, his features blotted out in the last rays of daylight. Pyrrha ran between her parents with the delighted squeal unique to toddlers. First, she grabbed her father's hand and pulled it before she broke off toward her mother.

"Go get daddy," Pandora said and the child would race back from where she came.

The chickens squawked each time she passed their coop, as though yelling at her to slow down. Rhea joined her for the first few passes but decided the effort was too great. The goat plopped down on the grass, a chunk of grass working in her jaws. Rex circled Pandora. He bumped her hands with his head and she stroked him. Pandora never gave much thought to the word perfection, but this must be as close as one could get. Laughter and love, her own Elysium on earth.

Rex froze, his back arched in alert, eyes focused to the right. Pandora followed his gaze in time to see a figure crest the side of the hill. A large figure. Prometheus. The utopian moment slipped away.

Pyrrha noticed her uncle and flew in his direction, her loud shout upsetting the chickens even more. Clearly, her daughter forgot all about last night's tirade, such was the whim of children. While she watched her brother-in-law scoop up her excited daughter, Epimetheus came to her side.

"What could he want now?" she asked, dismay evident in her tone.

"I don't know." Epimetheus' brow furrowed as his brother approached.

"Brother," Prometheus called, Pyrrha in his arms, "I have come to apologize."

He crossed the distance between them in a few strides, handed the girl to Pandora, and put his hands on Epimetheus' shoulders. "Forgive me for last night. I let emotion get the better of me and I am truly sorry."

"There is nothing to forgive. We are brothers, after all," Epimetheus said. "Come inside. Join us for dinner."

"Thank you," he turned to Pandora. "My humblest apologies to you, the woman who is such a devoted wife to my brother."

Pandora bowed her head in acknowledgment, a thousand questions ringing in her head. Why the sudden change of attitude? Did he still want something from them? Or had he settled his differences with Zeus and truly come to make amends? She balanced Pyrrha on her hip and entered the house in the wake of the Titans. Iris snuck her a concerned glance. The women held no trust for Prometheus.

The maid set out dinner, the table soon overflowing with lamb, olives, bread, cheeses, and figs. Prometheus complimented the spread. Amicable conversation flowed between the brothers, reliving memories before the time of humans, but also discussing the future and their own children. Prometheus said he hoped to have more children with Hesione, which prompted a long conversation on fatherhood.

Pandora remained quiet, adding few comments. At first, her guard was up, but as the meal progressed, Pyrrha took up more of her attention as she coaxed the fussy child to eat. Iris cut a date into tiny heart-shaped pieces, always a favorite of the feisty girl. The two women held their own conversation about Pyrrha's bath and what they needed for dinner tomorrow.

"I think we should celebrate," Prometheus announced. "Let's open a bottle of your best wine."

Epimetheus nodded at Iris, who went to fetch it from the pantry.

"What are we celebrating?" Pandora asked, her attention sharp on her brother-in-law again.

"Family, of course. And how lucky we are to have each other."

Iris returned with a small amphora of their best wine. She set it on the counter and reached for some cups. Pyrrha fussed in her highchair, tossing a plate on the floor. Pandora picked her up to comfort her before suggesting Iris take her for a bath. The maid left the room with a crying toddler in her arms, the wine forgotten.

"Allow me," Prometheus said.

He rose and took the three cups, took the resin stopper out of the container, and poured the wine. While he had his back to them, Pandora gave Epimetheus a quizzical look. The younger Titan shrugged, happy with his brother's appeased mood. Pandora eyed Prometheus. He returned to the table and set a cup in front of each of them.

"A toast," he said, raising his, "to family."

The brothers touched rims together. Prometheus drained his cup in one draft. Epimetheus followed suit. Pandora took a sip of her favorite wine, the amphorae leftover from her wedding day. Its taste brought back a flood of memories from that day, how frightened she had been of her future, the suffocating veil, her first glimpses of her new home. She savored another large swig of the sweet wine, but this time a sour aftertaste burned the back of her throat. Perhaps the drink had gone bad. No sooner had this thought crossed her mind, when Epimetheus crashed forward, his unconscious head lolling on the table. She tried to reach for him, but her arms would not move, her body held as rigid as a statue. Only her eyes moved by her will. They turned to Prometheus and an evil grin spread across his face.

"Get up," he commanded.

Despite her best efforts to disobey, Pandora's body rose from her seat.

"We are going on an adventure," Prometheus said. "Come."

He strode out the door, her unwilling feet trailing after. Pyrrha's giggles rang out from down the hall where Iris bathed her, unaware of the evil plot. Pandora prayed they would remain safe. Outside, wispy clouds hastened through the sky, the half-moon obscured by their deep gray masses. Prometheus hurried down the hill with Pandora's arm tightly in his grasp, an unnecessary precaution since her body compelled her to obey his orders. Her mind was under no such power and she quickly realized his plan.

The pithos.

He wanted to open it. What else could he need her for? The key vibrated hard against her chest. Somehow, he devised this scheme. With all her mind, she called for Athena, begging for protection.

Prometheus dragged her through the streets all the way to the temple steps. Once inside, a temple maiden approached to ask about their business, but cowered back when he roared at her to leave. Pandora listened to the terrified girl's footsteps echo down the stairs into the night. Would the girl get help? Would it even be in time if she did?

The Titan pushed her ahead to the platform where the pithos sat, the images in such a frenzy they were indistinguishable. Against her chest, the key grew hot. A warning. One she could not heed.

"Open it," he demanded, a gleam of triumph in his eyes.

Pandora tried to stop herself, willed her body to defy, but to no avail. The scene unfolded as if she watched from above, an observer rather than a participant. She climbed on the pedestal and pulled the key from underneath her tunic. The metal scalded her hand, the reek of singed skin filling her nostrils. Her heartbeat pounded in her ears, all other sounds drowned out. With a shaking hand, she inserted the feather-shaped key into the lock. Prometheus hovered next to her, his countenance a picture of desire.

With a turn, the lock clicked open. The Titan pulled out the stopper.

An enormous black cloud erupted from the jar, throwing both of them to the ground. Screams and wails rang, a cacophony of terror pouring into the space. The sound from her nightmares. Hideous wraiths swirled around her. Their ghostly arms reached toward her head, right into her mind. Anguish, desolation, and grief filled her thoughts, as though happiness drained from the world. Their piercing howls cut through the air, lodging in Pandora's heart.

All around her, the temple walls shook, chunks of rock falling to the ground. Prometheus ran from the temple, sidestepping debris. Pandora covered her ears. *My hands obey me again*, she thought. She caught sight of the stopper rolling across the floor nearby. She grabbed it and jumped up onto the pedestal, fighting against the sorrow, rage, and desperation that spewed from the pithos. With the last of her strength, she put the stopper back in and inserted the key. The last thing she saw before passing out was the great cloud of blackness whirling to the top of the temple and out into the night.

FIFTY-FOUR

Iris cowered in the closet, a screaming Pyrrha in her arms. Wind tore across the hilltop, the terrifying storm erupting out of nowhere. When the maid saw the rafters shake, she snatched up the girl and ran from the house. Outside, the ground quaked beneath her feet, black clouds raging overhead. She placed the child down on an open swath of grass, the safest area she could find, and returned inside to where Epimetheus lay with his face down on the table. Pandora was nowhere to be found.

"Epimetheus," she cried, shaking his enormous frame. "Wake up."

His head bolted up, his eyes cloudy as though he woke from a long slumber. A beam crashed onto the table, smashing it in two. The Titan jumped up, assessing the situation. Iris tugged him toward the door. He shielded her across the cracking threshold into the terrifying squall. Iris scooped up Pyrrha and searched for a place to take cover. Epimetheus grabbed her shoulders.

"Where is Pandora?" he shouted over the roar.

"I don't know," Iris cried, her words devoured by the wind.

The panicked animals bleated and clamored, tearing at their enclosures. Epimetheus searched for safety. He led Iris to a small crevice between two boulders. The gale flung branches and stones around at will. The large rocks provided the best cover he could find. Iris crouched down, the child enclosed in her arms.

Epimetheus ran to his animals, heedless of the fragments barraging his body. He opened the chicken coop and the sheep pen, urging the animals to flee. The roof of the barn blew off when he reached the paddock. His beloved horses reared up, white foam spewing from their mouths. The Titan opened the gate, and the creatures stampeded out. *Find safety*, he commanded. The steeds ran behind the crumbling house and scaled the path up the mountain. The remaining animals followed.

He sprinted back to Iris and threw his body over the boulders. While the storm railed, he tried to remember the events of the evening.

Prometheus.

His brother had come under the guise of making amends. They had toasted to family. Horror overtook Epimetheus. The wine had knocked him out. With Prometheus gone and Pandora missing, it did not take long to figure the situation out.

The pithos.

Prometheus made Pandora open it and unleash this tempest.

Minutes dragged on, the Titan clenching the rocks while wreckage rained down. Beneath him, Iris trembled, Pyrrha's cries ringing up faintly. How could he have been stupid enough to let his brother fool him? If the pithos caused such havoc up here, what happened in town? How could Pandora survive a calamity of this magnitude? He thought of her face, of their life together, of their love. How would he go on without her?

The storm died down at last, the black clouds giving way to a deep starry sky. Epimetheus stood and lit a torch to survey the destruction. The front half of the house collapsed in on itself. The splintered paddock face gaped with holes, broken staves sticking out of the ground like spears. A heap of mangled sticks and wires was the only trace of the chicken coop. He prayed his animals found safety.

Iris came to his side, Pyrrha on her shoulder. Before she could say anything, cries rang out, a torch flame illuminating the hilltop. Two people crested it and barreled across the grass toward them. Epimetheus recognized the men, but the sheer dread in their eyes gave him pause.

"You must flee," one said, with no recognition of who stood before him. "The village is gone. Wiped out. The dead are everywhere. Flee while you can."

Without another word, they ran across the field out of sight. Iris locked eyes with Epimetheus. Neither could utter their paramount thought. They stood in silence, the stars twinkling above, the cricket chirping once again, as though nothing was amiss. Epimetheus fell to his knees.

"She's dead. My beautiful wife is dead," he sobbed in anguish.

"We can't know that for sure," Iris consoled.

Pyrrha wailed at the sight of her father crying. While the maid soothed her, the Titan walked toward the side of the house. After checking the structure, he went in the door, returning a few moments later with some food, blankets, and supplies. Wordlessly, he erected a tarp near the firepit. Iris watched, rubbing Pyrrha's back while she slept. When he was done, he turned to her.

"You should be safe here. I am going to check on my animals. I need to be alone."

Iris placed the child down on a blanket. She laid next to her and wrapped another blanket around them. Exhaustion overtook her. As she drifted to sleep, she thought of Epimetheus and the tears streaming down his face when he left.

When the roar of abject misery rang from below, Zeus allowed himself a moment of satisfaction. At last, the pithos completed its task and all of mankind would suffer. Images of disease, famine, and violence played across his mind, each more gratifying than the last. Prometheus' overconfident humans would see they were no match for the gods. He watched the black cloud spread its plague across all lands with giddiness. Zeus had been right to place his trust in Hermes.

As though the thought conjured him, the messenger god appeared at Zeus' side. The King of the Gods clapped his son on the back. Hera, Ares, and Athena all materialized to find out the cause of the uproar in the world below. At the sight of the black cloud, Athena's heart dropped. The other immortals observed the gloom covering the world below with little interest.

"As I promised," Hermes gloated. "The jar is open and nothing connects you to the calamity, Father."

"Thank you, Hermes." Zeus replied, motioning for Ganymede to fill everyone's cups.

Once each immortal held a goblet of thick, amber liquid, Zeus raised his high. "To Prometheus and his wretched mortals."

While the others drank, Athena put her cup down untouched.

"Now your revenge against the Titan is complete," Hermes declared.

"Hardly," Zeus countered. "Prometheus withholds a name, a name I need to know. Ares and I have come up with a suitable punishment, an existence of pure pain."

While a pleased expression filled Ares' face, Athena gaped openly at her father.

"You planned another punishment for Prometheus? But you still let Pandora open the pithos?" she said in disbelief.

"There is no penalty too great for that arrogant Titan. He allowed the status of man to grow to a point where those bothersome mortals need to be kept in line. Opening the jar settles that score, but withholding the name of my potential usurper requires a crueler sentence," Zeus bellowed. "If you have a problem with my methods, that is your problem, daughter."

The King of the Gods turned to Ares, who eagerly described ideas for torment. Hera scolded Hermes over some trivial grievance. Athena's fellow Olympians forgot all about the havoc wreaked on the world, but the goddess of wisdom had to admit, she normally acted no better. After all, what did the fleeting life of a mortal matter in the end? Her gaze fell back to the reeling landscape below, and Pandora's face filled her mind. Athena transformed into an owl. She flew off to Epideme to see if there was anything left of Pandora's life for Athena to salvage with the special gift she had placed in the jar.

FIFTY-FIVE

When Pandora's eyes fluttered open, a hollowness filled her. Time had passed, but how much she could not say. Debris lay all around, pebbles and dirt rolling to the floor as she sat up. Broken columns ringed the chamber. Some leaned precariously on their neighbors. From fresh holes in the wall, a dim light from outside cast the space in eerie shadows. Pandora brushed her dust filled hair from her face and eyed the cracked pedestal which had toppled beside her. The unharmed pithos rested beside it, images still awhirl as though nothing unusual occurred. Only the key hanging from the lock spoke of the disaster.

Pandora crawled over to it. After finding that the key had cooled, she turned it in the lock and pulled it out. For a moment, she held the golden feather, suspended on its chain, such a harmless object for all it had wrought. With anger, she tossed it aside and rose on unsteady feet to pick her way through the rubble to the door. *Why has no one come to help?*

The answer hit her with the force of a mighty blow. Outside the temple, she beheld the village razed to the ground. Clouds of dust rose from the wreckage where buildings once stood. A giant crater yawed in place of the blacksmith's forge, the explosion damaging structures in a circumference of scorched earth. A tattered piece of cloth blew past her feet, the remnants of a market stall's awning now shattered. Smells of burning wood and flesh assaulted her as she numbly descended the steps. Never could she have imagined such destruction. All she had built, all she worked tirelessly for, gone in a matter of moments. What was left? And where were all the people?

Pyrrha.

The thought of her daughter broke her stupor. She rocketed off the temple steps and down the main road without a glance at the surrounding destruction. With frantic footsteps, she raced up the hill, hardly aware of the rocks cutting into her soles. Her lungs burned, each inhalation filled with dust, but her focus remained entirely on her child. She crested the hill and saw the splintered front gate. Panic took her across the meadow. A split fence encircled an empty paddock. One side of the henhouse hung off the hinges. With terror, she noted the house, with the front half of the roof caved in. She ran to the front door, but a broken beam blocked her path.

"Epimetheus! Pyrrha!" she cried.

"We're here," Iris called from the back of the house.

Pandora ran toward her voice. On the grass behind the home, Iris sat on a log, the picture of exhaustion. Pyrrha played with pieces of rock from the fractured wall, stacking them in piles to form a rudimentary village. She turned at the sound of Pandora's gasp.

"Mama," she squealed and ran to her. "Look what I made."

"It's beautiful," Pandora said, with a tight embrace. For one second, relief filled her, but the horror wormed back in. "Go finish building, sweetheart."

The happy girl toddled back to her creation. Pandora sank onto the log. A concerned Iris went to fetch a water bucket and insisted Pandora drink a few ladlefuls. The maid wet a cloth and wiped the grime from her mistress' face.

"Are you all right? Did Prometheus harm you?"

"Not exactly. He used a potion to manipulate me. He forced me to open the jar," Pandora admitted, the shock of it reverberating through her.

"We were certain you were dead," the maid whispered, her head turned away from Pyrrha.

"Where is Epimetheus?"

"He left, grief-stricken beyond comfort. He went up the hill to check on the animals. They fled there in the chaos."

She pointed at the back path. "They were terrified. The horses almost stampeded him and the chickens plucked out their own feathers. I've never been more scared. He said he wanted to be alone."

Pandora sighed, still trying to wrap her head around everything. "Tell me everything you remember."

"I was dressing Pyrrha after her bath when the storm erupted. First, I hid in the closet, but the house shook and cracked. I ran outside with her and put her in the grass. It was safer than the house, then I ran back in." Iris drew a steadying breath. "Epimetheus lay motionless, his head on the table. You were gone. I shook and shook him until he woke. We got out of the house and he shielded Pyrrha and me behind some boulders."

"Thank you, Iris, for protecting my daughter." Pandora held her hand, tears in her eyes.

"When the storm stopped, some villagers ran up and told us to flee. Their eyes held a crazed expression … they were not in their right mind.," Iris explained. "After they rushed off, the master sank down to his knees and cried. I tried to console him, but Pyrrha got upset. Epimetheus managed to get a few supplies from the house before he went. I slept on the grass with Pyrrha after the master went to help the terrified animals."

"Mama, hungry," Pyrrha said, patting her stomach.

"Can you find her something to eat? I have to go to Epimetheus."

"Of course, ma'am. But we will need to go to the village for some more supplies today to replace all we lost."

Pandora laid a firm hand on the girl's arm. "Iris, the village is gone."

She turned from the stunned maid and headed up the back path. The sun shone brightly, the birds sang, flitting from tree to tree. A soft breeze wafted across the long grasses, the stalks bending like elegant dancers. Whatever evil the pithos released, it held no sway here, which was some measure of comfort. Up ahead, she heard the nickering of horses. Rosa emerged from behind a bend, nudging Pandora with her snout. The animal went with her back to its companions, who spread out on a wide, uneven plain. Epimetheus froze at the sight of her. When he understood she was real, he broke into a run, swooping her up, his massive arms vise-like around her.

"You're alive," he whispered over and over, showering her with kisses.

"I am," she asserted. "But your brother used me to open the pithos. He wanted its blessings, but it held unspeakable evils. A giant black cloud erupted from it and destroyed all in its path. Everything we worked for, everything we built together, is gone."

FIFTY-SIX

The couple held each other for a long time, each full of apologies. Epimetheus railed against his brother for his treachery. Pandora despaired over the destruction of the village. The nicker of a horse brought them back to the present moment. Rosa nudged them with her nose. Most of the animals gathered around the Titan, confused but no longer frightened.

"Let's get them back home," he said.

Eyes downcast, they led the horses back down to the homestead. Chickens melted out of the brush, happy a state of calm had returned. Rhea and Rex now sat near Iris. They watched Pyrrha, who collected flowers for the maid to weave into a wreath for her head. The child's giggles at odds with the destruction all around her. Epimetheus assessed the damage to the house and other edifices.

"The front room is covered in rubble, but the back still stands. Once I clean it out, the ceiling will be a quick repair," he informed them. "You can still get water from the bathroom and we can cook in the firepit."

"I will fetch some more blankets from the bedrooms for us to sleep on," Iris offered.

"There's extra hay in the barn for bedding. Let me go get it." He stepped over a shattered piece of the front door.

"Epimetheus, wait," Pandora said. "I don't think it is wise to leave the jar down in the village. What if more evil is inside? I want to go get it and bring it back here to avoid further calamity."

Her husband nodded, his face grave. He turned and headed for the barn, shoulders slumped. Iris tried to talk her mistress out of going alone, but Pandora assured her she would be fine. After a quick snack of nuts and olives, she left for Epideme once more. What remained of it, at least.

On her descent, she gazed over the treetops to the lake. The limbs of a few cracked willows bobbed against the shore, but otherwise, the site was unscathed. The groves on the hill suffered more damage, a labyrinth of broken branches and upturned roots. She thought of the children with their games and laughter. Tears welled in her eyes at the once idyllic spot, now laid bare. Her feet dragged as though they weighed a thousand pounds, every step toward the village a greater effort.

At the town's entrance, splintered pieces of the gate pierced the ground amid piles of rock and dirt. Pandora found fragments of the town sign, once beautiful, now a jagged slab. Only the letters *P* and *I* remained intact on a fractured piece. She picked it up, rubbing the grime off it, and walked down the main street. For the first time, she noticed people, grubby and dazed, digging through different piles. Some called out names, others threw debris aside, and many wept, the devastation almost incomprehensible. Covered corpses lay in a line along one side street, mourners kneeling over the unmoving shapes.

"Pandora," a raspy voice cried. Chloe stumbled over to her, her youngest child on her hip with a bandaged head.

"My dear friend, are you hurt? How is Cressida?" Pandora asked, brushing dirt off the child's small arm.

"I am fine, only bruised. A large chunk of wood hit Cressida before I got to her. Thankfully, it missed her eye. My other two are safe." She pointed to where they sat, dazed and dusty. "Demetri broke his arm, but he still tries to find survivors."

"I am sorry, Chloe," Pandora said, stroking her child's head.

They walked toward the temple, the once splendid main thoroughfare rutted and clogged with debris. About halfway there, Pandora noticed the silence. All around her, people emerged from the destruction and made the sign to ward off evil, their hard stares full of anger. Paz emerged from behind a pile of what used to be her house. Pandora took a step in her direction.

"Witch," she cried. "Away with you."

"Paz, my friend, why do you speak to me like this?" Pandora stammered, feet frozen mid-step.

The old woman did not answer, only held her hand in the gesture held by the others. Chloe pulled Pandora's arm farther down the street, but she could sense the scowls of every person they passed burning into her back. Of course, their anger was justified, but they aimed it at the wrong person. Did they not realize how grieved she was about the loss of the town? Were they not her friends and neighbors? Everyone suffered, but could they not make it right together?

"Chloe, what is this all about?" she whispered when no one offered her anything but scorn.

"Last night, when the ground first shook, many of us ran outside. Prometheus sprinted out of the temple. He told everyone he tried to stop you, but you opened the pithos and unleashed the fury of the gods. He said even though you had more than enough riches and fame, you wouldn't rest until you knew what else was in the jar. That despite warnings from the gods, your curiosity got the better of you."

Too horrified to speak, Pandora could only survey the ruin of the village mutely. Prometheus had blamed *her*? In his cowardice, he would let her take the fall for his actions? The numbness which had engulfed her since the disaster transformed into rage, a molten deluge flooding her mind and heart.

"How dare he!" she shouted. "It was his plan all along. He wanted the gods' favor to appease them for his own wrongdoing."

"I believe you, Pandora," Chloe consoled. "I know you, and I know Prometheus. There is no doubt in my mind you speak the truth. However, Prometheus acted genuinely terrified and the rest of the villagers, something that came out of the jar changed a lot of them. Their minds are different, and not for the better."

"Then I will convince them."

She strode to a pile of stone and ascended. "Citizens, come, hear me speak."

The ragged corps of survivors staggered over, the injured supported by family and friends. Pandora found herself encircled by at least one hundred people, none of whom spared her a friendly glance. Smoke rose in the distance from newly erected funeral pyres, the stench of burning flesh heavy in the air. Pandora stared down at the faces of her friends and neighbors and suppressed a gasp at their befogged eyes, as though the specters from the jar had invaded their minds.

"We have all suffered from this disaster, but we can build back all we have lost together. I am still here to guide and help, committed to this town, to all of you. As I have always been."

"Liar," one man shouted.

"Witch," a woman hissed.

"I am not to blame. I promise you. It was Prometheus. He opened the pithos. Your anger is misdirected."

"Is it not true that only you could open the jar? Only you had the key," Paz accused.

"He gave me a potion. He forced me to open it. Don't you see? It was an accident."

"An accident?" a man with a bloody lip sneered. "My whole family is dead because of you."

Pandora tried to explain how Prometheus tricked her, but the crowd grew more frenzied with each second. They laid the full blame at her feet.

"She dishonored the gods with her curiosity. They told her to leave it alone, but she defied them and brought down their wrath upon all of us," one woman cried. "We must leave here and never come back lest the gods strike us down again."

"Yes! Yes!" the horde exclaimed.

"No, no," Pandora pled to deaf ears.

A rock hurtled across the sky and hit the side of her face. Fresh drops of blood dribbled down her cheek, falling in deep red spots at her feet. Before she could process what happened, another stone smashed into her arm. With a yelp, she jumped down from the pile and ran. The angry villagers followed, ready to vent all their frustrations on the person they held responsible for their anguish. Pandora did not want to lead them to the temple or to her home. Instead, she ran to the lake. Her small head start did not give her much time. She dove into the water, its chill stabbing into her, and swam across to hide in the cover of some overhanging branches. The mob clambered out of the brush onto the lake bank, but did not see her. After a few moments of shouts and curses, they gave up and returned to the rubble.

Pandora dragged herself up on the opposite bank and took cover behind a fallen log. The sun god rode his chariot to the pinnacle of the sky before he turned back toward the horizon. Light faded to orange and deepened to purple. When the half-moon rose, Pandora crept back to the village, still intent on retrieving the jar. She stayed in the shadows to avoid any unpleasant encounters, but after a few yards, something became clear. The bulk of the villagers of Epideme, once happy and prosperous, were gone.

FIFTY-SEVEN

Pandora picked her way over the rubble. The steps of the temple, rent with a vicious gash, yawed at her like the jaws of a deadly beast. When she ascended, they shook with a thunderous rumble, chunks of stone raining down from the unstable rooftop. Perhaps the entire edifice would crush her. This thought met with her indifference, and she plunged across the broken door into a gray gloom.

For a moment, she stood frozen, memories playing back in her mind. The derelict temple when she arrived, brought back to life by her careful guidance. Eager builders explaining each new phase of the restoration. The attentive hands of villagers adorning alcoves and walls. Travelers from far and wide praying before the pithos, the altar overflowing with offerings. The aroma of candles, the scent of flowers, the song of worshippers, all cast in the bright rays of sun. Each recollection assaulted her already shattered heart.

Now, in the ominous wreckage, only one object still shone.

The pithos.

On its side, but otherwise unharmed despite the carnage it wrought. As she approached, the golden images swirled, their usual dance across the inky background. Pandora kneeled next to it. In the Olympian temple, she and Iliana struggled to move it at all, but now her hands easily up righted it, no longer weighed down by the evil inside. She glared at it, every fiber of her yearning to smash it beyond recognition as it had done to her life. Her fingers tightened around a rock, its sharp edges biting into her palm. Her arm rose, ready to deliver the first blow, when a noise startled her. A faint clink rang from inside the pithos. After a second of silence, the sound repeated, stopped, then repeated, as though a trapped bird flew frenzied inside.

The rock slipped from Pandora's hand and she scrambled back, her heart pounding against her ribs. What evil remained in the jar? What if it got out? She could not let that happen. All thoughts of destroying it faded, replaced by the dread from her dream long ago. How could she bring this object home with her? How could she keep it near her daughter, knowing the horror it could unleash? But how could she leave it where someone else may find it, someone who did not understand the danger? Overcome with fear, she lowered her head into her hands and wept, her sobs muffled by the heavy dust.

A pale light roused her from her stupor. She lifted her tearful gaze to find a somber, yet beautiful figure, encased in an otherworldly glow, standing before her.

"Athena." The awestruck words fell from her lips and she bowed her head.

"Yes, my child. It is I."

"I didn't open it willingly," Pandora blurted. "Prometheus forced me with an evil spell. I never wanted to disobey you."

The goddess held up a hand and Pandora fell silent.

"Your will never mattered. Zeus crafted that pithos for one reason alone—to inflict evil on mortals, the prized creation of Prometheus. Now, disease, famine, greed, and all manner of disaster will plague humankind until the end of time. The volition of one mere girl is no match for the King of the Gods."

A cascade of emotion careened through Pandora. Disbelief, sorrow, and incredulity all distilled into anger that erupted with a force beyond her control.

"You mean I have been a pawn in this game from the beginning? All those I touched, all those I loved, all the obedience and gratitude I have shown the gods, all of it meant nothing?" She rose, her body trembling in fury. "And you knew the whole time and, rather than help me, watched it all unfold?"

Irritation flashed in Athena's eyes at the insolence and Pandora fell silent, dropping her head. What did it matter if she infuriated the goddess? After all, what power did the *volition of one mere girl* even have?

None.

"Pandora," the goddess said with a surprising tone of compassion, "I did all I could. I warned you not to open the jar, an order you followed fastidiously. But alas, I am not the only deity, and others who wanted the evils freed from the jar conspired against you."

"Is there no way to undo the harm? No way to put things right again?" Pandora's voice cracked against the lump in her throat.

"No. There is no way to return to the past. However, I did put one gift in the jar to help."

"Is that what I heard flitting about inside?"

"Yes. Open it and see for yourself," the goddess instructed.

Pandora picked up the key from the floor. Warily, she went to the jar and inserted it. With a nod of assent from Athena, she turned the golden feather and removed the stopper, her body clenched for an onslaught of malevolence. This time, nothing burst forth. Pandora peeked inside and saw a tiny golden dragonfly. It fluttered to the top where it perched on the rim before flying to her hand. The cuts on her palm immediately healed at its touch. She watched in wonder as it multiplied into hundreds, a golden cloud that rose and floated out the oculus into the open sky.

"What was that?" she asked.

"Hope," proclaimed the goddess.

"And it will reverse all the evil let loose by the pithos?"

"Sadly, nothing can do that. But it provides a faith that things can get better, that even the darkest moments hold purpose, and the worst of times can improve."

"*That* is a gift? That bleakness will pass? That suffering must be borne with only the idea life may improve? That sounds more like an evil to me," Pandora declared with bitterness.

Athena remained silent for some time before declaring, "I suppose it will be up to the individual whether to deem hope a blessing or a burden. Where some find comfort, others will find resentment. Prometheus gave man free will, therefore the onus to decide this does not rest with the gods."

Pandora wanted hope to spring up in her, to buoy her from her anguish, but her empty heart tore at her chest with ragged claws.

"I leave you now, my daughter. Destroy the pithos. Its purpose has been served. I will always watch over you. And Pandora," the goddess lifted Pandora's chin to her ageless eyes, "my wish is for you to find not only your hope but your peace as well."

In a flash of light, Athena vanished. Pandora stared at the fading glow long into the night.

FIFTY-EIGHT

Pandora gripped another rock, her scalding anger replaced now with desolate resignation. When shards of the pithos strewed the floor in jagged pieces, the images stilled at last, she felt no relief at its destruction. She should return home, but could not find the will to leave the broken temple. Emptiness filled her soul, the crush as strong as a tidal wave. Why had the gods used her so cruelly? How could she not have known this was their plan? After all, why had she deserved the supposed honor bestowed on her? The trap laid for her and Epimetheus snared them as easily as two ignorant rabbits.

Overhead, the moon descended, the night sky giving way to the steely gray of dawn, and still Pandora sat amid the ruin. Tears clouded her vision, the cracked columns and crumbled mosaics wavering like a mirage. She did not pray for whom would she pray to? The gods only listened when it suited them, granted favor on a whim, disguised guile as benevolence. Whatever wishes she had or ideas she planned did not matter. Any mortal who thought otherwise deluded themselves. Prometheus may have given humans free will, but they were not the masters of their own fate. No amount of adulation, bargaining, or even anger could change the ultimate power of the immortals.

She sat with her grief, a shattered woman in a shattered temple. The rosy fingers of dawn stretched across the sky. Far off, a rooster cawed. Pandora remembered the story of the young soldier, Alectryon, who fell asleep while guarding the door for Ares' affair with Aphrodite. His dozing allowed the sun to rise and reveal the duo's deception to the sun god Helios, who told Aphrodite's husband, Hephaestus. As punishment for this transgression, Ares turned the boy into a rooster, who must wake at sunrise every morning and crow a warning. Although she heard the account many times in her life, today the story held an additional layer of sadness. Another victim of an impulsive tantrum by a god.

"Pandora?" a voice whispered.

Iris stood in the fissured doorway of the temple, her eyes wide at the sight within. Pandora found the strength to rise and cross over to her maid, her feet as heavy as bricks.

"You must come quickly," Iris pled. "The master received bad news from a shepherd boy only moments ago. He is quite beside himself and calls out for you."

The maid held out her hand out and Pandora took it. At the touch, some sense filtered back into her numb mind.

"Pyrrha? Where is she?" The thought of her daughter roused Pandora.

"She is sleeping. All snuggled up with Rhea. I ran down her as fast as I could. We must get back to her and the master."

"Then let us hurry."

With one wistful glance back at her beloved temple, they made their way up the main road. A few stragglers remained in the village, rummaging through piles of debris for anything of value. Their fury from the day before had not faded. Each person stopped to watch the two women. Most made the sign to ward off evil. *As if it were that simple*, Pandora thought bitterly. Others scowled and hissed curses at her. As they neared the broken gate, a stone slammed into Pandora's back, then another. The pair quickened their pace against the hatred erupting around them. Pandora never set foot in the town again, never knew what became of Epideme or its citizens. Once her proudest achievement, she left her town with a sendoff reserved for the most malicious villain.

They ascended the hill, the path cluttered with downed limbs. Birds, who picked on bruised figs and olives, took wing when they rushed past. Breathless, they crested the hillside. Epimetheus leaned over the rails of the paddock, fresh boards interspersed with the weather-worn wood.

Pandora gestured for Iris to tend to Pyrrha. The maid never slowed, rounding the house out of sight. Pandora walked to her husband, who held his head in his hands, his stance the epitome of anguish.

"What happened? Iris said a shepherd boy came. What did he tell you?" she asked, rubbing her hand across her husband's back.

He lifted his head, his eyes red with tears. "It was no shepherd boy. It was Hermes. He came to tell me my brother's fate."

Pandora steeled herself for the news, but Epimetheus stared off into the distance. Hazel trotted over from where the horses knotted in a tight group and nudged Pandora's hand. She stroked her snout and whispered comforting words. The others followed, waiting in turn for the caress of their mistress, uneasy at their master's behavior.

"According to Hermes, Zeus found out the Titan, Themis—our aunt—told Prometheus a secret. When Zeus heard this, he hunted high and low for my brother. Prometheus thought I told the gods he held the secret. That is why he demanded our help. When I refused, he came up with his scheme."

Pandora sighed. "Prometheus thought whatever the pithos held would save him."

Epimetheus nodded, pain etched on his face. "Now Zeus has him chained to a rock in the Caucus Mountains. Each day, an eagle comes and eats his liver, and each night it grows back. He must endure this agony for eternity or reveal the secret."

"He still does not tell the secret? He endures this fate?" a horrified Pandora asked.

"Yes, for now. Prometheus knows the identity of a mortal woman. If this woman bears a child with Zeus, that child is the only one who would have the power to overthrow the king of the Olympians. My brother will never let Zeus have that information."

Pandora understood the significance of this secret. Zeus fathered children with a never-ending array of women. The

King of the Gods remained in peril as long as Prometheus withheld the name. Zeus' fury must be unmatched.

"But why involve us? Why give us the pithos?" Pandora asked.

"To punish Prometheus' favorite creation—mankind. The Olympians conspired to create the jar long before Zeus learned of my brother's latest deception. By unleashing woes on man, the gods are avenged for the fire my brother stole and the trick of his sacrifice offerings," Epimetheus explained. "They thought you would be unable to resist the enchantment on the jar and open it against their orders. But you proved stronger than they envisioned."

"In the end, we were only pawns in their game," Pandora stated. "Unwilling participants with no say in the outcome. Athena told me as much herself."

Epimetheus nodded. He wiped his tears with the back of his hand and pulled Pandora into an embrace.

"I've always lacked my brother's foresight. He warned me not to trust the gods, but I didn't listen," Epimetheus said, his voice warm against her ear. "But you are the greatest gift I have ever received, Pandora, and although we paid a high price, I'd like to think we could still have a pleasant life together here. We can rebuild and be happy again."

Pandora hugged him back, tears flowing at the hope he showed for the future.

FIFTY-NINE

Pandora and Epimetheus strove to pick up the pieces of their shattered lives. Within days, they repaired the house and barn. Pandora relished the work, a welcome distraction from all she had lost. Epimetheus returned to his animals, his eternal source of comfort. Iris helped Pandora replant the garden and tend to Pyrrha. The women did not speak of the dreadful night or what fate befell Iris' family. If her parents survived, they never sent word to their daughter. Guilt ate at Pandora when the girl randomly suppressed tears.

As dusk fell one evening, a figure rose over the hilltop, silhouetted against the setting sun. Pandora recognized the person at once and ran to her, Iris right behind her.

"Chloe," she cried, wrapping her arms around her friend.

"I can't stay long, Pandora," Chloe said. "But I needed to see you were all right."

"We are as good as can be expected. How are you? And Demitri? And the children?"

"We have been in a makeshift camp with some other villagers for the last month, about two miles away," her friend explained. "We plan to leave for Thessaly tomorrow."

"There are other villagers with you? Epimetheus and I should see them. Help them if we can."

"No, Pandora," Chloe said and touched her friend's arm. "You represent the greatest evil to them. I know it's not true. Believe me, I have tried to reason with some. Word has spread across the land of your evil deed. The mention of your name is forbidden."

"My name is forbidden?" Pandora whispered. The words caught in her throat.

"Whatever came out of that jar changed the villagers' love for you into hate. No one wants to rebuild Epideme or live anywhere near it. I seem to be the only one spared for whatever reason," Chloe confessed.

"Because our friendship ran deeper than evil," Pandora said. "I need to ask you one favor. Take Iris with you."

"No," Iris gasped.

"You deserve more than this isolated life. Go to Thessaly. Marry a nice man and have a bunch of children. Do it for me."

After a few more protests, the maid agreed. The women went into the house and packed a small bundle of clothes and food for Iris. Pandora wrapped some gold drachmas in a silk scarf for Iris to take. After teary goodbyes, Pandora watched the pair disappear into the night, wondering if she would ever have another visitor.

Only one other person ever came. Deucalion, Prometheus' son, came to live with them after his heartbroken mother returned to her sacred stream on Mount Parnassus. One day a Naiad popped out of the stream behind the house with the little boy. The water nymph handed him to Pandora and quickly swam away. Although confused at first, the boy delighted in the company of his cousin, who became fast friends.

No one else ever set foot on the hilltop. The foursome lived a life of tranquility tinged with sadness. Sometimes when the giggling children scampered on stumpy legs across the meadow, faith flickered in Pandora's heart. Other times, when loneliness set in on the hilltop, now shrouded from humans in the clouds, her heart burned as though branded forever to suffer.

Time passed. Pyrrha and Deucalion grew up, fell in love, and wished to leave the solitary confines of their home. Pandora and Epimetheus sent them into the world with blessings and a warning. In all the land, Pandora's name personified disaster. The blame for every misfortune, every sickness, every disaster, pinned squarely on her shoulders. The couple should keep their relation to her a secret. Pyrrha balked at first, indignant on her mother's behalf, but Epimetheus soon got her to see the danger of the situation.

Once in a while, the couple returned, with three children in tow. Pandora played the doting grandmother, savoring the laughter and kisses her grandchildren brought. More often though, she and Epimetheus were alone, all but forgotten, save for the infamous legend passed down from generation to generation, their solitary lives but faded petals of a summer bloom come autumn.

Over the years, Pandora tried to unearth hope from somewhere deep inside herself. Most days, it bit like the cruel sting of a wasp, but every once in a while, it soothed for a moment, an ethereal kiss to her heart, however fleeting. Though the couple's love never diminished, their ill-use by the Olympians blunted their spirits, quashing them down to lesser versions of themselves. Epimetheus assured her that all which transpired was the will of the gods, but icy fingers of regret grasped at her in unguarded moments, the will of the gods providing little solace.

Pandora never prayed, despite Athena's promise to always watch her. She did not believe the gods listened, and on the outside chance they did, how could she ever trust any of them again? All those years ago, when they gifted her the pithos, their magnificence awed her. Now, she thought them no better than a squabbling family of peasants, though with far more dire consequences. Some spell stopped time for Pandora on the isolated hilltop, the will of her Titan husband at work. No wrinkle touched her skin, no gray streaked her hair. Thus, her fate, though less dire than Prometheus', condemned her to eternally ponder an unending stream of what-ifs. Questions with no consoling answers now tormented a mind, once insatiable in its curiosity.

One afternoon, many years later, Pandora sat in the meadow, cool wind lifting her hair. Her mind wandered to the thought which vexed her most. That she could not set the record straight, that the Olympians used her as a scapegoat, gnawed at Pandora's soul. Not only for her sake, but for the sake of all women whom the gods victimized. But what hope was there for her story to be told?

No sooner did this notion pass, when a large dragonfly swooped past, the buzz of its wings ceasing as it landed on her hand. Images of her writing desk on Lemnos flashed across her mind, the sensation of clarity and peace the endeavor produced in her as a girl. The events of her life unfolded before her, the burden of regret released by the strokes of a quill, her mind freed from its internal prison of anger.

"Thank you, Athena," she said, as the dragonfly glided away.

She rose with purpose and crossed the property. The nickering of horses drifted in the air along with Epimetheus' soft voice to his beloved horses. For a moment, she watched him, arms over the rail, and memories of their early days flooded her with happiness. Tonight, she would sleep safely in his arms. For all their travails, his love never faltered.

Inside the house, she retrieved some paper, ink, and a quill. By recording her account, she regained some of the power stolen from her by the gods. Her full story could be told and bring hope to all who read it. With a new lightness in her heart, she dipped the quill in ink and wrote, for hope is a balm to all who embrace it.

ACKNOWLEDGEMENTS

It takes a village to publish a book and I am fortunate to have a wonderful team of people who help make my stories the best they can be. To my editor, Emma Jane Lounsbury from *EJL Editing*, thank you for your expertise, honesty, and guidance in polishing my words. To Keylin Rivers of *Fantasy Book Cover Designs* by Keylin Rivers, thank you for the beautiful cover and the time and patience you took with it. To Angelique Bosman of *RedFox Book Design* thank you for your formatting knowledge, which is always a life saver. To my beta reader, Jill, thanks for your continued support and friendship. To my house full of boys, thanks for giving me the time and space to fulfill my dreams. Finally, to my readers, thank you for allowing my stories into your lives. I hope you enjoy reading them as much as I enjoy writing them.

ABOUT THE AUTHOR

Jane loved to read from a young age, especially fantasy. Her Young Adult books, filled with fantasy, adventure, and a splash of romance, captivate readers of all ages with their strong, yet relatable female protagonists.

To date, she has published *The Stewartsland Chronicles* trilogy, *A Prophecy of Wings* (a Rone Award nominee and Reader's Favorite Gold Star winner), and *A Maiden of* Snakes (Reader's Favorite Gold Star winner and Book Fest Award winner).

Jane lives in a house full of boys, along with two spoiled cats, and a lovable German Shepherd. When she is not writing, you will find her reading, singing, at the gym or some combination of the three.

Visit my website and sign up for my newsletter for all the latest book news: